*In 1066 William the Conqueror defeated
Harold of England at Hastings—
and changed the course of Western civilization.*

In 1066, a woman watched the blood and carnage as
the tide of battle ebbed and flowed. She was a woman
of her time, chattel traded, for their own reasons, by
her father and brothers, a political pawn in the chess
game of power. She was Edyth the Saxon—and this
is her story.

Listen as she unfolds the chronicle. The years of her
childhood as the daughter of an Earl, of exile among
the Irish and the discovery of love in a strange
country where people sang their words and vowed
their allegiance to the strong, dark man who was her
husband. The years after the marriage ended with the
slash of a sword, when again she was commanded
to marry by her family, and the days and nights with
a new, and very different husband.

Come into the Eleventh Century and discover a
woman for the ages, a woman who saved those she
loved by daring the unknown.

The Wind from Hastings

Morgan Llywelyn

WARNER BOOKS

A Warner Communications Company

WARNER BOOKS EDITION

Copyright © 1978 by Morgan Llywelyn
All rights reserved. No part of this work may be reproduced or transmitted in
any form by any means, electronic or mechanical, including photocopying and
recording, or by any information storage and retrieval system, without
permission in writing from the publisher.

Cover art by Patricia Iemmiti

This Warner Books Edition is published by
arrangement with Houghton Mifflin Company

Warner Books, Inc., 75 Rockefeller Plaza,
New York, N.Y. 10019

 A Warner Communications Company

Printed in the United States of America

First Printing: March, 1980

Reissued: October, 1982

10 9 8 7 6 5 4 3 2

For Charles, *my Prince,*
Henri Llywelyn, *indispensable,*
Babian, *who was there,*
and
Henry Mooney Price

Author's Note

Saxon, Welsh and Irish names before the Conquest were subject to a number of variations in spelling and pronunciation. The Anglo-Saxon Chronicle refers to Harold Godwine's wife as Ealdgyth, for example; a name that many scholars have accepted. However, she is also variously referred to as Edyth, Aldith, Aldyth and Algifu. To simplify a confused situation I have limited her to two names, the Saxon Edyth and the Welsh Aldith. Other names of persons and places are those most generally accepted by modern scholars.

Hastings

WHEN THE WIND BLOWS from the Channel, it carries to us the smell of rotting flesh in Senlac Ridge. For days the Bastard's men have been burying the Norman dead, cursing as they work in the October sun and covering their faces with cloths against the stench.

Many of Harold's men still lie where they fell. Swollen and grotesque, they guard in death that awful piece of ground they could not hold in life. At night, when the Normans have gone back to their camp, the Saxon women creep onto the field of battle to find their men. It is difficult. The battle was daylong and savage; it took much butchery to kill the brave English. Angle and Saxon together, in death they have become the English. Mutilated beyond recognition, they sleep open-eyed on blood-stiff grass, and the keening of their womenfolk is piteous to hear.

We don't speak of that sound. We lie close together on the earth floor of the hut and pull our blankets over our heads, but still that cry comes through. Sometimes I think it will never stop, that I must walk all my days to the music of mourning.

Perhaps tomorrow the invaders will be done with their burying and march on to murder elsewhere. Then it will be safe for us to escape this place. As long as the Bastard and his men are in the area I dare not move or show myself. I can only huddle here with my children like a vixen gone to earth, waiting for the hounds to leave.

I am certain William of Normandy would give much to find me, doubly so with Harold's child in my belly. Surely he must know of it already; his spies are everywhere. There is no safety anywhere anymore. But was there? Ever?

At any rate, if my unborn child is a boy he is Harold's legitimate heir, the Atheling, for his father and I were truly wed in York Minster. The Norman Bastard would not want Harold's heir to live, to avenge his father someday and lay claim to the stolen throne of all England!

But for all William knows I am in safekeeping with my brother's household in Mercia; even all his spies cannot tell him I lie hidden within sight of his camp.

That was not my strategy, but Griffith's. Griffith, my lord and my love, dead these three years, yet I still see with your eyes and think with your thoughts. In Wales you once told me, "The safest place to hide is at your enemy's back." That is where I am, in a woodcutter's filthy hut with a tiny remnant of the King's household. Here I have much time to think, and to remember.

Remember the long and anxious journey to this place, fleeing through the haunted Andredsweald, knowing that doom lay ahead and yet driven by a compulsion to see it for myself.

Remember the day I knew I carried within my body the child of my loved one's killer.

Remember the awe and splendor of the wedding at York Minster, when I was married to King Harold of England, while his son by the woman he loved watched us in silence.

Remember the day of my Lord Griffith's murder, when I saw his head lifted dripping from his shoulders and brandished before my unbelieving eyes . . . No! I will not think of that!

Better to remember the quiet green and silver fens of East Anglia, the dawn light gliding my parent's home, the childhood of Edyth the Saxon. The little girl I once was, who lived in ignorance and dreamed of marrying a prince.

East Anglia

I WAS LITTLE MORE than a child when my father was outlawed for treason. Until that time my life was full of the sweet scent of marsh-grass, my brothers' constant quarrels and the clamor of meals by torchlight in the Great Hall. My brothers and I played at hawking; we raced our ponies across that rolling sea of grass called the fens and shouted insults at each other. I always won, for I was the best rider of all the children on my father's lands. No stige-rap was

11

needed for my feet, I could mount just by grab-
bing the horse's mane and vaulting onto his
shaggy back.

Surely Edwin and Morkere must have
hated me for besting them at boyish accomplish-
ments, even as they resented me for being my
father's obvious favorite. But then I could not
imagine being hated; life was good and I was
loved.

East Anglia is a beautiful place of far hori-
zons and close-up pools. In summer it is car-
peted with gillyflowers and green moss, forget-
me-nots and violet and butter-and-eggs. There is
a memory in me still, sweet as the ache of love,
of a heron silhouetted against the dawn sky
over the marsh.

That was so very long ago. But sometimes
—it is only yesterday.

My father was Aelfgar, Earl of East Anglia,
controlling the wealthiest and most populous
portion of the land, Northfolk and Southfolk,
that territory still governed under the Danelaw
and able to summon vast numbers of men to follow their thegn. As I grew out of babyhood and
began to swell with the ripenings of a woman,
Emma, my nurse, tried to impress on me the
great importance of my station.

"You will make a rich marriage, little
Edyth!" she often assured me. "The Earl's
daughter will be a sweet plum for a prince or

even greater! You will be chatelaine of a powerful house . . ."

"More powerful than this one?" I asked in
wonder.

Emma's eyes crinkled when she laughed,
and that always made me laugh too. "You can't
begin to imagine!" she said. "There are halls so
vast that all of the Earl Aelfgar's landhold could
fit inside them!"

That had to be a lie. My father's property
was the whole world, except for the western
shires and the sea! I always suspected adults
lied to children, but that made me certain of it.

"I don't want to be a . . . a . . . what you
said!" I told her defiantly. "I want to stay right
here, with my pony and my dogs, and my parents too, of course. If my father is so powerful,
no one can make me leave him if I don't want
to!"

There was a touch of sadness in Emma's
smile then. "My child, the Earl himself will
send you away, and congratulate himself on
having done well."

I had never heard of such betrayal! Furious with Emma, I dashed out of the small
chamber I shared with her and straight into my
mother's arms. The Lady Alveva always
smelled of the spices with which her clothes
were stored, and no matter how hectic our
household her voice remained gentle and soft.

13

"Edyth, childie! What's all this?" She raised my hot little face to study it with her sea-colored eyes.

"Emma says I must go, and my father himself will send me away!"

"Oh, now, I cannot believe she said such a thing!" There was a storm brewing on my lady mother's brow that boded no good for Emma.

"She did! She said I would have to learn to be a shatta-something, and live in a house bigger than our hall, and my father would be glad to get rid of me!"

The anger melted from my mother's face, replaced by a sadly tender smile that looked a lot like Emma's. "Ah, that's what this is about. She was discussing the marriage you will make someday, is that it?"

"Yes, but why do I have to do that? I don't want to do that!" I stamped my foot for emphasis, but the shock of the hard floor on my slippered heel hurt me more than it impressed my mother.

"Each person has a certain value, Edyth," my mother began explaining to me in her most patient voice. "A king is worth thirty thousand thrymsas, which is the penalty owed if he is slain. A ceorl is worth but two hundred and sixty-six thrymsas, which is his value to his thegn as a hard-working freeman. A great earl, like your father, has much value, because he

14

can support his king with men in time of battle, and because he can defend his holdings and all who live on them."

All of this boring talk of "value" made little sense to me, and I could not see what it had to do with my father's sending me away. But I knew better than to interrupt my lady mother; gentle though she was, she would box my ears and send me back to Emma for a thrashing.

"A woman has value as well," she continued, "though it is not reckoned in terms of money. A woman is valuable for the children she can produce and the honor she can bring her husband. And the daughter of a noble house is most valuable, for she brings as her bride-gift the allegiance of her father and all her father's power."

All this talk of grown-up things was making me uncomfortable, and the wool of my shift began to itch. My mother ignored my squirmings.

"Likewise, when a daughter marries, her father hopes to obtain the support of her new husband's family and power. This is how you will repay your father for your siring and your raising, Edyth. You will marry well, and provide him with some strong and useful ally."

At last I began to understand what she was saying, but I was not much pleased by it.

Where, in all this exchange of value, was there to be anything of value to me?

"Do you mean I shall marry some tiresome stranger, and go to live far away, and everybody will be very happy about it but me?" I asked, outraged.

My lady mother tried to reassure me. "Would you call the Earl Aelfgar tiresome? It was my parents' desire that I be married to him to unite our families, and he has always been a good husband to me. I am well fed and finely sheltered, and wherever I go freemen and socmen do me honor. That is greater happiness than most people ever know, Edyth, and I could wish nothing better for you."

Obviously my mother thought I should be grateful for this blighting shadow thrown across my life, but I could not share her opinion. Wrapped in my blankets at night, I viewed the prospect of marriage like a sour fruit bit into by mistake. Growing up did not seem to be a very desirable thing.

Yet in time the woman's body took control of the child's head. As the tides of life began to ebb and flow in me, as my breasts formed and a joy like drunkenness seized me betimes, I began to think of men in strange new ways.

The muscles standing taut in the arms of the Earl's page seemed suddenly beautiful, as

16

if I had never seen them before! The shape of men's limbs in their hose, even the newly husky laugh of my brother Edwin, had an exciting quality about them that both frightened and fascinated me.

"What is happening?" I whispered to myself in the night.

I began to notice that when we had guests at our table, which was frequently for every meal, my lady mother seemed to enjoy herself very much. The men flattered her and offered her choice titbits from their own bowls, and much laughing and winking went on. A delicious kind of by-play took place which my father both noticed and approved, basking in the glow of having a lovely wife. Beauty was legendary in our family; my father's own mother, the Lady Godiva, had set the standard (although the adults spoke of her in whispers when I was near).

The relationship between men and women took on a glamour, a fascination for me, and I began to suspect there were excitements beyond hawking and ponies.

Taking notice of my frequent dreaminess, Emma continued my education. "If you keep your skin fair and don't lose all your teeth, you will bear your prince more children," she advised me. "Men couple more often with honey than with sour milk."

17

"This coupling . . . Does it hurt?"

"You've seen animals coupled, childie. Does it seem to hurt them, or do they seek it gladly?"

I thought on that. "Both it seems. The stallion mounts his mares with joy, but the cats wail and scream in the courtyard!"

"The wailing and screaming is part of it, to be sure; 'tis some creatures' only way of expressing their feelings. But if the coupling were not a pleasure, all living things would not seek it so eagerly."

"But the coupling is just to get children, is it not?" I looked closely at her worn old face, trying to penetrate the mysteries that had begun to intrigue me so much.

Emma looked right past me. She seemed to gaze into some world of her own that I could never share. I felt locked out, the way I did sometimes when my parents' eyes met and a silent language passed between them. They were inside a golden circle from which all else was barred.

"For the daughter of a great house the coupling is to get children, yes," she told me. "But for simple folk like me, it can be done just for the pleasure of the thing. The servant and the ceorl have few enough of life's joys; it is the kindness of God that we can enjoy each other."

One unfairness piled atop another! Could

18

only the peasantry get any pleasure out of coupling?

"If you are very, very fortunate, childie," Emma promised me when I complained, "the man who is given you will be young and lusty and give you much happiness in the marriage bed. And many children too, of course!" she added hastily.

My nightworld began to change. I lay on my pallet, eyes squinched tight, and peopled my chamber with young and lusty boys whose eyes looked at me hotly, the way men looked at my lady mother. I had dreams from which I awoke squirming, my flesh all a-tingle, desperate for my nameless prince to come and claim me.

Looking down the table to me one suppertime my father announced to my mother, "The time has come, Alveva, to put our young filly there on the market. Soon she will be rolling her eyes and twitching her tail, and I shall have to stand a guard outside her chamber!"

I was a little embarrassed by his jesting. I was no mare in heat, and I hated being reminded that I would be bartered like any other piece of property. But that was not to happen, not then. The next messenger who rode into our courtyard was not from a marriage-minded noble.

Spring was quickening the land, turning brown to green again, and I sat on my little stool in the Great Hall, weaving ropes of greenery together to decorate the Maypole. A thudding of hoofs sounded in the road and was greeted by the customary challenge from the warder at the gate. The answer came with a ring of authority. "We are the King's men!" cried a strong voice, "bearing a message from the Witan for the Earl Aelfgar of East Anglia!"

My father and Edwin went to greet them while my mother hurried to order mead and pastries brought for our guests. It was no hardship for me to set aside my garlanding for a while; the task had become tedious as all tasks do to a child near grown, and visitors excited me. Of late I had been thinking overmuch of strange young men riding up our road. The spring wind was full of promise; any traveler might bring magic with him! I smoothed my hair and gown and stood waiting. Waiting.

At length my lady mother returned from the kitchens and looked around in surprise; it was unlike the Earl to stay in the road with guests. Even the servants looked apprehensive. They moved back into the shadows of the hall, as they were wont to do when the jesting became too rough at table. My mother looked round her at them, then put on her "You are well come here" smile and went to the door, her heavy skirts gathered in her hands and her keys jangling at her waist.

She stood for a long moment just inside the doorway, and as I watched, her smile froze on her face. The men's voices did not reach me, but my mother could understand what was being said, and her very posture began to frighten me.

Unable to wait alone, I crept to her side and stared down the steps into the forecourt. My father and older brother were at the foot of the stairs with the steward and a few of the housecarles. Facing them was a small party of the King's men, still mounted on their sweated horses. The obvious leader of the group was tall and fair, with the blunt features of a pure Saxon. His clothes were almost excessively fine, intended to awe the commonfolk, and no man so splendid looking had ridden in at our gate in my memory.

It still shames me to realize that I was so impressed by his appearance I forgot everything else; while my world was being destroyed I was gawking at a velvet tunic and a plumed hat. And part of my mind was not even on the man, but on the possibilities of using that gorgeous plume in my own hairdress!

My mother's moan of anguish broke the spell. I turned to her, and the expression on her face was enough to knock the giddy girlishness right out of me. She shoved me aside and ran down the steps to stand with my father, her hand clinging white-knuckled to his arm. Edwin, usually brash and outspoken, stood quite subdued on my father's other side. His eyes were fixed on the face of the man with the plume; they all listened with dreadful attention to the herald's final words.

"Therefore, by order of the Witan for Our Sovereign Edward, in this Year of Our Lord 1055, let it be known to all men that Aelfgar, son of Leofric of Mercia, is outlawed from this day, is relieved of his Earldom and must give over immediately to his Sovereign Lord all his holdings and possessions."

Even to a girl that was plain enough. Outlawed! In our own courtyard, embraced by familiar walls and with the fens growing green all around us, we were suddenly dispossessed! The bluebells and primroses piled in baskets to trim the Maypole were no longer mine. The crusty loaves of bread in the ovens, my dear little merlin on her perch in the falconry, perhaps even the contents of my clothes chest —all of these belonged now to the King!

I had missed hearing the charge, but I understood the sentence all too clearly. The sight of my father's grayed face and my mother's stricken eyes made it unbearable; I twisted away from the door and ran mindless to my chamber.

It was just a small room, let into the timbered wall of the hall, but it held much that was dear to me. My goosedown pallet with its warm woolen blankets; the carved clothes chest that had contained my lady mother's dowry; the combs and trinkets and pots of creams that had begun to interest me more than children's games. My chamber had no door to protect me, only a woven hanging suspended from a rod. Fear and shame came right in with me and attacked me as I lay huddled on my bed.

The daughter of a great earl was a safe and protected person, with servants and clothes and a way of life made comfortable by her father's power.

But what could happen to the daughter of an outlaw? We would have to leave the fens, leave England itself, flee to some strange and distant place, be poor and humble . . . It was too horrible!

"Disgraced!" I cried to myself. "Outlawed! How could he do this to me? It's time for the May Day, young men will be coming to dance with me, a prince might have offered for me . . . Oh, Father, how could you do this!"

It was so enormous I could scarce conceive of it. The only scandal in our family, at least the only one I had ever heard about, had been caused by my grandmother. A lady famous for her beauty, she was wed to the great Earl Leofric of Mercia, and was much admired by noble and vassal alike. When Leofric levied an excessively heavy tax on his subjects, my grandmother, the Lady Godiva, took their side. In jest, he told her he would abolish the tax on the day she rode naked through the town.

My grandmother must have been as stubborn as she was beautiful. To the Earl's dismay, she took his joke as a challenge and announced that she would indeed, ride naked through Coventry, covered only by the fall of her unbound hair. She insisted that that would be enough protection for a righteous woman, but my realistic grandfather was well aware that even the lightest breeze would lift the red-gold locks and give the townsfolk a view that only he was entitled to enjoy.

So he decreed that all citizens of Coventry should stay inside their cottages that day, with their shut-doors tightly fastened, on penalty of having their eyes put out. Grandmother made her ride, only one or two imprudent souls defied the decree and suffered the consequences, and the Earl Leofric rescinded the tax. But the Lady Godiva was still the subject of whispers in our household, and I could never decide whether to be proud of her or ashamed.

And how should I feel about my own father? To be named in the Witan, the King's own council, as an outlaw! Why was such a thing done? And how could a mere girl-child ever hope to learn the truth of it? If a man dishonors his family and his name, do his children still owe him allegiance?

The questions were too difficult for me. Emma's training was to make me a wife and mother, but at whose knee could I learn to be an outcast?

There was no resisting the law of the Witan. They could make kings, by Saxon law, and unmake earls just as certainly. The Witan was the true power at Winchester, for saintly old King Edward was a gentle man who laid too light a hand on the reins of authority. If the Witan had outlawed my father there was no appeal, no escaping the sentence.

Trembling, I lay on my bed and tried to see into the altered future. (How many times since has that happened to me? My whole life is turned around in the wink of an eye, and nothing is as it was before. It is a curse, though Griffith would laugh and call it a challenge.)

At last Emma came in with my candle. Dear Emma, nurse to me when I was small, friend to me when I was tall. Childhood rhymes speak truly. She sat by me and put her hand on my tumbled hair.

25

"Have they forgotten you, childie? Here you are in the dark, all worn out with crying and without a bite of supper in you! Saints' blood, has the world gone awry?"

"Oh, Emma!" I wailed. "It has, it has!"

"Childie, you must learn something important, and now is a goodly time to do it. When the world is knocked heels over head, it always rights itself in time. If it is raining on you, there are still places where the sun shines, and it will shine on you again. Never give in to despair, my lady; all you must do is go into the sunshine. Find the place where it is."

That sounded like a lot of empty cheer to me. "How can I, Emma? My father is outlawed, we are all disgraced forever, all that we have is forfeit to the King!"

"Whatever your father has done may be a disgrace to him, childie, but not to you. Only you can disgrace yourself."

It was all very well for her to talk, but what could a mere servant understand of disgrace or shame? Pah!

Emma was no help at all; she could only talk about things getting better when it was obvious they would only get worse. When I could lie in my chamber no longer without knowing what was happening, I wrapped a cloak about me and went to the hall. A velvet cloak, it was. I remember wondering if it was the last velvet cloak I would ever have.

Edwin sat alone at table, where supper had been served as I hid in my chamber. If my parents had eaten anything there was no sign of it; they were gone and the table was clean in front of their stools. My younger brother was absent as well, so Edwin sat in solitary splendor, gnawing a mutton joint. Disaster had not ruined his appetite.

He glanced at me from beneath the tangled ledge of his brows. "Most of the supper is gone."

"So I can see. No matter, my stomach's as hard as a stone. Edwin, how can you eat now?"

His gray eyes were as cold as the fens in winter, and I do not think he was being intentionally amusing when he replied, "But I always eat now. It's suppertime."

"Don't toy with me! You know what I mean!"

Edwin wiped his mouth on his sleeve. "You mean to work yourself up to a temper, that's what you mean. Father may find it charming, but it won't get you anywhere with me."

One of the torches sputtered and spat a flaming particle of pitch to the floor.

Brothers are intended by God as a sort of

plague, like floods and locusts. I tried to keep my temper, congratulating myself on the effort. "Please, just tell me what's happening!"

"Very little, really. The servants will scarcely bother to stir themselves from the kitchen and stillroom, Morkere is off somewhere vomiting, and our parents have gone to the buttery to quarrel. So I am left with you, like a boil on my nose." He cut a great hunk of cheese and stuffed it into his face.

"Edwin, I have to understand this! Why is the Earl outlawed?"

"You did not hear?" He looked astonished.

"Not all of it. Just the part about the banishment, that I heard. And that we were dispossessed. But why?"

At that moment the manshell of him cracked, just a little, and I caught a glimpse of the frightened child within. He grew pale and darted nervous glances into the shadow spaces between the sputtering torches. I came as close then as I ever would to loving my elder brother.

"The charge was treason," he said hoarsely.

"That can't be!"

"The Witan found him guilty. Of making treasonous statements in public, saying the

King is unfit to govern and the Danes insult the English throne by planning to have one of the Godwines crowned when King Edward dies.

There was the kernel of the thing, and I began to understand. Since babyhood I had heard my father at table arguing the same point. He and my lady mother were of the old, pure Saxon blood, which had been the nobility in the east before the Danish warriors came to our shores. My grandmother Godiva was of the House of Alfred, called the Great. Bitter was the resentment of the Saxons against the Danish kings who had ruled our country for three generations, until the death of King Hardecnut in 1042.

Then a Saxon of Alfred's blood again assumed the throne. But he was no mighty warrior in the old tradition. King Edward was an ascetic, a man who wore hair shirts beneath his royal robe and spent too much time in prayer and pious acts. The real rulers of England were still the Danes, and the Danish-supported Earl Godwine of Wessex raised the most powerful voice at court.

The Saxons, who had long mistrusted the Earl Godwine and his Danish wife Gytha, went about with their hearts in their hose. My father had become a focal point for their grumblings, and our Great Hall was a place where the deeds of Alfred and Aethelwulf were sung again and again on long winter nights.

To a child there is enchantment in the telling of old tales, and I secretly enjoyed thinking of myself as a real princess of England. Never, never did I imagine overthrowing the King, nor did I think my father and his friends meant to do such a thing. But how can children know what big folk mean?

It was not quite as bad as my worst imaginings. True, by sun-come-up most of our servants had vanished, melted away like snow by the heat of our disgrace. But we were not thrown into the marshes to starve. We were allowed to take our clothing and beds, and my lady mother kept some of her jewels and her dower chest. Emma and a few others remained faithful, including the Earl's grizzled squire Owain. They had been together many years and the bonds between them were close. Owain was a Briton from Wales, the mysterious mountains to the west, and when he spoke his native tongue it sounded like water gurgling over stones.

It was Owain who rode down the coast and arranged a ship for us. He knew of men in Wales, and across the sea in Ireland, who would be inclined to be generous to an enemy of the growing power of the Godwines. My father

was determined to resist banishment, and I
was glad of it. I heard him question Owain
long and long about the fighting ability of the
Welshmen. A proud, strong man was the Earl
Aelfgar; if he had meekly accepted outlawry
for all of us, I could never have forgiven him.

Within the week we were boarding a ship
to sail to Ireland.

The ship was a merchant vessel, a creaking thing that smelled of wet wood and rotting fish. It gave me such a sea-belly I was
afraid I would not die, but soon that passed
and I was able to stand at the rail with my
father. My mother was so shaken as to be no
use at all. One moment she raged at him for
his foolishness, the next she cried and clung
to him and moaned of her losses. (Though in
truth she had lost but little. She had her health
and her family, even some of her personal trea-
sures. I have seen much more loss than that,
since.)

Edwin and Morkere stayed apart from my
father as much as they could on the cramped
ship. Already they seemed to be drawing away
from him, building shells around themselves so
they could remain indifferent to the pain of
others.

My father planned to leave us with sup-
porters in Ireland while he and Owain traveled
to the court of the Welsh Prince. Aelfgar,

former Earl of East Anglia, would there do homage to the Welshman in return for men-at-arms.

The thought of my father journeying to that wild land was frightening, but even more so was the idea of his raising an army against the King and the Godwines. Nor could I understand why the Welsh Prince would be willing to join him in such a venture!

"Girls are taught little of history, as it is not necessary for them to know the past," my father explained. "But the telling of it will help pass the voyage. Your sea-belly is all gone, is it?"

"Oh, yes, sire!" I answered proudly, knowing full well that Edwin and Morkere were still wretchedly ill, somewhere below. Ha!

"Well done. So . . . first you must understand that the Welsh will never accept English rule, although the King longs to unite them with England."

"Why not?"

"For the same reason that Danish rule is unacceptable to us Saxons. We were here first. The Saxon ruled England before the Dane, but even before the Saxon was the Celt. Once all this land was theirs. They fought against the Roman invasion a thousand years ago."

This was astonishing news to me! I could not hold in my mind the sum of a hundred years. People who lived, and fought, and died

32

. . . a thousand years ago? They were farther from me than the moon in the sky!

"What happened to them, those Celts, when the Romans came?"

"They fought bravely, but they had only skins for armor and clubs for weapons. The Romans carried spears and rode fast horses; they drove the Celts from the heart of the land, back into the wildness of the mountains. They settled there and called themselves the Cymry. In the old Celtic tongue that means Sweet Singers. Through all the years they have lived there, in the land we know as Wales."

I do not like the way men have of talking all around a point. "But why should the Welsh help you now?"

Like my lady mother, he took his own time and would not be hurried. "A great disaster occurred in Rome, a mighty nation very far away, and the Roman soldiers went home. Then the Cymry came down from their mountains, only to meet the first Saxons coming to settle here from Germany and the Low Countries. The Celts and Saxons fought mightily for many years. In the monasteries there are still parchments written in those times by one Gildas, a historian. He tells of the Celtic hero Arthur, who drove the Saxons from England at the Battle of Badon.

"When Arthur died, however, the Saxons

returned, and at last conquered through their great numbers. The Cymry returned to their mountains."

"I'm sure I'm very sorry for them," I said, dutifully, as he seemed to expect. "But that explains nothing!"

My father gave me the kind of look men reserve for ignorant women—when they have kept them ignorant and are annoyed by it. "Of course it does, Edyth! The Cymry—the Welsh —still feel that England is rightfully theirs! They may well be persuaded to join in an overthrow of Edward and the Godwines, in hopes that they will be able to snatch the throne themselves."

"Oh," I said. Standing on a storm-tossed ship, looking at a cold black sea and rushing forward into the unknown, I could not be very sympathetic with all these people who plotted to control England. All I could imagine desiring was a bed that stayed still, and a drink of water that did not smell of fish.

Ireland

IN CRAMPED AND SMELLY quarters we sailed along the Saxon Shore, around the southern coast of England and westward to that desolate point the sailors call Land's End.

With good reason, I thought. I stood on the tossing deck, my feet braced against the roll of the ship, and listened to the sailors' cries and the endless creaking of the sails. For once I was most glad to be a female. The sea life was not for me; I could find nothing about it

35

that I liked except the occasional exhilaration of a spanking salt wind in my face. But everything was so splintery—decks, walls, tables—and the noises of the living ship went on and on.

How do men rest in a world where nothing ever rests?

"Do you like the sea?" I asked Owain once, catching him as he emptied the Earl's slop jar over the side.

"In Wales we live between the mountains and the sea; if you don't like one you must learn to care for the other. But I prefer the mountains." He flipped the slops over the rail with an expert twist of his wrist, stepping aside to avoid the backward spray as the wind caught it.

"Are the mountains quiet, Owain?"

"Tomorrow we'll turn northward, I think, and soon you'll see them for yourself, my lady. They are quiet, I suppose, but it is the silence of sleeping giants. Not like this rowdy bitch, the ocean!" He waved his free hand at the dark and tossing water.

I did see Wales, rising out of the sea in a glory of lifted stone. The gentle swells of the marshes had left me unprepared for such sudden, savage beauty. Wales seemed to climb right out of the sea and reach for the heavens, holding up the sky on emerald-topped shoulders.

"It's beautiful!" I breathed, enraptured, to my lady mother. "Do come and see!"

"It's a barbarous place," she moaned, "and we are going to another one. Bring me a cloth for my head!"

We put in and exchanged much cargo at a place called Aberystwyth, on the Bay of Cardigan. Owain tried without success to teach me how to pronounce Aberystwyth, and at last gave up with laughter. "The Cymry do not speak the language so much as they sing it, my lady, and your song is a squawk. I think one must be born in this land to master the tongue."

"But it sounds so lovely when you say it!"

"Only to some, my lady," he shook his head sadly. "Only to some."

The last and most dangerous part of our voyage was straight across the Irish Sea. We were assaulted by huge waves that smashed against our ship in solid walls, until Morkere screamed with fear and even the Earl looked pale. Buffeted hour after hour by water and wind, I thought never to reach Ireland alive.

When even Emma had begun to despair, of a once the water sweetened, and one of the sailors came to tell us we were putting in at the mouth of the River Liffey. Edwin, my father and I went up on deck for our first look at Ireland.

The River Liffey flows past Dublin town, and the harbor is an exotic place. Voyagers from all over the world must put in there—we saw ships and flags of every description. Edwin was most excited by the tall dragon ships of the Vikings, needing only the elaborately carved heads which the warriors fastened to the prow before battle to turn them into monsters from a nurse's bed-tale.

"Dublin is called 'Ath Cliath na cloc'— Dublin of the Bells," the Earl told us, "and it is through the good offices of the Earl Leofric that we have sanctuary here. See that you behave yourselves, both of you, as the children of a noble Saxon house, and always treat our hosts with the utmost courtesy!"

I had no intention of doing otherwise, although with Edwin no one could be too sure. In East Anglia I had begun to be a woman, but in this strange and frightening new place I was glad to go back to being an obedient child again, thankful I had elders to tell me how to behave.

Some sort of official personage came to greet us, and with much bowing to the Earl and excessive reverence all around, he got mother and me into a rather primitively fashioned litter. The rest of our party were mounted on shaggy Norse ponies with very rough gaits; Morkere could be heard whining all the way.

We went through narrow streets, past houses of clay and rude circular huts of wickerwork. The better buildings had windows with shut-doors, but all had roofs of thatch. Some of the houses were washed with white lime; some were painted in shades of blue and yellow and ocher. People along the streets stared at us with open curiosity, as we did them, for there was a great difference in the apparel of a Saxon earl and that of Irish commonfolk.

The women wore a simple dress of wool or linen; the men, short tunics and an odd little skirt. Strangest of all was their hair. Both sexes dressed their hair in thick plaits with metal balls at the ends. I could not help remembering my brief infatuation with the idea of braided hair and a gorgeous plume.

"I'll leave you with the Lady Maeve, cousin to Dermot Mac Mael-nambo, King of Dublin and Leinster," the Earl had told us. "The Irish have kings all over their land and are much divided. This same Dermot once gave shelter to our enemy, young Harold Godwine, but it seems he's ready enough to give us welcome now."

Irish hospitality is a thing of such legend that even in East Anglia we had heard of it.

Doubtless Dermot was amused to offer sanctuary to both sides of warring factions. Irish humor can be hard to fathom.

The Lady Maeve greeted us graciously in her cousin's name. Her house was of timber, neither as large nor as fine as our hall, but I saw straightway that she had many beautiful things. Her table was set with goblets of glass, the first I ever saw, and Morkere broke his on the first night. He threw it from the table because he did not like the strange taste of the food. The Earl looked at my mother, my mother looked at Owain, and Morkere was taken outside somewere.

There were cups and plates of silver, knives of staghorn and squares of fine linen just for wiping our mouths! That was what Edwin liked best; he minced about and dabbed his at his lips until I wanted to hit him. "Can't you behave yourself, Edwin?" I demanded of him quickly after that first supper.

"I am behaving myself, sister dear! I am learning to adjust to the customs of the country just as quickly as I can and I would urge you to do the same."

"You're not adjusting, you're just making fun of them!"

"Perhaps they don't know that," he tossed off, and I saw that the cruel streak in my brother was strengthening with age.

Our first Irish meal was unlike the roasts and boiled meat we were accustomed to at home. It was also much better than the vile stuff given us aboard ship, though we had not eaten overmuch of that! Cooks in white caps and aprons of linen served us trays heaped with wheat cakes, bowls of oatmeal and boiled eggs. There was warm milk still a-foam from the cow, and honey scented with clover and thyme. Maeve and her retinue were delighted with a joint of some stringy, herbed meat, but I could not stomach it. Only my father ate a goodly portion, as the laws of hospitality required.

When we could eat no more we were sent to bed, with Emma and the boys' body-servants to tend our needs. The Earl and his Lady remained talking before the fire with the Lady Maeve.

This fire was not on a raised hearth in the center of the hall, as is our custom, but set against the wall. The smoke of the burning peat which the Irish use for fuel was left to find its own way out through the thatch of the roof. As a result, the walls were sooted black, and everything was permeated with that pungent odor. To this day I have only to close my eyes and summon the smell of peatfire, and all of Ireland comes back to me.

That night we slept between linen sheets, with embroidered coverlets in heathen patterns. Not yet accustomed to sleeping in unfamiliar beds, I had Emma lie with me and hold me.

"Emma . . . ?"

"Sssshhhh, childie. Go to sleep."

"But I want to know! Emma, is my father not disgraced here? We are being treated so honorably I do not know if the Irish think my father good or bad!"

Emma shifted her bulk in the bed. Sheets were a novelty, and I do not think she liked them. "Quit fretting what folk think of your father, my lady. Haven't you been raised as a noble? That means you are proud of your many great ancestors who did noble deeds; your strength must come from them."

My lady mother was a noble, too, and her strength seemed to have deserted her completely the day her husband was named an outlaw.

"Where does your strength come from, Emma?"

There was a long silence. Then, "Myself, I suppose. That's all folk like me have."

I would give a lot of thought to that later. But it did not answer my question that night. "What about me, Emma? Can I be proud here, as I was proud at home?"

Her voice scolded me. "You can be proud anywhere, my lady! You are Edyth of the line of Alfred; no one can take that away from you!"

Satisfied, I slept.

The Earl Aelfgar sailed for Wales within the week, feeling certain that he had acquired some Irish allies. The rest of us, save only Owain, who went with my father, remained in Ireland all that year. We were not shamed in that green and rainy land, but treated as honored guests and made very comfortable. In some ways, the noble Irish live with more luxury than we Saxons. Yet in other ways that are surprisingly coarse.

The Lady Maeve could not dress her own hair, never having done so in her life. Each morning she sat before a fine mirror of polished metal while her maidservant combed her hair with a jeweled comb taken from a special comb bag of soft leather embossed with gold. She put red powder on her cheeks, blue upon her eyelids, and rubbed her teeth with a hazel twig dipped in salt. When her toilet was completed to her satisfaction, she went out to the stinking cow byre to milk the cow.

I thought the Lady Maeve very old, for she was at least as old as my mother. In truth, she must have been about five and thirty, which age does not seem so great to me now. She was very tall and deep-bosomed, her greatest beauty being a mane of heavy hair the color of

43

dark red oak leaves. She had surpassing
strength for a woman; I saw her move a huge
chest across the room when her own steward
could not. In the evening, when we were oft-
times entertained by a storyteller, I came to
recognize her for the heroine of many an Irish
tale.

The Celts have a special attitude about
their women. In Irish tales the heroines are always beautiful and courageous queens. In Scot
Land, I have heard, the fashion is for women to
be beautiful and mightily proud. In Wales,
women besung by the bards must be beautiful
and delicately tender. (I, the Saxon, am none
of these things; yet when my Griffith loved me
I was all of them!)

Those months in Ireland were a learning
time for me. In my ignorance I had thought
all people other than my own uncivilized,
barbaric. My lady mother thought that and
never changed her opinion. Yet in Ireland I
found a civilization so ancient, even the bards
could not say when it began. When nothing but
birds and fishes owned East Anglia, the Irish
already made gold jewelry so fine it was carried to every distant land. Laws they had, and
the old Druidic religion, and a land so rich no
man need go hungry.

I had been taught those things deemed all
a lady need know: sewing, weaving, the use of

herbs and spices and the brewing of mead, how to tend the sick and do honor to guests. But Maeve's children could read! I swear it is true; not only her four strapping sons, but even her two daughters could look at a written thing and name every word! Even her steward, a savage-looking fellow with black hair and shoulders like a porter—that man could read! It was a thing so widely accepted that no one ever asked me if I could or not. Fortunately.

One bluelit afternoon, with rain pattering on the thatch, Maeve's son Brian and I sat before the fire with the chessboard balanced on our knees. Chess is a game that has all of Ireland in thrall, from the noblest household to the poorest hovel. Where they learned it I know not, but it is a constant occupation, and many cattle and sheep are wagered on the outcome of the battle between the courts of Black and White.

Brian was a forward fellow, letting his leg press against mine every chance I gave him. And I gave him a few. I was doing so well with the game that I became suspicious, for the thing was uncommonly complicated, and I knew I had not learned it well enough to beat him.

"Brian, are you letting me win?"

He gave me a wide-eyed stare with big blue eyes like his mother's. "Why would I do that, lady?"

"Courtesy to a guest . . . ?"

He laughed, but with a false sound to it. "Never would I do that, Lady Edyth! It is not courteous, but rude, to allow your opponent to win. That would insult him."

For some reason my temper flared. "You lie! You are letting me win, so by your own words you are insulting me!"

He raised a hand in protest, but I was a-shake with excitement and would not give him a chance. "You insult me in other ways as well, you knave! You stare at me too boldly when you think I'm not looking, you find too many excuses for laying hands on me . . . !"

As I leaped to my feet to give emphasis to my words, the chessboard clattered to the floor. The cunningly wrought knights and bishops and yeomen scattered everywhere, as many a real court has done, and the hapless white king rolled straight into the fire. As many a king has done.

Quarrels among the young were taken lightly, but the careless destruction of a family treasure was cause for severe reprimand. It fell to my lady mother to chastise me.

I have said little about my lady mother, for, in truth, there is little to say. She was a handsome woman with wheaten hair, but was so quiet and deferential to my father that she had little color in our household. After the

Earl's banishment she became timid and nervous, slow to speak and quick to cry. Her cowing encouraged my brothers, to disobey her openly. Lacking the Earl at her side, she became the shadow without the sun.

After supper she came to me, twisting her hands nervously in her skirt as she did much. "You have injured the ancient law of hospitality, Edyth," she said in her soft voice, "so you must give up a treasure yourself."

In truth I had little, only my own jewelry and clothes. Already I was thinking in terms of the dowry I hoped to need, and nothing could be spared. I answered as best I could, telling her my possessions could not be spared to replace a rather foolish toy.

Her sad face grew sadder still. "I see you are selfish as well as bad-tempered. You are of an age when the blood runs hot, so mayhap you will outgrow your temper. But the vice of selfishness can ride you all your life. I feel shame that the daughter of Aelfgar would begrudge one of her trinkets to someone who sheltered us in our trouble."

What she said was painfully true, but I would not have her think so of me. I used the only weapon in my defense.

"Lady Mother, by year's end we will be restored to the earldom! Father is sworn to that; even now he raises troops to win back what is rightfully ours! When we go home I will be of an age to marry—indeed, I am now. So you see, I cannot give up the few valuables I possess. I will need them, and many more, for I must go to my husband well dowered!"

The poor lady could not summon the heart even to insist; she just left me alone. Later, I saw that she had given her own favorite brooch to the Lady Maeve, and I felt ashamed. My outburst of temper had cooled as quickly as it flared, and all I had to show for it was my mother's reproach and my own embarrassment. In the sanctuary of my bed I reflected on the folly of rash actions, and the wisdom to be found in a gentle demeanor. It was as Emma said, only I could bring shame on myself.

On the day next I sought out Brian and apologized. The words stuck in my throat, which made me seem more meek than I felt, but Brian appeared pleased. He accepted my plea with grace and was charming to me all that day.

Another lesson learned, thought I. Men prefer soft women. Life is more pleasant when we are more pliable. So.

After that I took care to see that there were no more outbursts of temper, and if a rebellious spirit flared up in me, I nursed it in the quiet of my own bed and did not inflict it

upon others. My brothers behaved otherwise
and seemed to be always in trouble.

Where would I be today, had I not learned
to be compliant and yielding?

We were well into the season of Christ
Mass when word came at last of the Lord
Aelfgar. The Lady Maeve and her steward were
in the town, Edwin was lurking somewhere
around the docks, and my lady mother and I
sat in the late afternoon gloom, mending
clothes. Our wardrobes were beginning to show
signs of much wear, but our position was
thought too precarious to allow the purchase of
new cloth. I was thinking bitterly that soon I
would be dressing in rough cottage wool when
we heard a knock at the door.

No member of the household would knock!
We exchanged nervous glances; then I leaped
to my feet and raced to the door.

In the muddy forecourt a dark and handsome man waited with perfect composure,
though his clothes were common and stained.
When he saw my face he broke into a radiant
smile. In his transformed features I saw a like-
ness to my father's Owain—our visitor was a
Welshman! He proved me right by beginning
to speak in a musical voice that tripped nim-
bly over the Saxon words and turned them
into something like song. (How sweetly they
sing, the Cymry!)

"Greetings to the house of Maeve Mac Mael-nambo, and the compliments of my prince to the family of Aelfgar, Earl of East Anglia!"

I heard my mother gasp behind me. Even our Irish hosts had not referred directly to my father as Earl of East Anglia. Flustered, I bade our visitor enter without asking either his name or rank. My mother remembered her manners even if I did not; in a twinkling she had him seated at the hearth, a servant fetching him beer and cakes, and was questioning him eagerly.

"You come from the Prince, in Wales?"

"Yes, my lady, I just arrived this day after a most unpleasant voyage in a dreadful Irish coracle. My Lord Griffith, son of the Prince Llywelyn, sent me at utmost speed to inform you of the victory of his forces and those of the Earl Aelfgar. My Lord Griffith feared you would be distressed and worried, and he would not leave ladies in that condition."

My mother and I exchanged glances, and her eyebrows were lifted almost into her hair. Such consideration for women was not a common thing in our acquaintance, even among the nobility. What sort of man was this Griffith that he would dispatch a messenger all the way across the water to reassure his ally's family?

"My good fellow," began my lady mother, "I do not believe I know your name . . . ?"

"I am Madog son of Gwyn, my lady, and servitor to the Court of Gwynedd." He spoke with great pride, his chin held high, not at all as one of our servants would have spoken. I felt some confusion; was our messenger of noble breeding, then? (It was only in Wales that I learned that all Welsh speak that way. Like the Irish, the Cymry believe that every man is a king. It makes it difficult to determine station.)

Madog began straightway with an accounting of all that had happened since my father had arrived at Holyhead with a force of eighteen Viking dragonships whose alliance he had won!

The monks at Holyhead had arranged guides to take my father to the Welsh Prince's court. The dragonships with their cargo of fighting men sailed on to the port of Caernarvon and were disembarked there. Thus it was that, in a few days, the Earl and a very sizable complement of men-at-arms arrived at the court of Gwynedd. The Prince greeted them with hospitality, even lodging the Vikings with his own servitors. He listened to Aelfgar's story sympathetically, although he could not refrain from commenting many times on the treachery

51

of the English court and on the barbarism of the Godwines in particular.

How odd it was that the Prince of the wild Welsh thought Saxons and Danes barbaric!

"But how did the Earl come by the Viking dragonships?" I could not resist asking.

Madog chuckled. "I understand that the Vikings prefer fighting to food and drink. The Earl recruited them right here in Dublin harbor, with a promise of much bloodletting and a share of the spoils."

"But they will be fighting against their own kind!" my lady mother protested. "It was the Danes who spoke against my husband in the Witan and had him outlawed!"

Madog looked pityingly at us women, who could not understand simple warfare. "Men always fight most savagely against their own kind; it is easier to stir up grievances against someone you know."

The Earl had put his proposition to Prince Griffith, and they agreed to join forces "after the Lord Aelfgar offered sufficient inducements," according to Madog. The joint force set out with little delay. It was agreed that the most vulnerable target, that which would hurt the English most, was the town of Hereford. Before the Earl Ralph's family had risen from dinner in his castle, the village was attacked. The raiders pillaged the town, putting it all to the torch, and even sacked the pretentious cathedral of the Bishop Athelstan, an outspoken foe of the Welsh. By daylight on the twenty-fifth of October, a train loaded with booty and captives was making its unchallenged way back to the safety of Wales.

The horror of the English court was easy to imagine. A new Welsh uprising, led by a Prince with a reputation for war and an exiled Saxon Earl who obviously still possessed power! Harold Godwine went straightway to Gloucester in the King's name.

He was able to put together a fighting force and march them westward, but the hastily assembled English fyrd was ignorant about mountain warfare and could never even get close to Griffith. At last Harold settled for refortifying the ruined town of Hereford and went to Winchester to advise King Edward to negotiate for peace.

The Lady Maeve returned just in time to order torches lit and hear the last of Madog's recital. The last, and the best.

"And so, it is my happy duty to inform you that a treaty has been concluded. My Lord Griffith is given all that border land which has long been in dispute, and the Lord Aelfgar is restored to his title and holdings!"

So long had we waited for these words, we could not believe we had heard aright. Madog had to repeat himself twice before my mother would accept it, then she burst into such a storm of weeping we were all frightened for her. Poor Madog was most perplexed to see his glad tidings merit such a reaction, and Maeve was distraught—as well she might be, now that we were suddenly made persons of great importance once more. Only when a scented linen had been applied to my mother's temples did she regain some composure. By that time the Lady Maeve had become so solicitous of her guest's health that her hovering was making us all nervous.

Then Edwin and Morkere returned and the news had to be repeated for them. With each telling I became more convinced that it was true—and also that there was something still to tell. The Lady Maeve set out a splendid supper for us and even brought in a paid minstrel, which showed that she was as unsure of Madog's status as I. When we were all fat with eating—I found my appetite much improved— I drew Madog aside to question him about my father's safety.

"The Earl Aelfgar is truly well, my lady," he assured me. "Not one wound did he receive. Only one of his Vikings was killed, and he was knifed by a wench he raped in Hereford."

I chose to ignore that lurid detail. "I rejoice that my lord father is well, and I thank your Prince for sending you to tell us the good news."

He smiled a little ruefully. How I enjoyed the way his dark eyes admired me! "I must confess, my lady, that being the herald of victory was not my only mission."

Aha! I was right! "And what other have you?"

"Your safe conduct, Lady Edyth."

I was startled. "My safe conduct! Do you not intend to provide us all safe conduct back to East Anglia?"

"No, my lady, I understand the Earl Aelfgar is sending a ship for his wife and sons that will take them to England. I am to bring you to my Lord Griffith."

I went cold with shock. "What are you saying?"

His smile became gentler, a little amused. "Your father has affianced you to wed my Prince, in return for his support. That was the sufficient inducement I mentioned. You will accompany me to Wales to marry Griffith ap Llywelyn, prince of Wales, King of Gwynedd, Powys, Deheubarth and Morgannwg."

And the unfamiliar names rolled from his tongue like a peal of bells.

Wales

THE HOUSEHOLD was thrown into disarray by Madog's news. We had gone from being poor to rich again within the length of a cat's tail; it meant a lot of adjustments for everyone.

The Lady Maeve had always treated us well, I thought, but after hearing the news of the Earl's restoration she made such an effort on our behalf that her previous hospitality seemed slight by comparison. It was interesting to observe the difference.

"Power," Edwin commented, "is most no-

table in the effect it has on others. For myself,
I feel exactly the same as before, but I seem
to appear much improved to the girls of the
household!"

As my lady mother and the boys readied
themselves for the return to East Anglia, I felt
myself set apart from my family for the first
time in my life. There were preparations to
make for me, too—extensive ones. Although in
actuality I hardly possessed a thing, I had to
be properly dowered for my Welsh Prince.
Seamstresses were hired, bolts of cloth bought,
and finery appeared as if by magic to be heaped
into the dower chest. The Lady Maeve gave of
her finest goods, though I have no doubt she
expected to be repaid in still finer coin by the
Earl Aelfgar.

I found myself confronted with a whole
new bag of fears that I had never faced before. It is one thing to dream of a prince,
dreams being your own creation and easily controlled. But to face the actuality of the thing
is something else. The child in me wanted
to go back to the safety of the dream, the
adult in me was extremely fearful of the coming reality. How to imagine a man, a place, a
completely unfamiliar life?

Worst of all, there was no one to confide
in. Emma was of the opinion that I was very
fortunate and should count my blessings.

"Then you go in my place," I offered her sulkily.

"Not me, childie! I'm no use to a prince!"

"You should be glad of the chance to start a new life on your own," Edwin commented. "I have no doubt that our lord father will continue to get himself involved in these skirmishes with the Godwines, and it will only mean more trouble. You'll be well out of it."

I doubted that, since it seemed Prince Griffith was our father's chief ally. But there was never any point in arguing with Edwin; his opinions were begotten in stone and only grew more unyielding.

I took my doubts to my lady mother. "How shall I behave in Wales? Are they so very different from us? Will they like me?"

She stared at me as if I had no right to ask such a question. "You will behave as the daughter of a noble Saxon, that is enough. They are all barbarians, anyway; it matters not what they think of you."

"But what about the Prince?" I persisted. Will he like me?"

"Lord deliver us from plague!" my mother exclaimed. "He agreed to take you, didn't he? So I suppose he shall like you well enough, you're young and comely and you can bear him sons."

I realized I was annoying her, but I had to

58

ask anyway. "What if I don't like him? What if he's gross and mean and treats me badly?"

Her eyes were pitying when she looked at me, but there was no answer in them. "I told you before, Edyth. You are the daughter of a Saxon Earl, you come from an old and honored lineage. You will behave always in keeping with your station. Now let us have no more of this nursery whining!" With her own restoration to being a person of circumstance, my lady mother had regained much of the backbone she had seemed to lose.

That was another thing to ponder. Was courage and dignity a pose, at least for some? A mask they assumed when they were unchallenged, a mask behind which a frightened child might hide? If adults could hide like that, what about me? Behind what mask could I conceal my own fears and cowardices?

A ship was being sent for my family the way we had come to Ireland, down the Saxon Shore. So it would be many weeks before my mother and brothers left the household of the Lady Maeve. For me time was growing short. As soon as I was properly prepared and dowered, I was to leave straightway for Wales with Madog.

How hard it was to go! How dear each familiar face suddenly became; even haughty

Edwin and sullen Morkere were at once magicked into my sweet and beloved little brothers whom I might never see again! Perhaps I had misjudged them. I could even forgive Edwin, and chuckle to myself, when I heard him boasting outrageously, "My sister is going to marry the King of Wales, you know. She will be more important than anyone in Ireland!"

When our ship at last nosed out into the harbor and I set my face to the east, I felt that I was leaving my own self behind on the shore, like the skin of a locust split asunder.

That trip was different from the one to Ireland. Now I was the important personage on board, and I saw that it made quite a difference. Foods were specially prepared to tempt my appetite, and even my Emma was treated almost like a lady. Madog seemed always to be hovering at the rim of my vision, anxious to be of service. It was "my lady this" and "my lady that" and "Please advise the Captain that my lady wishes . . ." I had of a once acquired much authority; I was a person to be pleased and feared!

I began to understand in some small measure why it is that men seek power.

Then I stood at the rail and saw the coast of Wales rise from the ocean once more, beautiful and forbidding, and my heart pounded in my throat unbearably.

We sailed past Anglesey and Llandudno, heading for the mouth of the river the Welsh folk called Clwyd. Our destination was the Castle of Rhuddlan, Griffith's foremost stronghold. The bitter wind of the Irish Sea became sweeter as we neared landfall, and the gulls wheeling to meet us sang a haunting song that seemed different from their raucous cries in Dublin harbor.

"They feel the hwyl come upon them," Madog told me.

The what? How could I ever learn this language?

Madog was patient. "The 'hoo-ill,' the spirit of the land. It is a pride and a glory, my lady; it affects every living thing in the land of the Cymry."

"Perhaps it doesn't apply to Saxons," I remarked.

It was not a bustling city where we cast anchor; it seemed more a poor fishing village. The coastline was not so rugged here; as we approached I could see that the land beyond appeared to be a great upland plateau. A huddle of modest huts stood back from the shore, dark buildings of timber and wattle.

"That is the tref, the village," Madog explained. "These folk do some fishing, but mostly they farm the uplands and keep some sheep. They will all be turning out to see you, my lady. The arrival of our Prince Griffith's bride will be the occasion of much feasting."

Madog spoke truly. Before a smallboat could be put down to take us ashore, a crowd had gathered on the beach, vomited out of every hut and hovel.

They were dark, the Cymry, with wild locks that blew in the constant wind, and they moved with the grace of flowing water. Dressed in robes of rough wool, knotted about the waist with thongs of leather, men and women together they came to greet us. As the bottom of our boat scraped against the shell beach, a dozen pairs of eager hands seized it and dragged it forward.

"Sweet Mary!" breathed Emma behind me. "They are a wild, dark people for sure, my lady! You are given to wed a savage!"

I had been thinking something of the kind myself until Emma spoke, and glancing aside I saw the red stain of a blush on Madog's cheek. He had been good to me; I would not have him embarrassed by my nursery-maid. Something perverse took hold of me and overrode my fear.

"Be silent," I commanded her as I would not have dared a month before. "We know Madog and the Earl's Owain, and they are men of much quality! Already I like this land, and these people are my . . . my husband's subjects.

We will be friends." I looked into the nearest pair of dark eyes and smiled my brightest smile.

The shout that went up was so sudden it affrighted us all. The Cymry could not understand my Saxon tongue, but they understood a hopeful smile well enough. They lifted me out of the boat with a mighty heave, snatching me right past the astonished Madog and the oarsmen, and lifted me to their shoulders!

They splashed through the scallops of foam at the sea's edge and ran with me inland, toward a place where a huge pile of wood was built up. Men lit torches and held them to the stack until it ignited, sending a tower of fire into the twilight sky. All around me was the music of voices singing, chanting, with words I could not understand but with tones of joy and happiness.

They set me down gently on a low block of carved red sandstone, a sort of small altar set up at the tide's limit. Although it was still too cold for the blooming of flowers, garlands had been made of shells and leaves and braided hair; these were hung around my neck while all nodded approval. The women reached out their hands and touched my cheeks and the yellow of my hair and looked at each other

63

wonderingly. The Cymry women were smaller than Saxon women, their bones fine and delicate; in spite of my furs and velvet I felt like a great lump compared to them.

All the men wore robes of varying lengths, tattered about their calves. My eyes missed the clean look of our Saxon garb, the short tunic and colored hose with cross garters. But I found the men handsome of face and form; they did not repel me as they danced about me, singing.

Then Emma came scurrying up the beach, frantic as a mother hen after a lost chick. "My poor lady, what have they done to you?" she cried, wringing her hands over my imaginary misfortune.

"I think they have done me homage, Emma," I told her as calmly as I could.

"So they have, my lady!" called Madog cheerfully. He did not seem at all upset by the rowdiness of my reception. "Saxons are not usually welcome here, but this woman, Angharad"—he gestured to the matron whose stare I had met with that first smile—"she has the Sight. Your soul cannot lie to her; always she knows the truth of a person. She has accepted you and that is enough."

I was much flattered by my welcome, but at the same time I felt a touch of contempt for people who would base their acceptance of a stranger on such a slender thread. How easily these Welsh must be fooled, I thought. Then.

The feasting Madog had spoken of began. The bonfire was used like an oven, haunches of meat with pikes thrust through them were being held in the flames to be roasted. Flagons of mead were passed from hand to hand, and I was given a big wad of bread with a fish paste spread upon it.

The ship was being unloaded by torchlight. From my seat of honor on the sandstone I saw my dowry trunks deposited on the shore, and each new one was eagerly inspected by the villagers. They never touched them, however, just circled round them pointing and exclaiming. My hastily assembled trappings of wealth were making an impression.

"The bonfire light will be seen by the watchguard at the castle," Madog assured me. "Eat lightly my lady. Soon they will be coming to take you to Rhuddlan."

Even as the wind freshened from the sea and Emma began rummaging in the chests to find me a warmer cloak, they came, a long procession of men, winding down the sloping face of the headland to the white beach where I waited, heart a-thud once more.

First came a troop of fierce-faced warriors, bearing shield and glaive. They marched single file, which I was to learn later was a wise maneuver in a mountain land. They were followed by a band of courtiers, much more richly dressed than my welcoming party from the beach. They were mounted on the most beautiful ponies I ever saw, clever little beasts with large liquid eyes like deer.

Emma looked fearfully at the procession as it approached. "There is no litter, my lady!" Shock was in her voice.

"I understand that the Lady Edyth can ride well," Madog commented. "Prince Griffith was muchly pleased by that. I am sure that a fine mount has been provided her."

I had to look down and toy with the garland around my neck to keep from laughing outright. I fear it was not concern for my dignity that prompted Emma's upset. More likely it was her horror at discovering that she herself must walk or ride a pony. On formal occasions my nurse had always shared the litter with me. "I am a woman grown, Emma," I reminded her. "I no longer require you at my elbow; I am sure the Prince's men will find you a suitable place." My speech befit my new station, but I was hurt by the hurt in her old eyes.

I was greeted straightway in the name of Griffith ap Llywelyn, Prince of Gwynedd and Ruler of All Wales. With much deference and ceremony I was given the reins of a little gray horse who won my heart the first moment, and when I forgot my new dignity and vaulted onto his back I was given my second spontaneous cheer of the day.

In all the exictement there was one disappointment. In my girlish dreams Prince Griffith had come to greet me, but not in the flesh. After all my anxieties I would have liked it much if he had been there, that I might see him straightway and know my fate.

Up we went and up, good Madog riding at my side. We followed a path cut in white limestone that glowed eerily in the torchlight, with a great hedge of hawthorn and ivy springing up beside us. I glanced at its black bulk.

"Is it safe for so large a party to ride abroad by night, Madog?" I asked my companion.

He seemed quite insulted. "This is the land of Prince Griffith, my lady! No man living would dare to offer harm to you here! You are more safe now than a babe in her dam's arms!"

I was not so sure about that. In east Anglia, or in Ireland, for that matter, the creak of carts loaded with chests of rich belongings would have been a sore temptation to cutthroats and thieves. But Madog's tone suggested the mere mention of such a thing would be an insult here, so I kept my peace.

Only in the echoing vault of my own head did I send up a small, voiceless cry: Ah, Father, what have you sent me to? I am afraid, sire; come take me home again and make things as they were!

Such prayers are never answered; they are almost too foolish to mention. Only the sleepy voices of the cuckoos in the hawthorn hedge answered me.

Up and up, and on and on. Being Cymry, our party soon began singing to the music of harps some of the courtiers carried. Wild and lovely the music was, and passing strange. Not word one did I understand, yet it seemed my heart could understand all of it, and in that time the fear at last left me for good. The doors to the past were shut to me, and I was coming into my own world.

The moon came out, peeking shyly at first through trailing tatters of cloud, then pouring such a pure and intense light down upon us that the torches of the servitors were unnecessary. Looking ahead, I saw that we were tapping the headland, and the rolling plain spread before us, lush fields, dark woodlands, great outcroppings of stone. Across the sweep of the land a mighty shape huddled in shadowy dignity before a distant mountain.

"That is Rhuddlan, my lady," said Madog with simple pride.

Rhuddlan Castle was a massive timbered fortress, with no such friendly air about it as our Saxon manorhouse possessed. It was built not for hospitality but for protection, and the width of its walls and size of its watchtowers gave mute evidence of its strength.

Strange to say, it did not seem forbidding to me. Emma told me later that she crossed herself when she saw the place, but I only had a sense of peace. Bathed in moonlight, its air scented with hints of the oncoming spring, Rhuddlan opened its mighty wooden arms to welcome me, and I went gladly in.

We rode through gates set beside a square gate tower and entered a courtyard of earth and slate. Grooms ran out to catch the horses' bridles, and glad voices shouted greetings. I heard the rumble of the baggage carts being taken off into the darkness at my left.

A herald much like Madog in face and stature trotted up to us hotfoot, turned and faced the large rectangular hall which centered the fortress and cried, "The Lady Edyth the Saxon!" in perfect Saxon tongue. Then he repeated my name in Welsh, a lovely rippling that sounded most like "Aldith."

The doors of the hall were thrown open, and a man stood alone, his back to the light from within. I could not make out his face, but his imperious bearing as he stood there was all the identification he needed.

The herald confirmed it. "Prince Griffith ap Llywelyn!" he cried.

An assemblage appeared behind him in the doorway, watching eagerly as he came slowly down the steps toward us. Is he young or old? Fair or foul? I strained my eyes with peering.

The party around me fell back as he advanced, leaving only Madog at my side. I sat as straight as I could on my pony, whose reins I had refused to abandon to a groom, and tried to look as I thought a proud Saxon lady should. Whatever my bridegroom might be. I was determined that he should think he had chosen well in me.

It took him hours and hours to reach me. I thought surely the cock must crow daybreak before he was close enough that I could see his face. Madog leaped agilely from his mount and stood beside it in a formal salute, knuckling his forelock and unsmiling.

I just sat there. Only when he reached my pony's head did I lower my eyes and bow to him, murmuring, "Your servant, Sire," and wondering if he could understand the Saxon tongue.

"Well come, Aldith," replied a resonant voice. I looked up then and saw his face clear in the moonlight. The dark auburn hair lying thick-locked about his temples, the high-bridged nose with nostrils flared like a nervous horse, the tender, smiling mouth and jutting fighter's chin. I looked right into the eyes of Griffith and Llywelyn and saw the other half of my own soul.

Griffith

W E ENTERED the Great Hall together. He did not touch me, nor I him, but I felt his presence at my side like a dark fire. The members of the Welsh court were assembled there to see the Saxon woman Griffith had bought with his men-at-arms, and their acceptance of me was not given like that of the peasants on the beach. I looked straight ahead, my head held high, but I could feel their eyes probing and measuring me from all sides.

He took me to the head of the main feasting table, where a high padded stool with a back ornamented with gilded leather marked the King's place. (I was to learn that he was, in truth, considered King in Wales, though he was known as the Ruler of All Wales and always referred to as Prince Griffith.) There he turned and repeated the herald's introduction of me by my Saxon name and then in his own language. The courtiers bowed and we sat down to the feast.

Tired in my bones I was, though I did not realize it until that time. The table piled high with food did not tempt me, and I felt my eyes stinging with weariness and the effluvia from the torches. I sipped mead or ale, I knew not which, from a goblet of some dark wood, and I tried to get the feeling of my surroundings. But I could not. I was only aware of the man who sat beside me.

"Eat some of this bird, Aldith," he urged me. "It is roasted with honey and herbs; it will restore your strength." He spoke to me as a father might to his child, caringly, and in truth, he was almost of an age to have been my father. The lines of wind and laughter were deeply etched about his brown eyes, so that the heavy lashes seemed to pull his eyelids down of their own weight. He spoke the Saxon nearly as well as Owain, and with the same lilting accent.

Griffith was not overtall, being of a height

with me, but among the Welsh he was tall. Broad of shoulder and deep of chest, the upper part of his body was built as a warrior's should be. But his hands fascinated me as I watched him cut portions of the meat for me. His fingers were long and slim—they moved with the grace of a girl's—and his every gesture was beautiful.

He saw me looking at his hands and smiled at me. It was as if he heard my inmost thoughts. "I play the harp, Aldith. When it is time, I shall play the songs of the Cymry for you and teach you to sing them."

I was embarrassed. "I cannot sing, my lord. Everyone says I have the voice of a raven."

He threw up his head and laughed. The courtiers did not join self-consciously in his laughter, as they would have among the Saxons. In Wales a man's conversation was private and not to be entered into without invitation. "You are of the Cymry now, Aldith, and therefore you must sing. We will do what we can to make it sweet."

I tried a small smile. "You set yourself an impossible task, my lord."

"I often do," Prince Griffith replied easily.

All through our supper he told me the names of this or that person at table, together with a history of their deeds or a short description of their virtues. Sometimes he invited them to speak directly to me, but not often, as only a few knew the Saxon language.

"Tell the Lady Aldith of the marriage rite we practice here," he instructed the Bishop from nearby Saint Asaph's. Bishop Iorworth was a well-educated man, as all Christmen need be, and Saxon was but one of the languages he spoke right well.

"By our law you will remain under the government of your father and male relatives until the marriage is effected, my lady, but you are now in the Prince's protection. He is responsible to your father for your safekeeping until he possesses you totally. The essence of our marriage rite is the formal bestowal of the bride by her kindred. Naught can be consummated until this is completed."

But I knew from Madog that the Earl Aelfgar had returned hotfoot to East Anglia, to consolidate his victory and take control once more of his properties. Bewildered, I turned to the Prince.

"Cannot a marriage be completed without my father?"

"Of course not, Aldith; it is not our way. A joining of two tribes is more important to the tribes than to the Church. We wish the blessings of the Church, of course, but by Welsh law it is not necessary. You will not be wife to me until your father says, in my presence, 'Maiden I have given thee to a husband, and I have paid him a fee in recognition of the rights of all his kindred who have lost you from their tribe.'"

"You will spend the time wisely until the Earl Aelfgar concludes his affairs and comes here, my lady," Iorworth told me, "in learning the ways of our people. The Cymry can never completely accept one who does not speak their language or know their customs; it is well for you to learn these things before the wedding."

Griffith leaned forward and put his beautiful hand on mine, actually touching me for the first time, and all of my body seemed magically rooted to the spot where our two skins met! "Likewise, Aldith," he said, "we will have a chance to learn each other, and see if we are pleased."

What a great weight went from my heart then! The Welsh law must be very different from the Saxon custom if my happiness was to be a consideration!

"You will find that our laws are most fair to you," the Bishop assured me. "Your husband will not have the power of life and death over you; he may not even beat you save for those serious offences specified in the Codes. You will have limited control over your joint property and certain personal possessions which are entirely yours and cannot be taken from you under any circumstances. Most important, Welsh law gives considerable protection against arbitrary divorce."

Divorce! I shrank on my stool and felt a trembling in my limbs. Never had I known of a wife who was put away by her husband, but I had heard of such things, and it seemed to me a very great calamity, a disgrace like outlawry, to be declared unfit by the man to whom you were given!

Griffith saw my distress. In a gentle voice he said, "The ancient rule that a man may put away his wife, if so minded, is still valid. If a king's wife should bear him no heir, for example, it is a matter of much consequence. But our law takes care that it should not be frivolously put into operation by providing for a substantial payment to the divorced woman."

"Only for the first seven years of the marriage!" Bishop Iorworth interrupted. "After that, a man must give his wife half of all his possessions if he divorces her. We would not have our women made poor or shamed before the community."

And my lady mother had called these people barbarians! My weariness overcame me at last; I felt my spine go soft within me and wished for nothing so much as to lay my head down on the table and go to sleep.

Again Griffith foresaw me. With the raising

of his eyebrow he brought a servingwoman to my side and sent someone to fetch Emma. I walked in a daze from the Great Hall to the private chambers, where I was put in a fine room with its own window and fresh grasses laid upon the floor.

So changed was my life from anything I had known that at first I felt like a very small child again. Prince Griffith got me tutors in the language and the Laws. The Welsh people set mighty store by the Laws handed down from King Hywel the Good. Unlike Ireland, in Wales only the Christmen read and write, so these laws are handed down by mouth from one generation to the next. But they are most strictly observed! Among the Welsh, a man's word is his bond, and if he breaks it even in small ways he is shunned by all the community.

My tutor in the Laws was Cynan, a cousin of Griffith and as such honor-bound to him in all things. "The tribal feeling is very strong here, my lady," he told me. "Unlike the Saxons and the Danes, who slay one another out of hand, father against son, we believe that our strength is in the unity of the family. Kinship is reckoned exclusively through the males, but as the wife of Griffith ap Llywelyn you will be expected to know all the family pedigree and pass it on to your sons."

78

"And if I have no sons . . . ?" I made bold to ask.

Cynan smiled. "You will, my lady. You are young and strong, and our Prince is very virile. He has many sons hereabout."

"He was married before?"

"Not to a great house. His children are by his concubines, but under the Laws we do not disinherit such children. And you may be assured, my lady," he added hastily, "Prince Griffith will set aside his concubines out of honor to you when you are wed!"

It was Griffith himself who told me of my most noteworthy predecessor. On a radiant spring afternoon, when I had gone for a ride on my gray pony with only the loyal Madog for companion, Griffith rode out to meet us and sent Madog on some made-up errand.

"Are you happy in the land of the Cymry?" Griffith asked me seriously as soon as we were alone.

"Yes, I think I am very happy. I am a little surprised by that; I was not sure."

He laughed. My Griffith laughed a lot. "Neither was I sure when I asked your sire to send you to me. But, having seen you, I am most pleased. It was time for me to make an alliance outside our kingdom; I would play a part in the world that lies beyond the mountains and perhaps see my sons as rulers in all of Britain one day."

It was the right time. "You have sons already? Cynan spoke of them."

How sensitive he was, how quick to shield me from imagined hurt! "I have sons born of youth and a man's needs, Aldith. I have no heir to Gwynedd and Wales."

"But you were married before, my lord?"

He gazed into far distances. "I took for wife the wife of a rival I defeated. She was beautiful, and I thought it made my victory over him complete. But it was not a good thing, Aldith; we were not suited. Had she not died I might have had to set her aside, or awake some morning to find her dagger in my back."

A shiver of horror went up my spine. I felt a quick sense of loss and tragedy for that killing that—thank God—had never happened.

"Do you think we will be suited, my lord?" I asked, keeping my eyes turned down so that he might see the sweep of my lashes and the curve of my cheek.

Griffith laughed again, the black mood gone from him in a moment. "I am taking time to be sure!" he said. "When we are wed I shall expect you to stand at my back, covering it, not stabbing it. So I would court you now and make a friend of you, Aldith, that I need not fear in the future!" He put his hand on my sleeve. "And you, what do you think?"

I could not flirt or dissemble with him. He seemed to know me too deeply; there was no way but truth. "I pray we will be suited, my lord, for the thought of marriage with you pleases me and I grow anxious for my lord father's return!"

"Everything need not wait until then, Aldith." He was not smiling now, his eyes were deep and burning.

"But the nuptials . . ."

"Yes, that must wait. But you and I, we can learn to know each other better as we wait. I would like to know the texture of your lips, my Aldith, and see how well the curves of your body fit mine. It is not an unreasonable request, do you think? In the interests of learning our suitability to each other?"

His breath heated my cheek as he leaned near me, gazing at my lips and dropping his voice to a murmur. With all my being I longed for him to hold me, kiss me . . . and yet I was afraid! The moment was sacred, it might be too easily spoiled. I might say something foolish and seem ridiculous to a mature, empassioned man; this was no stripling boy to be fended off with arch words, teasing play.

"My lord, I don't know what to say!"

"Say nothing, sweet Aldith. Let our bodies get acquainted and our thoughts rest." He tangled his fingers in the braid of hair wound around my head and pulled it down with one sharp tug. "Your hair is lovely. It smells like sunlight." He lifted a lock of it to his lips.

When he put his arm about me and I felt his fingers at the neck of my shift I drew away without meaning to. "What's this, Aldith? Squeamish already?" He said it in a gently teasing way, so as not to insult me, but I feared I had displeased him.

"It's not that, my lord. I am only . . . unsure."

Griffith pulled a little away from me and looked at me intently with his eyes that saw every thing. "Tell me frankly, girl. Have you been with a man before?"

I was embarrassed at such a question! "No, my lord! Surely my father told you I am a maiden!"

He waved his hand. "To be sure, but all girls are virgin to their fathers. I am asking you, Aldith. Have there been some boys you sported with, perhaps? Just a little?"

"I do not know how to answer that question, my lord. But I cannot lie to you. I have . . . flirted, betimes, and teased the boys a bit."

"But are you a virgin?" he insisted.

"Yes," I told him, proud of the fact that as

a bride I was untouched and yet disturbed by something in his voice.

"Ah well, so be it." There was a definite note of regret in the Prince's voice, though I could not understand why! "I am glad you are a maiden, Aldith. That is right and as it should be, of course. Your father would have done wrong to offer me used goods. But still"—he shrugged his shoulders and gave me a child's mischievous smile—"it does limit our sport!"

I felt all churned up inside. There had been a promise of wondrous excitements in his voice, his touch; and yet it was all to be denied me because I was that most desirable thing, a virgin! How could one ever cease being a virgin under those circumstances?

Griffith continued to seek me out from time to time, when he had a few moments to spare from the business of Gwynedd, but he treated me thereafter with great gentleness and a respect I did not totally desire.

Fortunately my hours were well filled otherwise. My tutor in the Welsh language was a woman, a lady-in-waiting given to me by Griffith. She spent much time patiently explaining to me the peculiarities of the strange Cymry tongue.

"It is pronounced Hloo-ellen, my lady!" she repeated to me despairingly when I had mispronounced the name of Griffith's father for the

dozenth time. "You must put your tongue between your teeth and blow lightly around the
sound. Now try again! It would shame Llywelyn's son to hear you say it thus!"

In time I mastered the tricky sounds; I
called Gwynedd Goo-in-neth and the name of
our nearby river Cloo-id. I learned the words
for food and drink and bed; I learned how to
ask for my pony and how to address the various
members of the court. I even tried to think in
Welsh, as my tutor assured me that was the
best way to join myself with the Cymry. But it
was hard, hard! In moments of stress I still
thought the Saxon words, and when my pony
trod upon my foot, it was a Saxon curse I bel-
lowed!

But I had some success. One day Emma
said to me, "Sometimes I scarcely recognize
you, my lady! With your hair all streaming
down your back like that and your feet bare and
brown, you look like one of these . . ."

"Don't say it!"

"One of these Welsh people," she finished
smoothly. We had had a severe discussion, at
least on my part, about her habit of referring to
the Cymry as savages.

"I'm pleased you think me so, Emma," I
told her. "I hope my Lord Griffith will see the
change in me as well. Surely we will hear soon

of the coming of the Earl Aelfgar to give my hand in marriage; I want to be worthy."

"Oh, my lady, you are worthy!" Emma told me, a quaver in her voice. "But to spend the rest of your life in this empty place!"

"Pish! You were the one who thought it so fine, me wed to some nobleman!"

"Aye, but I thought it would be a Saxon noble, my lady, one of your own kind!"

I felt a sting of protective rage. Toward Emma, for her implied insult to Griffith, and toward myself, for caring about a servant's opinion. "Prince Griffith is my own kind, Emma, far more than any lad who might have come running hotfoot to seek my hand in Anglia! Now, speak to me no more of this!"

As my knowledge of the language improved, I was able to learn more of my bridegroom's history from the members of the court, who seemed pleased by my interest. They told me of his sire, Llywelyn ap Seisyll, a great and noble Prince. They told me of Griffith's youth, when he had been considered little but a sluggish loafer on the fringes of his father's court.

One New Year's Eve, driven out-of-doors by the taunts and reproaches of his sister, whom he loved, Griffith had an experience which changed him into a bold and determined warrior. New Year's Eve is a night of signs and portents; it is said a man may learn on that night what to expect for the coming year. Lazy and reluctant to stir himself overmuch, Griffith chose to seek his own signs by the easiest method—eavesdropping. Leaning against the wall of a house where a company was intent upon the process of boiling chunks of meat in a cauldron, the young Prince heard the cook swear a vile oath.

"By the death of life!"

"What's the matter? What's wrong?" cried other voices.

"Here is one piece which, however firmly I drive it down with my fork, always persists in coming to the top!"

Griffith drank in the words, convinced that they bore a prophecy of his own future. From that moment he was a changed man. What taunt and reproach could not do was brought about by the spur of ambition and the hope of greatness.

Within a short span of time he began building a reputation as a courageous warrior, an unconquerable spirit, and as a man of unshakable confidence. He would allow none to triumph over him in love or war. Yet men spoke of him well, as a man of wit and generosity, a man easy in his own person and thoughtful of others.

When he inherited his father's kingdoms

of Gwynedd and Powys he set out to enlarge his holdings, and he did so well over the years that he was considered ruler by all the Welsh. He had won back many lands held by the English and had slain in battle my own great-uncle Edwin, brother of the Earl Leofric. By the time of our engagement he was all-powerful in the land of the Cymry. At distant Bishopstree he had another residence, where it was rumored that he kept a woman or two until the day our wedding feast would be celebrated.

This last piece of information made me burn with the prickly heat of jealousy. I dared not discuss it with the Prince, but on the day he boarded one of his own ships which lay at anchor in the mouth of the Clwyd and set out on an inspection tour of his kingdom, I jerked all my bridal finery out of the chests and hurled it to the floor in a fit of temper. Not since Ireland had I allowed myself such a display.

Emma and my servingwomen set themselves calmly to making order out of the mess, but for the rest of the day they made certain to stay clear of my foot which might kick and my hand which could slap.

Then Griffith returned and was as warm to me as before. When we sat for supper that first evening in the hall, he reached out and put his hand on mine, the dark ruby in his ring blazing against his brown skin. He was tanned by sun and wind and more beautiful to me that ever, though I was too shy to say so.

"When I was gone, Aldith," he said straightway, "I put in order my domestic affairs elsewhere." His eyes bored into mine. "You understand what I am saying? I am sure someone has spoken to you of it?"

Unable to answer, I cast down my eyes and nodded.

"It is just as well, I would have no secrets between us. But know this; I have provided for all of those who are my responsibility, though I need have no more commerce with them. The children too, they will be properly reared and will be no disgrace to the house of Llywelyn." He paused, then his second hand reached out to join his first and cradle both mine gently within.

"The Earl Aelfgar will leave East Anglia this day week," he continued, "come to give you into my keeping. I would have nothing hurt you or make you regret our betrothal, Aldith. I will come to you completely yours, as I demand that you be completely mine."

He reached out and put his fingers under my chin, cradling it in the warm cup of his hand and lifting it until my eyes met his. "I am a possessive man, Aldith. Know that now, I will

88

not share one smile of yours, one touch, not even one dream! Do you agree to that?"

I was glad the courtiers habitually ignored one another's private conversations! For I wanted to say to Griffith, "How could I smile, or touch, or dream of another, when you have filled up all the empty spaces inside me already?" But I could not do it, the poetry of the Cymry had not yet loosened my cold Saxon tongue to make such a declaration possible. I could but nod again, like some halfwit child slow to learn a lesson, and hope Griffith could read the words written on my soul.

It all happened. Just as Griffith had promised. My lord father came to Rhuddlan with a large party of his relations, all come to witness my marriage to the Welsh Prince. We were wed in the chapel at Rhuddlan, and I wore a gown of violet silk, with my hair unbound in the Cymry fashion. The Earl Aelfgar said those words required by the Welsh law as he put my hand in Griffith's; Griffith took the massive ruby from his little finger and put it on my third one.

All around us they stood, the Cymry I had come to love and know even as my own kin. Dillwyn and Trevor and Cemaes, Morgan and Dafydd and Rhys. Angharad up from her hut by the sea, and Madog and Owain and Emma, too. All my people, forevermore.

Then we were alone at last, in the private chambers of the Prince, with nothing but the cheery spirit of the fire in its kettle for company.

Griffith put his hands lightly on my shoulders and smiled. "How you tremble, little one!" (Though I was as tall as he and met his gaze on the level!) "Are you frightened? We all fear the unknown, and we are surely about to confront the unknown in each other. But it will be all right, I will not hurt you. Do you believe that?"

"Yes," I whispered.

"It is my responsibility, as you are virgin, to see that you overcome your fear and learn to feel pleasure in me as I shall in you. Tell me truly, have you ever seen a man naked?"

That was a foolish question! Surely everyone had seen nakedness; children run unclothed in warm weather, sparing their mothers much weaving and needlework. And it is no great feat to spy on a servant bathing in a stream; I had done that aplenty.

"I have seen children, my lord. And servants, in a stream."

"Now you are about to see me in the hide my mother gave me, Aldith, and it is not seemly that you be so formal. When I came naked into the world I was dubbed Griffith, and that only. So I would be to you henceforth."

"Yes, my . . . Griffith."

He chuckled. " 'My' Griffith has a fine

sound to it, little one. Let us proceed with your education."

Taking my hands in his, he guided my fingers so that I helped remove his clothing. As the garments fell away I became aware of a new sensation, replacing my timidity—I felt the prickings of curiosity.

When Griffith ap Llywelyn stood before me, naked in the firelight, I felt no fear at all. He was beautiful, and there was no shame in him. In response to his dignified gift of himself, I gazed my fill of him in wonder and thought of nothing else.

He stood straight and proud, my Griffith, with his shoulders back and his chin lifted. The line of his throat was supple though his neck was thick with strength. There was a soft sheen to his skin that made me long to touch it, and I wondered fleetingly if he oiled his flesh.

I raised my eyes questioning to his and saw, from the patient waiting in his face, that more was expected of me. So I took a deep breath and gazed full upon his manhood.

And it was not at all frightening! Unlike the sword the stallion plunged into the mare, this was a small and fragile-seeming bit of pink flesh, so vulnerable and soft I almost laughed aloud at my earlier fears. It lay curved over the bag of the scrotum, which I saw was just the size to fit in my two cupped hands. I don't know what expression crossed my face at that moment, but I heard Griffith's sudden sharp intake of breath. And to my wonder that sleeping and insignificant part of him grew before my very eyes, stretching and quivering as it leaped out toward me! This was the miracle, then, this rich flowering of beauty and power. Through what must have been iron self-control he had shown himself first to me in such a way that I was not affrighted, merely curious and interested. But at my reaction his manhood had broken through his will power and presented me with the male in all his formidable majesty.

I gave him a shy smile and reached out to touch the broad shoulder glowing in the firelight. The moment I touched him I saw the pulse leap in his throat, and I realized that in some way he was as vulnerable to me as I to him. My heart flooded with tenderness.

"I love you, my Griffith!"

And then the time was come when I was truly made wife to Griffith ap Llywelyn; all doors were opened and all walls let down. And in our joining I knew that we were not two, but one.

In this new realm I could happily have spent a lifetime. But the strongest flesh weakens, and at last I fell asleep in his arms, sore and happy. When next I woke a tray of meats and fruits had been set beside the fur-covered pallet where we lay. As I had been hungry for his touch, so was I starved then for food, and we ate together like ravening wolves and laughed at each other till he kissed the juices from the corners of my mouth and all began again . . .

And always he talked to me in that marvelous musical voice. His body made love to my body, his voice made love to the Aldith in my head, so that I was not alone in any way. He spoke of my beauty, whispered his passion, groaned with our mutual rapture. When we rested he built my future with his words, so that I could see our whole life together spread before me as I lay in his arms. He asked me about myself and listened intently to my answers, even as his fingers memorized the curve of my cheek. Sometimes he spoke love to me, and sometimes he quoted poetry, and I swear I could not tell one from the other.

Griffith, Griffith, so much did you make of us one person that I still breathe with your breath, your heart beats in my breast!

Rhuddlan

MY NEW LIFE was truly begun. In one day
(and a night) I had moved in rank from stu-
dent to First Lady in Wales. And chatelaine
of Rhuddlan, too: keeper of the keys to the private chambers, the stillroom, the strongroom,
and the solar. My domain included the kitchens,
a chapel, barn and stables, a kiln-house for
drying grain, a cow byre, a small house for Griffith's falcons, the porch where we dined on
starry summer nights, and the privy.

Also within Rhuddlan's walls were the watch towers and sleeping huts for the men-at-arms and the servants' chamber and hall, but these were none of my affair. Emma did love to bring me tales from the servants' chambers and I did love to give ear to them, though I pretended for the sake of my dignity that I was impatient with such tittle-tattle.

But the part of my new kingdom I loved most was not within stout timbered walls; it was best seen from the back of my gray pony. The rich and rolling valley of the Clwyd, its colors always changing beneath the racing clouds—that was dear to me. The distant purpled hush of mountains. The songs of the thrush as we lay on our pallet of furs in the early morning, when pearly light came streaming in through the solar's wind door, open to air and sky. The funny manmade mountain they called "Toothill" upon which Rhuddlan stood.

The valley of the Clwyd was rich land, so fertile that many of the Cymry had given up their traditional occupations of hunting, hawking and fishing and taken to tilling the soil. Landowners plowed with a heavy wooden plow and a team of eight oxen; a whole community went in together in this endeavor, sharing the oats, barley or wheat they raised. I loved to ride along the edges of the fields, listening to the cries of the callers who walked backward leading the oxen, singing their commands like bards.

"It seems the whole world is here!" I said to Griffith once. "Everything we need is grown hereabouts or provided to us as the court's share from the tribes. It is not like East Anglia, where we purchased from traders so much of our goods."

"It is wrong to be dependent on others," Griffith replied. "Each tribe of the Cymry cares for itself; no man can cut off its food supply or take away its clothing and fuel. We do without some of the luxuries of the great towns, perhaps, but we are free." His face grew very serious. "Remember that, Aldith. It is a great thing to be independent, to have no foot on your neck." There was a real sadness in his eyes that surprised me.

"Surely no man is so free as you!"

My Griffith gave a bitter laugh. "Few men are so enslaved as I."

"But you are Ruler of All Wales!"

"Mmmmmm," said Griffith, stroking his neatly trimmed auburn beard.

I waited. I had learned that those "Mmmmmms" of his meant he was about to deliver himself of an important thought and wanted all of my rapt attention.

"So I am, Ruler of All Wales. That is a title I went after like a hungry bear, sweeping aside everything that got in my path. And would do so again, just as fiercely! Make no mistake about that, Aldith; my ambition is not quenched, nor will it ever be. Unfortunately.

"For I can tell you this, little one. At sundown the landowner puts away his plow and oxen, the fisherman leaves his nets and weir and goes home to a good supper and an easy sleep. But for a Prince sundown means only that the torches must be lit, so that he can see better the problems he must grapple with. There are always friends to be made, enemies to be starved off, decisions and choices and dealings until the mind scurries like a trapped rat.

"We live well here at Rhuddlan, Aldith, but I pay for each cow and oat and piece of gold as surely as if I wrested them from the land myself. No plowman works as hard as I; no beekeeper keeps such hours. I have not just one flock to guard but many! I must protect them all from invasion, administer the Laws and hold court to settle rights and wrongs. It is a tiresome task that is never completed, for as soon as I put down one problem two more rise in its place." He shook his head in a weary way.

97

"If the business of kingship is so tiresome," I asked, logically, I thought, "then why do men seek to rule?"

Griffith took a long time answering, and his voice was soft when at last he spoke. "Each man has a vision of himself, Aldith, a picture in his head of the way he wants to think of himself. I was the son of a great Prince; my vision, when it came, was to be a greater Prince than my father. I saw myself as a man who could not be beaten, and it gave me much pleasure to think of myself in that way. And so I have lived my life, striving always to be the best, the strongest, the most powerful."

"But it hasn't made you happy? Is that what you are trying to tell me?"

His face lighted marvelously, and I felt a wash of relief. "Ho, Aldith, it has made me very happy! Sometimes. I have you! And honors and opportunities and the respect of men. I meant merely that I pay a high price for all that, my love, and that I will never be free of the goad of ambition or the responsibilities that go with it."

Sometimes, he had said. Sometimes he was happy.

But sometimes he was not. Warned, I noted the times when his expression was grim and there was no laughter at table. I saw his

98

hands shake with fatigue at times, and many were the nights I lay alone on our pallet till cockcrow while he conferred in the hall with ministers and soldiers.

And sometimes he was away for long periods, and the wind from the sea sang sad songs around the towers.

When Griffith was at Rhuddlan, he broke with ancient custom and had me always seated at his right hand at the feasting table. But when he was away, with his household cavalry and his cup-bearer and his physician and his footholder and all the rest of his retinue, then I was banished too. Instead of taking my meals in the Great Hall with the ranking members of the court, I dined in our own chamber. I could hear the male voices raised in song or quarrel, but without Griffith I was no part of them.

During that time I felt almost an outcast again, denied the company of men I had come to like and admire. There was Emlyn, the court judge, kindly and sober, and Gwerstan, our chapel priest and Griffith's secretary. Rhys the chamberlain and Caradog the steward. And a goodly number of others besides. All men who talked with me and asked after my health and seemed to enjoy my company when Griffith was there. But when Griffith was away on the business of his kingdom, those of the court who re-

mained behind were a closed company, kind
and polite to me always but never including me
in their number.

Even though this was the Saxon way as
well, still it rankled me. I complained a bit to
Griffith.

"I am your Lady whether you are here or
naught; don't I deserve a place at table in your
absence?"

"It is the custom, Aldith!"

"It is not a fair custom!"

"You are still a child, Aldith; you have not
had enough experience to judge what is fair
and what is not. The ancient ways were established by wise men who had good reasons. It
is not seemly for you to question them." Griffith
was using his stern, adult-speaking-to-a-child
voice on me, but it did not always work.

"When will I cease being a child? When
will I be old enough for my own ideas to be
respected, Griffith? I am not a fool. I can think!"

Griffith began to lose patience. "I know
you can think. I would not have a wife who was
stupid, she might give me stupid sons. But you
should think a woman's thoughts and not try to
meddle with the traditions of men." There was
a rough note of anger in his voice and a glint in
his eye that warned me not to press too hard.
My beautiful, poetic Welshman had a savage
temper once he lost it; he had not yet lost it

with me, and I was reluctant to have him begin over such an issue as my dining arrangements.

But, nevertheless, it was not fair!

The affairs of the outside world were not unknown to us in our private world; Griffith came back from one of his trips with the news of the death of the Earl Leofric of Mercia, my grandfather.

"The Earl Aelfgar will accede to the earldom of Mercia," he announced, "and a new earl will take his place in East Anglia."

I was happy for my lord father. Taking his sire's place as Earl of Mercia would give him much satisfaction. But who would sit in the hall where I grew up?

"It is not yet decided, Aldith, and I suspect the Saxons and Danes will do much quarreling over the bone before one of them makes off with it!" The quarrelsomeness of the two factions pleased Griffith; he liked to see dissent among all those who would call themselves the English.

As it fell out, the earldom of East Anglia went to Gyrth, the fourth son of Earl Godwine, and all of Oxford Shire was adeed to his portion as well.

"Ho!" Griffith exulted. "There will be hot hearts over that bit of business! The Godwines strengthen their control almost daily, it seems." He turned to me and smiled. "I daresay we will be hearing from your father again soon, little one."

We did. Two messengers came hotfoot from Mercia, begging the support of the Welsh Prince in a new uprising against the Godwines. This time my father proposed to obtain mercenaries from Norway as well, promising them the same looting privileges that had enlisted the Vikings in Dublin.

"It will be tedious," Griffith sighed.

"Then why do it?"

"My dear, if I don't keep them terrified of me, the light-fingered English will continue to nibble away the land along our border. Besides, who knows what crumbs may fall to us along the way!"

"I hate the thought of your going off to do war, my love!"

"Nonsense! War well done is a fine and profitable business."

"But you could be killed"

"In that case I would be a hero, covered with glory as well as a shroud! But come, Aldith, do not pull such a long face. Your Griffith will come home to you safe enough, I vow!" He put his fingers under my chin and tipped my lips up to meet his, thinking to make me forget battles and killing. It almost worked, but not quite.

"Be sure you do come home safe to me,

Griffith. I would not have your son growing up fatherless."

Griffith took half a step back and looked at me. "My son? *Our* son? Aldith, are you sure?"

"Emma thinks so, and your own court physician is agreed."

He threw back his head and gave a mighty bellow that so frightened the hounds sleeping at the hearth that they fled from the room. "A son! A son!" He grabbed both my hands and whirled me around in a mad caper that left us both breathless and laughing. "An heir to Gwynedd from my Aldith!"

The very next day heralds were sent out to the folk round about to give the good news. Gwerstan blessed our unborn son in chapel, and Emma whispered to me that some of the Cymry who still set store in the old ways were sending their own prayers of thanksgiving to pagan gods. She disapproved.

Griffith assured me that that was no sacrilege as far as he was concerned. "Christ of the Cross and Epona the Horse Goddess, I would ask the blessings of every benevolent spirit on our unborn babe, Aldith."

"You would traffic with pagan gods?"

"Christianity is the true faith, surely, and I would run a sword through any man who denied it. But the gods of the woods and water were here long before the coming of the first man to the land of the Cymry. Their place has not been taken by the region of men; they still have their own laws and are deserving of respect. I pray each day to the God of the Christians, but I do not challenge the power that hurls the lightning."

Griffith had many deeps in him. In a lifetime I could not have learned them all. If we had had a lifetime.

So my Griffith left me to attend the business of war, and I was left with the business of women. Day by day my belly swelled with the fruit of our lovemaking until the babe growing inside me even crowded out some of my loneliness for my absent lord.

"He will be a fine, lusty boy, my lady" everyone assured me.

"He must be; Griffith wants a son so much. But how can I be sure?" Then I remembered Angharad, the woman from the beach who had "the sight." I sent Madog to fetch her to me.

"Angharad, it is said of you that you can see things unknown to others. Is that true?"

She gave a simple nod of her head. "I can tell some things, my lady."

"I would know—truly—if the child I bear is a son or no. Can you tell me this thing?"

She gave me a gap-toothed smile. "Spit, my lady."

I was startled. "Eh?"

"Spit! Into your palm, like this; then give me the taste of it."

I never heard of such a strange thing! But she seemed so sure of herself that I did as she bade me, though I felt extremely foolish.

After her hot tongue flicked across my wetted palm she shut her eyes a moment and then nodded. "Aye, my lady, you carry a son. Be certain of it."

The days were long; the summer moons waxed and waned. It was not Griffith's custom to wage war in the wintertime, so I hoped he would return to Rhuddlan before our child was born. I was worried about him, but there was nothing to be done for it; such news as we got made it seem that the war was a sizeable one, and that the Prince was acquitting himself well, as always.

We heard that a fleet came from Norway led by one Magnus, son of Harald Hardraada. "Hardraada is a giant!" the message bearers said. "He is reputed to stand full seven feet tall, and his son Magnus is near to his sire's height. He will wreak fearsome devastation on England!"

Griffith and my father seemed to have picked for themselves a frightening ally. I waited with apprehension for each new titbit of information, always hoping and fearing together.

"You will do yourself harm, my lady!" Emma remonstrated with me. "You should think only of the coming child!"

"Mayhap. But I want to know, Emma, I want to know!"

Emma shook her grizzled head and muttered, "It is a curse, this 'wanting to know.' Why can you not be content with women's matters?"

"My husband's life is my affair, too! I would not be shut all day in a chamber, ignorant of everything beyond the door! Who knows what might be sneaking up on me unawares? As a child I was ignorant, Emma. I do not want to be that way anymore."

In time we learned that a fleet came from the Orkneys, the Hebrides, and Dublin, all intent upon attacking England. But the winter came on early and savage that year, frost killing the crops even before the harvest, and the storms that raked the coast eventually forced the invaders to turn back. Griffith came home, bitterly disappointed, with news that the Earl Aelfgar had once more been outlawed and that his own adventures against England were temporarily halted.

It was not seemly to appear to rejoice over my husband's failure, so I did so in private. I felt pity for my father, of course, being now dispossessed of the earldom his own father had held so long and well. But I was mightily thankful that my love had come home safe to me, to stand by my bed at the lying-in and hear our baby's first furious cries. It was a son, of course.

We christened him Llywelyn.

Then we had more good news: The English king, the saintly Edward, had decided to make a grand gesture of magnanimity. Once more the Earl Aelfgar was restored, and the holdings in Mercia returned to him.

"It is safe enough to do that now," Griffith commented when we heard the tidings. "The campaign took much out of Aelfgar, Aldith; he is like an old dog with pulled teeth. I fear he will make no more trouble for Edward and the Godwines, and they know it as well. When he is gone Mercia will go to your brother Edwin, and the struggle will begin anew."

"I doubt it," I said dryly. "Edwin will simply ally himself with whichever seems to be the strongest side, and that will be that."

"You do not understand politics, Aldith."

"I understand my brother."

Aelfgar was Earl in Mercia for four more years. In the autumn of the Year of Our Lord 1062 word was brought to us of his death as I lay abed giving birth to our third child. Llywelyn and his little brother, Rhodri, were too young to understand the death of a grandsire they had never seen, but even amid the birth pangs I felt the death pang of my father.

Once my father's dying would have been a loss past all imagining or bearing. How strange to find that the miles and the years cushioned me from it, made it a thing which had happened to someone dear but no longer indispensable to me!

We spoke of it as our new daughter took milk from my breast, and Griffith watched with that contented look of a man who already has sons. He could well afford to enjoy the beauty and delicacy of this tiny female person who chewed my nipple and rolled her eyes at him.

"Were you much grieved when your father died?" I asked Griffith.

"I felt his loss, to be sure. He was a noble man and a good sire to me. But in a way it was just as if he had stepped aside and left a place for me to fill. I continue in his stead, and so Llywelyn ap Seisyll is not lost; when I am gone our son will do that for me, God willing."

"It is not the same with daughters," I commented sadly.

Griffith looked as if this were a new thought for him. "No I suppose not! But your father's blood flows on in your children; mayhap you would like to name this new girl with a name from his family!"

What a generous idea! "His mother was called Godiva . . ." I began.

Griffith frowned. "Yes, I've heard of her. Perhaps another name might be more, ah, seemly?"

I thought a moment. "Agatha?"

"It has a hard sound."

"Emma?"

"Please, Aldith, your maid is named Emma!"

At last we named the child Nesta, after a famous and beautiful Welsh princess who happened to be an ancestress of Griffith's.

But the peaceful time was short for us. When Nesta was six weeks old my dear Emma fell ill with the burning sickness, and before the babe was weaned we held a Cymric funeral for her on the plain before Rhuddlan. Emma would not have approved of the old Welsh customs by which her passing was mourned, but it did my heart good to know that her bones rested within earshot of my children's laughter as they played.

In spite of the deaths, the coming Christmas festivities were muchly anticipated; court mourning for the Earl Aelfgar was to be put aside in celebration of the holy time. The cooks prepared a great feast, and Griffith invited all his kinsmen from as far away as Deheubarth and Morgannwg. Then I sat by his side at table;

then was I honored and admired and my opinions much listened to!

"Your Saxon wife does you credit, my lord," commented one of Griffith's numerous cousins. "If I were to close my eyes, my ears would tell me she was born within our own borders."

"That may come to pass, in a way," smiled my Prince. "It is well known that the borders of countries are not immutably fixed; someday we may see East Anglia within the borders of Wales, may we not?"

All of the company laughed and cheered at that, and I raised my goblet in toast with the rest, though I privately wondered what King Edward and the almighty Godwines would think of such a boast.

I found out soon enough.

Even as we sat at table that feast day there were those among us who could not be trusted, men jealous of my Griffith's power and anxious to ingratiate themselves with his enemies. I cannot understand it! Griffith was a goodly Prince, fair and generous to all his people. Yet for his very virtues some men hated him.

The wreaths and garlands we had hung in the hall were still glossy with life when word came from Chester. I was sitting at my loom, I recall, giving instructions to Gwladys, Emma's replacement. We heard a mighty commotion outside and much running about, and I sent Gwladys to find out what was the matter. While she was gone I sat frozen, remembering the long-ago sounds of the King's men come for my father.

But it was not Gwladys who told me what it all meant. My Griffith himself came storming into our chamber, black as a thundercloud, bellowing to have the chamberlain and the captain of his guards sent to him.

"My lord! What is it?"

"Godwine," Griffith snarled, and the look on his face was one I had never seen before. It was the face of hate and war. "Godwine has attacked Chester."

My thoughts were numbed. "The old Earl?" I could not picture him leading troops, he must have been well nigh in his dotage!

"Not the Earl! His son, Harold, leads men against us, and the cub is much more dangerous than the tiger who sired him! They have swept aside all resistance and are marching upon Rhuddlan this very moment! Rhys? Rhys! Attend me at once"

Rhuddlan—under attack? I simply could not shape my mind around such a thing. All my life I had heard the names of the Earl Godwine and his sons, but they had always been "the enemy" distant and apart from me, a situation to be dealt with by politics or battle. Now they were bringing the battle to Rhuddlan! our home!

Shock upon shock. Rhys came at last, hotfoot and out of breath, to report that there had been some kind of a defection among the household guards, and our troop strength was muchly reduced. "By the gods!" thundered Griffith, "that damned Godwine has dipped into his bottomless purse and lured my own men away from me! I'll slice him into sections for that! I swear to you, Aldith, by next Christ Mass we will feast on Harold Godwine stewed and served in a pudding!"

A counting of heads convinced Griffith that Rhys was right; not enough armed men remained at Rhuddlan to defend it. "Will you stand and fight here anyway?" I asked my husband. "You can defeat a mere Godwine even without troops, I know it!"

Even in that extreme moment he paused to give me a quick, tender smile. "So I could, my love, and I bless you for your faith. But there is one weapon to Harold's armory I cannot face."

I was indignant for his sake. "What weapon!"

"You, my Aldith. You and our children. I cannot risk battle with you here. I will not take a chance with your lives. We must do as the

112

wolf does when he is outnumbered, seek a safe den and fight when we have a position of strength once more."

Horrified, I reached out and touched his arm, feeling the muscles clench and unclench as he made fists of fury. "Flee Rhuddlan, Griffith? Is that what you are saying? We will abandon Rhuddlan to Godwine?"

"Only for now, Aldith," he assured me. "Only for now."

In a matter of hours Griffith, the children and I, with a few servants and our most trusted courtiers, were miles from Rhuddlan and riding a-gallop for the mountains to the west. As the land began its first gentle rise beneath us, Griffith pulled up his steaming horse and turned his face in the direction we had come. What I saw mirrored in his eyes horrified me. "Don't let the children look!" he told me hoarsely.

All along the eastern horizon was the glow of fire, from the mouth of the Clwyd where Griffith's ships lay at anchor to the Toot-hill itself. Harold had put all to the torch.

How cold the west wind was! Snow stung our faces and whipped around us, blinding the horses. At night we slept on the hard ground, wrapped in our cloaks like soldiers. The boys were brave in their ignorance, thinking it was

113

some exciting new game we were all playing,
but I worried for the baby's sake. She was so
small, so dainty!

Griffith was making for Caerhun, where he
hoped to put together a force of men capable of
fighting Godwine. Madog thought he would
have a better chance of getting enough men at
Conway, but Griffith rejected that.

"Conway is on the coast, and Godwine is
bound to send ships there looking for me. If I
am to be hunted down like a dog, I do not
choose to fight with my back to the sea; I am
no great swimmer, Madog! We will go instead
to the mountains, where I know a hundred secret places and ten thousand friends will aid
me!"

We struggled on and on. The boys realized
it was no game and became exhausted and fretful; the allies Griffith hoped to find seemed to
melt away even as we approached. So savage
had Harold Godwine's attack been that he carried all before him like a storm wind. Griffith's
peace had made the Cymry soft; they were no
longer used to fighting in their heartland. The
Godwine seemed invincible.

At Caerhun we learned there would be no
army raised in that region. "It is rumored that
Tostig, Harold Godwine's brother, approaches
already from Northumbria. There are ships of

Godwine's landing up and down the coast, taking hostages and demanding tribute." The patriarch of the tribe at Caerhun was sympathetic but badly frightened. "We are not able to fight such a force, my lord!" he told Griffith. "Aelfgar is dead, his men are of uncertain allegiance now. And the Irish, the Norwegians—they are too far away! By the time they could assemble an army and bring it across the seas all Wales could be in flames! Besides," he added, giving Griffith a sly look from beneath his brows, "it is said that the tribes to the south are not totally in sympathy with the Prince of Gwynedd anyway. It is well known you have no hereditary right to rule there, my lord, having taken control of that country from, ah, men you defeated in battle."

"So what do you suggest, you cowardly dog!" Griffith was white-lipped with rage. "Should I send my submission to Godwine and his lily-livered King? Should I turn over all of Wales to Edward Milk-Mouth? Pah!" He spat in contempt, and if most of his spittle hit the face of the patriarch of Caerhun it may not have been an accident.

That night we sheltered in a cave in the forest. With a stone rolled into the cave mouth to conceal most of the glow of our fire, the place was warm enough and dry. I lay in my Griffith's arms, and the scent of the smoke was sharp in my nostrils, like the peat fires in Ireland. Furs and boughs formed our bed, a supper of cold mutton and oatcakes filled our bellies. Strangely enough, though I was frightened, I was not unhappy. In those hours Griffith was more mine than he had been many times at Rhuddlan. With our children sleeping nearby I still had everything that really mattered.

But we could not stay there. Scouts saw soldiers on the road, and we were off again, hares running before the hounds. We went ever deeper into the wild places, while winter melted into spring and the promise of summer greened the land.

Many times we were promised aid that never materialized. Occasionally Griffith would gather enough men to stage an attack on the nearest English-held post, but we were so sorely outnumbered by that time that the best he could hope to do was to inflict some damage and get away with a whole skin. It was the defection of those Griffith had believed loyal that hurt him the most, even more than the destruction of Rhuddlan and his other holdings.

"I have always been a loyal man, Aldith!" he mourned to me in his dark hours. "Loyal to my heritage, loyal to my friends and allies. Could I not expect loyalty in return?"

"I heard once, my love, that you commented on the treachery of the Saxons and the Danes. Perhaps such things are commonplace with all men, even the Cymry?"

"No!" He smacked his first upon his knee. "I will not believe that! I would not have it so! Honor is sacred among us, it *must* be. So often that is all we have."

Oh, my love, I would have spared you the final treachery if I could.

It was in the eighth month of the year, after a hard summer of running and fighting and running again. I felt that I had learned to be an Irish warrior queen in truth and had begun to fancy myself in that way; the children had grown hard and smart beyond their years and the few friends we still had had proved their loyalty thrice over. We had built ourselves a camp of sorts, by a waterfall and a clear mountain pool, and Griffith and I were enjoying a rare moment of peace. We sat together on a sun-dappled rock, paddling our feet in the pool like children and laughing. From the rocks above us came the voice of Madog, who was acting as sentry.

"There are men on the path, my lord."

Griffith gave a sigh and lifted his feet from the water. I could see the drops fall, separate sparkling little jewels, from his toes. "Soldiers?"

"I think not, my lord, they are dressed as Cymry. It is . . . yes . . . no . . . yes! I believe it is some of our own men, my lord, come back to us!"

The pleasure in Madog's voice found no answer in my Griffith's face. He stood up swiftly, peering down the path, and I heard the gasp of his indrawn breath. "Aldith, quick! Go find Gwladys and the children and hide! Hide, do you hear!"

"But Griffith . . . !"

He gave me a mighty shove that sent me stumbling away from the pool. "Don't argue now, woman, of all times! Those are not friends; they are traitors who left us as far away as Caerhun! We are betrayed!" With a despairing cry he grabbed for the sword which never lay far from his hand. I raced up into the rocks, my bare feet cut and bleeding and caring not, and at last I found Gwladys and the children in a thicket where they had gone hunting birds' eggs.

The sounds of battle came clearly up to us as we crouched in the brush. Some Welsh voices we heard, but many more spoke the Saxon tongue. And the cries of pain began straightway.

"God-a-mercy, what will happen to us if the Prince is killed?" Gwladys whispered to me. Unlike Emma, she was a Celt and did not always look on the bright side of possibilities. Hearing her, Rhodri began to whimper, and we had much ado to quiet him.

The commotion of battle lessened. With pounding heart I wriggled my way forward on my belly until I could look between two saplings directly down to the area of our campsite. There I saw the one thing in all the world I could not bear to see. My Griffith stood, erect and proud and still barefoot, in a ring of Saxon soldiers. Around him on the ground, dead and dying, were the bleeding remnants of our little band. Closest to his Prince lay faithful Madog, with the arm that still carried his sword hacked clean from his body and lying by itself in a crimson pool.

A Saxon with a sneer of victory on his face stood before Griffith, and in his shadow lurked the cowards who had betrayed their Prince and led Godwine's men to this old hawking place of his.

"Griffith of Gwynedd?" the Saxon intoned mockingly. "I have an invitation for you. Harold Godwine requests your attendance at his supper table tomorrow."

"I would sooner dine with the pigs!" Griffith flung back his head and glared at his captor.

"Ah, you misunderstand. You are not invited to dine. You are, let us say, to provide the *entertainment*."

"I will provide no sport for the Godwine! You cannot frighten me with torture!"

"I have no instructions to torture you," said the Saxon coolly. And with a sudden, savage swing, he raised his hideous battle-ax and cleaved Griffith's head from his body.

The man caught it by its auburn hair, even before it hit the dirt, and he held it up at arm's length for the cheering men. "The centerpiece for Harold Godwine's table!" he cried.

Harold

SOMETIMES IT IS POSSIBLE to be hurt so badly that you don't feel anything at all. It was like that for me for a little while. I was fully aware that the sun was still high in the sky, birds twittered in the trees and the rocky ground on which I lay hurt my ribs. But an unseen blanket was wrapped around me; no grief or agony passed through. My eyes saw Griffith die; my soul did not feel it. For a little while.

There was so much blood! I had not believed there was that much blood in a human body! I lay there whispering "Jesus and Mary, Jesus and Mary" to myself, I don't know why, watching the blood spout from my husband's body and feeling only a sense of relief that the children could not see it from where they crouched, hidden with Gwladys.

Then all at once something snapped in me. I have no memory of getting up or scrambling down the hillside. I was aware of nothing until I staggered into the center of that murderous band and began hitting blindly at everyone in sight. Screams of hate and rage tore from my throat. I felt possessed of a thousand devils. Nothing could hurt me, nothing could stop me! I knew only that I must punish them, tear and rend them with my teeth and nails until the thing was undone somehow and my Griffith was alive again! It had to be!

I was seized around the waist from behind by that same Saxon housecarle whose ax had just slain my lord. I kicked—it gave me some satisfaction to feel my heels striking his shins— but even in my madness my strength was no match for his. Oh, my Griffith, I was not strong enough to be the warrior queen you deserved, but I did my best, my love!

"What's this!" I heard his voice exclaim. "A Welsh wildcat come to kill us all!"

The men around him laughed, making mock of me, but I did not care.

"Murderers, murderers!" I screamed at them.

"Not murderers, lady!" exclaimed one of the Saxons, putting on an offended voice even though he laughed at me. "This is an honorable act of war. We have slain the troublemaker Griffith and restored the land to peace."

I struggled to reach behind me and rip the ears off my captor, but two other men grabbed my flailing hands and held them fast. To my horror, I saw that one of the men was Rhyderch, a former member of our own household guard. In my contempt I spat in his face.

"You do not call this murder, Rhyderch? You who have betrayed your Prince with the foulest treason, do you not think that makes you his murderer?"

Rhyderch stuck out his weak little chin obstinately and tried to look as if he were a man. "Not murder, my lady! I have aided our Saxon friends in the destruction of the Welsh tyrant, and I am proud to take credit for it."

There were no words for the fury I felt, so I screamed without words. My mind searched the Welsh vocabulary I had learned so diligently and found no name foul enough to call Rhyderch and his kind. But the Saxon tongue abounded in them.

"Maggot in dog dung!" I shrieked at him

in the language of my childhood. "Ball-less abortion of a humpbacked whore!"

"What's this! The Welsh wildcat is a Saxon!" The man holding me shifted his grip and spun me around to face him, that I might see the light of triumph in his eyes. "We have caught ourselves Griffith's wife, the Lady Edyth! Is that not so, Rhyderch?"

"Aye, for what it's worth," responded Rhyderch. His Saxon was as poor as my Welsh was good, but the housecarle understood him well enough. "The daughter of a twice-convicted traitor and herself a traitor to King Edward, she's not such a prize."

"You're a fine one to talk of traitors!" I exploded.

"Yes, shut your mouth, Rhyderch," the Saxon said. "You enrage this witch much more and I may not be able to hold her. In fact, I may let her loose at you!" They all laughed at that. He gave me over to be held by his men and stepped back to get a good look at me.

The strength of my madness was draining from me, leaving my stomach heaving and my knees weak as water. A roaring came into my ears like the distant voice of the sea, heard from the towers of Rhuddlan. I tried to fight it off, but a swirling mist enveloped me and they all went away, Saxon and Welsh alike. I sank into a darkness where there was no Griffith.

The world came back to me very slowly. I lay on a rough blanket on the ground, face down, and my ankles and wrists were bound with something that scratched my skin. I wanted to vomit, but my belly was empty, and I would have swallowed my own tongue rather than give those men the satisfaction of seeing me shamed.

There were voices above and behind me.

"What shall we do with the body, sir?"

"Dig a hole yonder and bury it; I have no orders concerning its disposal. Bury it deep so that you need build no rock cairn to protect it. I want no one to find his remains!"

His remains! It was my Griffith's body they were putting into the ground, in an unmarked grave in the mountain fastness of Snowdonia. There was something right about that. It was not a royal burial—the Cymry funeral rites would not be done—but at least my lord would sleep undisturbed in a place he loved.

Then I remembered. He would not sleep entire. My body convulsed with pain, and I wept bitter tears onto the Saxon blanket.

"She's awake, I think."

"Let her be." It was the voice of the captain, he who wielded the ax. There was compassion in it. "There is no comfort for her in this day. The best thing we can do is to leave her alone to mourn her dead."

"What will be done with her, sir?"

"She will go with us to Tremadoc Bay, where we rendezvous with Godwine's flagship. My Lord Harold will be much impressed with the trophies we bring him."

"The head is not a trophy!" exclaimed a Welsh-accented voice. "You gave your word, Gareth!"

"So I did. Very well, it shall be a sign from your people that they wish to make peace and will submit to the King."

I shuddered. How my Griffith would have hated having the head of his body used for that vile purpose! Griffith, who never submitted. Griffith, who had fought so long and gallantly to unite his people as the independent Welsh.

The children!

It came on me like a blow. With Griffith's death every other thing had gone out of my mind; it was as if nothing existed but him and the loss of him. Then they were back again, all that was left of our love, and I knew that they were nearby and in danger. I twisted around on my blanket and tried to see what was going on.

The Saxon captain, Gareth, stood close by, supervising the breaking of our camp and the packing up of booty. Little enough it was by then: our ragged clothes, our weapons, cooking utensils and the small chest of coin and jewels that was all we had left of the wealth of

126

Gwynedd. I saw one of the Saxons gather up the violet silk which had been Griffith's wedding gift to me and smooth it against his rough beard.

"There are toys for a child here, sir," one of the men reported. "And these are an infant's clothes."

Gareth was on his knees by my side, bending down to peer into my face. "Where are they, my lady? What have you done with the children?"

"They could not be here!" exclaimed someone. "Small children could not have made the trip to this desolate spot. They must have left them on the other side of Llanberis Pass!"

I felt contempt for any man who might think the children of Griffith ap Llywelyn too weak for mountain climbing! But I knew better than to open my mouth and brag; let them think the children were elsewhere.

Gareth kept his eyes on mine. "Where are they?" he said sternly.

I glared at him and clamped my jaws shut.

"Search!" he cried. "We will not leave this place until every rock is turned over and every crevice plumbed. I tell you Griffith's welps are here, and they must be found!"

There was no way I could save them, nothing I could do but lie helpless and heartsick.

127

I heard the Saxons scrambling about in the rocks, awkward and swearing, and I wished they might all fall and break their necks.

Ill wishes do no one any good. They found the children eventually and brought them to Gareth, together with a trembling but defiant Gwladys. One of the Saxons had a rueful smile and a swiftly closing enpurpled eye. "She hit me with a rock, but I wrestled her down," he reported cheerfully.

"Good job. It is close upon sundown; we will camp here for the night and leave by daybreak; some of Griffith's rebels may still be alive in these mountains. The sooner we get out of here the better I shall feel."

So they brought us down from the mountains, to the deep blue bay where Godwine's Saxon ships rode at anchor. I cannot say we were treated unfairly. At Gareth's order Gwladys was allowed to tend to my needs and dress the children; she bound up my hair for me and saw to it that my appearance did honor to my husband's memory.

Part of Griffith came with us also. In a wicker basket, strapped onto the back of a pony who carried no other burden. I tried never to see that pony.

A landing party met us at the shore. Like Gareth and his men, they wore a body armor of boiled leather, replacing the links of mail I re-

membered from my childhood. Gareth had
caught me eyeing it once and commented, "It is
an invention of Harold Godwine, much lighter
and easier for mountain warfare. He has many
strings to his bow, our Harold."

Our company was drawn up along the
beach as the landing party set out from the foremost ship. The boat carried a gonfalon at its
prow, a flag hanging from a crosspiece and bearing the golden emblem of the Fighting Men,
which was Harold Godwine's personal device.
Beside his banner stood Harold himself, legs
braced against the rolling of the boat, the first
man to leap out and onto the conquered Welsh
shore.

In childhood I may have see Harold Godwine at some feast day, though I do not remember. I had heard whispers that he was handsome
above other men, but as he looked nothing like
Griffith ap Llywelyn I found him ugly. He was
of an age with Griffith, somewhere in his early
forties, but there all resemblance ended.

The brute stood a head taller than the tall-
est of his men, so that one could not look honestly into his eyes. His hair, cropped short for battle, was as gold as the Fighting Man; the face
beneath it might have been chiseled from stone,
so firm and unyielding it was.

His eyes were blue, icy as the Irish Sea.
The lashes and brows were gold like his hair,

but so pale against his sunburned skin that he appeared to have none. He looked like what he was, half Saxon and half Dane, all arrogance. He returned his captain's salute and listened gravely to his report, glancing once toward the pony who stood waiting with his dreadful wicker hamper. Then he nodded and strode briskly over to me.

"Your servant, madam," he said formally. His voice was not deep and rich like Griffith's, it was roughened by too much shouting in battle.

"God strike you dead," I replied.

"What a tender greeting! My man has told me you were not appreciative of being rescued from these savages."

"These savages, as you call them, are my people!"

"How loyal of you!" he said dryly. "I like that. Loyalty is a quality in very short coin these days. Perhaps sometime you will tell me how Prince Griffith managed to win yours."

"I would not tell you if your beard were on fire!" I spat.

"Then I must keep my beard away from the hot coals of your temper, my lady," Harold said. He turned his back on me abruptly, with great rudeness, and began ordering the preparations for boarding ship.

To my annoyance we were treated civilly

130

enough on board. I would have preferred something I could fight, a reason to scream and struggle. Gwladys, the children and I all had to share one small cubbyhole, to be sure, as a warship is not equipped for family travel, but at least we had a private place to sleep and decent food was brought to us.

The children and Gwladys, their stomachs used to Welsh fare, rebelled at the beef pies and stewed eels I remembered from Saxon tables. Then too, they all suffered much from the seabelly. But that was never to bother me again; the first voyage to Ireland had cured me of that forever.

What happened to the Welshmen who had led Harold's soldiers to us I do not know. They did not accompany us aboard the Saxon ship, and I never saw them again, to my great relief. It was easier for me to forgive Gareth and his ax, or even the spirit of Harold Godwine that guided it, than to forgive those treacherous cowards who traded their Prince's head for King Edward's peace.

We sailed south across the Cardigan Bay and past the westernmost tip of Wales, then turned toward the sun into the Bristol Channel Harold was making for Gloucester, to meet with the members of the Witan and tell them personally of his triumph.

On the night before landfall he sought me out, sending Gwladys and the children away that he might speak with me in private.

"I have nothing to say to you, Godwinesson," I told him contemptuously as soon as we were alone.

He was not bothered. "There is no need for you to speak at all," he said. "Women's words have no weight with me. I inform you of my plans as a courtesy, nothing more. I assure you, madam, there is nothing you can do to thwart me!" His cold eyes flashed such a sudden, hot blue that I was startled. Was there some way I could thwart him, then? Was he warning me off? If I could find the way, how gladly would I see all Harold Godwine's ambitions reduced to rubble about his ankles!

"At Gloucester I will produce the . . . token . . . we carry with us, and sue for peace on behalf of all Griffith's former subjects. Then, if you like, it will be given Christian burial."

My eyes threatened to fill with tears, but I dashed them away. I would not give this man the satisfaction of doing me a favor! "Do what you like with it! It is Griffith no longer; nothing of him lives in that bloody relic you acquired with treachery! His soul is immortal, his spirit is safely housed in his children; you cannot use his empty shell to play games with my sympathy."

There was a certain grudging respect in Harold's eyes. "You have a strong heart, madam. Do you throw sons as brave as yourself?" His eyes raked my body from breast to hip and back again. "Yes, indeed," he murmured as if to himself, "Griffith chose well. Three children in a short span of years, and all alive and sturdy. Two sons, and a body to bear many more."

I stared at him in horror; his thoughts were too frankly writ upon his face. "You think I would bear you children! I would kill myself on the instant before I let you even touch me!"

His smile was amused. "Oh come, Edyth. There is little you could do to prevent me if I chose to take you here and now. At a word from me, guards would be here to hold you for me, if that were necessary. Though it would not be; I have taken stronger wenches than you."

He leaned, perfectly relaxed, against the bulkhead of his ship, I could see that he was enjoying this crude play, and my hatred only spiced the pot. I determined to bite my tongue and give him nothing more.

"You are of a noble house," Harold commented idly, "for the line of your father is as old and honored as mine. You have kinsmen whose alliance would be of much value to me. You might be valuable as a wife."

I was as deeply shocked as I have ever been. Under the circumstances how dare he make such a vile suggestion! How could he hope to force me to share a marriage bed with him after killing my Griffith!

Besides—my thoughts ranged back over the years—was he not already wed? In my girlhood I had heard something, surely, about a wife to Harold Godwine? And was there not a touch of scandal to the story? I struggled to remember.

"What you speak of is not possible!" I lashed out at him. "You have a wife already. Would you add bigamy to all your many sins?"

The fierce blue eyes clouded, and I saw that at last one of my own darts had struck home. "Keep silence! I commit no crimes against God or the Church! The woman of whom you speak was hand-fast to me only, we were never wed formally. She is of peasant stock; our children cannot sit on the throne."

With that one statement he revealed to me the utmost reaches of his ambition. It was true, then; Harold Godwine did indeed intend to be King of England, and even his long-time relationship with the mother of his many children would not be allowed to stand in the way of that goal. A hand-fast wife was bound to her husband in every way but in the eyes of the canon law. Harold would put her aisde to get heirs whose bloodlines were above reproach.

"And your children by her?" I asked, anxious to wound him further now that I had got my knife into him a little way. "What of them?"

He was quick as a cat, Harold. He stole my weapon and turned it against me in the winking of an eye. "And your own children, madam, what of them? Mark you well, they are in my custody and power. If I choose to execute them tomorrow as a danger to the Crown, no man can say me nay. Think of that, Edyth!"

He spun on his heel and left me alone, the echoes of his words resounding from wall to wall.

The weapon Griffith feared most was at my throat now.

From that moment on the boys were kept from me. Gwladys brought Nesta to me to suck, but I never saw Llywelyn and Rhodri. "They are safe, my lady," Gwladys assured me. "I see them myself, and they ask for you and send you love." But it was not the same as having my own arms around them.

A guard stood, night and day, where my every movement could be seen. I was allowed on deck each day to walk and take the air, but only during such times as the boys were safely out of sight. When we put in at Gloucester and Harold went ashore, I was kept closely guarded below-decks.

Fortunately, one of my guards felt sorry for me. It was he who brought me news of the

world beyond our prison ship. "Harold Godwine
has put into Gloucester and glory, my lady!"
he exulted. "News of the subjugation of the
Welsh has already reached here; the people are
drunk with excitement, and it is said Harold
will be proclaimed Vice-King by the Council!"

"What does it mean, Vice-King?"

"It ranks above the title of atheling, my
lady. It is a sure sign of King Edward's favor
and forgiveness."

Forgiveness? "Why should Harold Godwine seek the King's forgiveness?"

"It was his father, Earl Godwine, who tor-
tured to death King Edward's brother Alfred
many years ago. Even when Edward married
Godwine's daughter he could not find it in his
heart to forgive that, for all his piety and chari-
ty. Although the Godwines rose to power until
they controlled the Witan itself, the curse of Alfred's death has ever hung over them. Mayhap
this new Welsh peace will put an end to the bitterness at last. King Edward has much to
be grateful to Harold and his brother for."

Murder and treachery; it seemed they ever
ran in tandem with power and the struggle for
it. Would that be the legacy of my sons, elegant Llywelyn and sturdy little Rhodri full of
chuckles?

Harold Godwine came to me again, but
he did not come alone. This time he brought

with him two of his men, one of them Gareth of the ax. I smiled when I saw that.

"Are you so afraid of me you need protection, you murderous son of a murderer?"

Harold's expression did not change. "You have a savage tongue, Edyth. Mayhap I will take the time to cure you of it, and of all the foreign ways you learned with your Welsh Prince. But there is not time for that now. I came to tell you that I ride for Worcester tomorrow with the Bishop Wulfstan."

"What concern is that of mine?"

"None," he said shortly. "But I thought you might like to know that I have divided Wales between Griffith's half-brothers, and they have all sworn fealty to Edward and to me. I go to tell my Lord King of these things and receive his blessing."

I did not ask him about the head. I did not ask him for word of my children. I asked him nothing; I gave him a face of stone.

"I have been undecided as to what to do with you," Harold continued, gazing at the wall above me as if I were of no consequence. "Your brother Edwin sits in Mercia now, know you that?"

I shrugged. Indifference is a woman's weapon, better than none.

"And your brother Morkere is come of age as well, and makes known his claim to land

and title. Mercia is the only territory of great size in all England not under my influence, Edyth; I would like to feel that Earl Edwin has some reason to support me in the event of an attempt on the throne by some foreign usurper."

"I can assure you there is little love lost between me and my brothers," I informed him. "If you plan to hold me hostage to insure my brothers' allegiance, you make a mistake."

"I plan to do no such thing," Harold assured me. "I doubt it will be necessary. If my judgment of his character is aright, I think Edwin will come to me in time. But I think it would be wise statecraft to keep you under my thumb, nevertheless. I should not like Griffith's widow and his wolfpups set loose in the countryside. I would not feel my back was safe."

"So you will stay awhile with me, as my guest, Edyth. I hope that will be satisfactory with you?" He did not bother to listen for an answer. "And at such time as your brothers seek a star to follow, perhaps we shall all be one happy family, eh?"

"Your guest!" I said contemptuously. "You mean your prisoner!"

"I mean what I said. You—and the children, of course—will stay with my mother, the Lady Gytha, at one of our houses. I can assure you that you will have every comfort save only the ability to leave when you like. I would not show disrespect to a fallen foe's widow, Edyth. Griffith was a brave man and a worthy opponent; I want you to know that I am aware of that and I honor him for it."

"We don't need your honor! We don't need anything from you!"

"Nevertheless, madam, you will take what I give," said Harold.

On the morrow, preparations were begun for us all to depart the ship, Harold and his men riding north, and I to be met by a party of Saxon housecarles who would take me to Harold's mother—and the start of my imprisonment.

An armed guard walked me from the dock to a place where two covered litters awaited us. I was seated in one before they brought my sons from the ship; looking through the draperies. I could see them. Nesta stirred in my arms, and I clutched her close to me, looking down at her little face in the rosy half-light that filtered through the cloth.

A clatter of hoofs sounded from the High Street and was met with a mighty cheer. By that sign I knew that Harold Godwine was riding through the streets of Gloucester as a hero. Then my sons came up and were put into the other litter. A wall of housecarles closed around us, the litter swayed, and we began our journey.

Wessex

As HAROLD GODWINE WAS Earl of Wessex, he
controlled all that portion of land in the south of
England from West Wales to the English Channel. The Godwines owned a goodly number of
houses throughout the countryside, and as it
was Harold's intention that I should be in his
mother's custody (he called it "safekeeping"),
he was sending me to her residence of the moment at Chichester.

Our way lay through the southern shires, a
land I had not seen before, and very different

from the sunny Anglian marshes. We traveled through peaceful green valleys and wooded pastureland where swine grazed; we crossed rolling meadows and skirted hills that were ridiculous in comparison to the mountains of Wales. All about us lay a rich and fertile land, readily obedient to the blow, and I began to realize the wealth of the Godwines.

One midday we stopped at a river fording to break our fast with bread and cheese, and the boys' escort allowed them to play for a little while at the edge of the woods. Llywelyn and Rhodri had won the hearts of their guards, and often I saw the rough housecarles playing gentle games with the little fellows, games which were surely not a part of their orders.

But on this day the guards' vigilance must have slackened, for the adventurous Rhodri had vanished into the dark mouth of the forest before anyone missed him. I was watching Gwladys mutilate a perfectly lovely loaf of bread when of a sudden there came a wail of pain and outrage. Guards or no, I was on my feet in a twinkling and running toward the trees.

"Mama! Mama!" Rhodri came stumbling toward me, his chubby little arms outstretched and his face reddened and scratched by brambles. I scooped him up and held him tight against me, feeling the little heart race like a rabbit's. One of his escort reached us and tried to take him from me, but no one could have done so at that moment.

"Are you hurt? Did an animal attack you? God, child, are you all right?"

Rhodri went on wailing and sobbing, but the answer came to me in the calm voice of my elder son, standing patiently to one side. "It is the stinging nettle," said Llywelyn. "I told him it was in there—it is everywhere about—but he wouldn't listen."

I began to laugh with relief. The Saxon guard, unable to understand Llywelyn's explanation, looked vexed, so I made a quick translation for him. Then he laughed too, a thing which changed Rhodri's tears of pain to tears of rage. No doubt he felt his grave injury was not properly appreciated!

Rhodri was allowed to ride in my litter the rest of the day, and I endeavored to make up to him the grave insult to his dignity. Gwladys lacked a salve for stinging nettle, it not being much of a hazard in the mountains, so we were grateful for the supply of some from the purse of one of the housecarles.

By such small adventures did we approach Winchester. A great city, Winchester, with some seven thousand souls, a cathedral and a market justly famed. Once it had been the capital of all Wessex, but times had grown portable—the center of his land was wherever

Harold was. Still, the city thrived and attracted produce and pilgrims, and I would have muchly liked to see it.

To my great disappointment, we left the High Road before we caught more than a glimpse of the town ahead of us, and we skirted it altogether. Only later did it occur to me that perhaps there were those in Winchester who might have been willing to aid the widow and children of the Welsh Prince; perhaps Harold still feared my dead husband's power. It comforted me to think so.

Each night we slept at a house belonging to the Godwines or one of their thegns. As we traveled farther and farther from the land of the Cymry, there grew in me a great sense of isolation from my heartland, and the sight of my children was more dear to me every hour. I hugged Nesta to me so tightly betimes that she cried, and Gwladys would scold and take her from me.

We passed through the shires at harvesttime; at one small farm where we stopped for water they were celebrating the feast of Harvest Home. A ceorl came out of his cottage and invited us to join in their merrymaking.

"Please, Osbert!" I begged the housecarle who captained our party. "It would be a treat for the children!"

Like the others, Osbert was not unmoved

by Griffith's little princes. "Very well, my lady, but mind you, it is a favor. Don't try to take advantage!"

What possible advantage could I have taken of such an opportunity? A helpless woman with small children, guarded on every side and lost in the heart of a strange country. I must confess the thought occurred to me, but it was too formidable an undertaking for me to consider seriously.

Harvest Home was the triumphal occasion of the year. To people who lived entirely by the efforts of their own hands, it was more important than Easter or the Christ Mass, I think. A corn dolly was made from ripe grain, dressed and decorated in a cunning fashion, and the farmers gathered round her to sing and dance. There was nothing of Christianity in this tradition, it was the ancient customs from pagan times, and I saw Llywelyn watching with wide eyes.

Osbert dropped on one knee beside my son to explain the ritual to him, and for that moment Osbert was almost as dear to me as lost Madog or Owain.

"They will sacrifice something, a sheep or an ox, and its blood will be sprinkled on the ground to insure next year's harvest."

Llywelyn's quick mind had begun to grasp the Saxon language, although I had nev-

er spoken it to him in Wales, but his tongue
stumbled badly over the words. As a gesture
to Osbert, however, my noble boy did try to
answer him in kind.

"The blood . . . it will make things grow?"

"Aye, son, that is the belief."

Llywelyn pondered a moment, then asked
a question which stopped my heart and froze
Osbert's smile upon his face.

"My father's blood; I saw it, on the
ground. What will grow from that?"

Osbert shoved the little boy toward me,
not unkindly, and turned his face away.

The countryfolk shared their feast with
us, a bounteous spread of beef, bacon and
wheaten cakes. Reed baskets were piled with
eels and lampreys. There were golden mounds
of cheese and butter, and in addition to mead
we were offered stout ale and perry in wood-
en cups. They did not know I was widow
to an enemy, but had they known it I am certain they would have treated me just the same.
Simple people in robes of goat hair and rough
wool, on that day their joy was so great it
overflowed and must be shared with everyone. Joy is like that. Sorrow is a solitary indulgence.

And so we came to Harold Godwine's seat
at Chichester. Or rather, I should say, at
Arundel, for it was there that the greatest of

his manor houses stood. Even from a distance the size of it was impressive, looming through the trees. We had come down an open way between two vast forests, and as we neared the sea the wind swept to us like a familiar friend. For the first time in many days Gwladys smiled, for a moment, but the smile was wiped from her face when she saw Arundel rising ahead.

"It is a fearsome place!" she groaned.

"Nonsense. It is a manor hall, such as the one where I was born. And there is no need to be a-tremble, Gwladys; they will not eat us. The country roundabout is adequate to feed the Godwines very well."

My brave words to my servant were from my lips and not my heart; the sight of Arundel frightened me as well. In truth, it was much larger than my father's hall at Thetford, and it was fortified somewhat as Rhuddlan had been.

We approached between two watchtowers, and the men who came to meet us were all armed. Osbert made his report to their captain, then servants came from within the hall to unpack us and escort us inside.

"The Lady Gytha, is she here?" I heard Osbert inquire of a porter.

"Aye, she is in her chamber and has not been out all the morning. Doubtless she will greet her guests when the mood strikes her."

That did not bode well for our welcome!

Harold Godwine's hall was as big as the hall at Rhuddlan—nay, bigger—and its richness was that of a king. Or a man who intended to be king. The timbered walls were stoutly made and chinked, and the sea wind was shut out by a Magnificent array of tapestries, some as high as two spearshafts. Purple and crimson and blue, fiery with gold threads, they took my breath away.

One had only to look at the number of feasting tables to realize the size of this vast household. And each table was draped with linen, after the Irish fashion, and covered with a wealth of gold and silver plate.

The fire which blazed night and day upon the hearth at the center of the hall was fed by wood unfamiliar to me, and the smoke was different from our sea-coal fires at Rhuddlan. I had come to yet another world, more hostile than any before, and I squeezed down inside myself and was afraid.

I was taken to a pleasant enough chamber, although it had neither hearth nor window, and there I slept on the first featherbed in all my life. An uneasy sleep under Harold Godwine's rooftree. Nesta slumbered on my breast, Gwladys lay at my feet, but no one shared the darkness inside my skull.

About cockcrow a page came to me. "The

Lady Gytha bids you God's day, and asks that you come to her chamber," the lad intoned in a piping voice.

"Dress me well, Gwladys! The violet silk, if it will hold together for one more wearing, and Griffith's medallion on my breast. I would not have this woman think me beneath her station!"

I might have spared myself the effort, and my violet gown the final wearing which saw its seams give way forever. Gytha, Lady of Godwine, thought everyone beneath her station, and it would not have made the slightest bit of difference had I worn gold samite and a crown of diamonds.

"You are Edyth the Saxon?" she began straightway, eyeing me up and down.

"I am Aldith, widow of Griffith ap Llywelyn!" I replied with some hauteur.

"There is no more Griffith Llywelyn, and his kingdom has sworn fealty to my son! Therefore you are once more a Saxon, and his vassal. You would be well advised not to vaunt your Welsh connection here; it is of no importance to us."

I found myself speechless with rage and could only stand a-tremble, glaring at the woman, until I had my tongue under control. The things I would say on my own behalf could not be said, for my children's sake, but the effort to bite them back cost me dear. I contented myself with taking her measure with my eyes, but I was not reassured by her looks.

A powerful matron, broad-hipped and gray of hair, Gytha was still in the strength of her maturity, and the remnants of beauty lay in her bones. The Danish accent still flawed her Saxon speech, and her eyes were Viking eyes, sea-watchful and savage. Her body had born a litter of warriors; I saw them in her face.

"I am not your willing guest, madam," I said coldly, "but I must insist you grant me the dignities of my station."

"Your station is whatever my son decides," she replied. "But I do not dishonor a guest, willing or otherwise, so you have no need to insult my hospitality by demanding fair treatment."

Our relationship was not well begun.

That night I had a dream, a nightmare, which was also a memory and a foreboding. I saw again the road from Gloucester to Winchester and that place of evil omen we had come upon. We had ridden for many miles through a lush and smiling countryside, dotted with ceorls' cottages and tapestried by late summer roses. And then, of a once, our way opened out onto a great drear plain, almost level, but with low-rising sweeps.

The spot was the extreme of desolateness, especially in the gathering twilight. The plain was dotted with mounds and fallen columns of stone, ancient tumuli beyond the telling of man. Druid circles, the housecarles whispered among themselves, and the pious made the sign of the cross.

A cold, sad wind was blowing as we paused on the Salisbury plain and looked at the ruin they call Stone Henge. No one spoke; even Gwladys fell silent with the hush of the place. I felt then a sense of timelessness, of deeds long past and deeds yet undone, and I felt that my small life had no part in any of it. The stones watched, uncaring, and kept their secrets. The clouds raced over us to their rendevous with the night, and a chill struck into my soul I thought I should never lose.

All this came back to me in my dream that night in the hall at Arundel. That same sense of doom no man could avoid, that same cold. It was said that blood sacrifice had been done at Stone Henge, and not the blood of cattle and pigs, either. In my dream the scent of blood came to me again, and I thought it blew to me from the future.

Gytha did show me one kindness: a mother herself, she understood my need for my children and did not keep us apart, though I doubt not that was her son's intention. They made the adjustment better than I; at least Rhodri did, and for the baby one home was very like another. Llywelyn was another matter. Very much his father's son, he had a tendency to worry a thought until he had got all the meat off its bones. I cannot count how many times he asked me the same questions.

"When will we go home, Mother?" "If Father is dead, am I Prince of Gwynedd now?" "Will I fight for Wales when I am older?"

I was of two minds as to the answer to that last question. Of course I wanted my son to be brave and noble, a worthy successor of his father's heritage. But a legacy of blood and death, of ambition never satisfied—how could I wish that for my son?

No such considerations bothered Gytha. Her ambitions for her own sons knew no bounds. Her conversation was larded with references to "My son Tostig, Earl of Northumbria" and "My son Gyrth—he holds your father's former seat at East Anglia, you know!" And every opportunity was made to speak of Harold Godwine's glorious future, which was to be exactly as the late Earl Godwine had planned it.

"No man in Christendon is so fit to be King of England as Harold!" Gytha would exclaim often in the hall, without fear of contradiction. "King Edward is old. His marriage to my daughter is chaste and without issue. Edward the Atheling, nearest in blood to Edward, a mere child, and his life has been spent in a foreign land. The Witan will never give him rule of this land when the threat of invasion is so constant!"

At one of these occasions, shortly before Christ Mass, Harold's brother Leofwine was present. Leofwine was the least blessed of the Godwine sons, holding only the earldoms of Essex and Kent, but he was as outspoken as the rest of that brood. "Tostig is the King's favorite, not Harold," he reminded his mother. "Think you not the King's wish will carry some weight with the Witan?"

Gytha swept his opinion aside with a wave of her brown-speckled, beringed hand: "It will be Harold," she said with certainty. "It will be as he desires."

"Desire!" Leofwine shouted with laughter. "If desire were the guarantee of a crown, half the kingdom would wear one! Would you say my lady mother, that Tostig's desire is lesser than Harold's?"

Gytha's thin lips pursed. "I would not. But Harold knows how to measure his desire and spend it out as he needs it, while Tostig is eaten alive with his. Harold will plan and do all things in the light of that plan, and I fear his brother will always act rashly."

Gytha had a fierce loyalty to all her children, but I never heard her be other than objective in her assessment of them. She had the qualities of a good general, did Gytha; she was realistic about strengths and weaknesses.

Leofwine was smaller and darker than the rest of that brood, and his eyes were twinkly like my Rhodri's. If I could have found it in me to like one of the Godwines, I would have liked Leofwine. He was always pleasant and courteous to me, and he flirted with the baby and made her laugh.

"What is Harold going to do with this Welsh prize, Madam?" he called over his shoulder to Gytha as he bent over Nesta's cradle. "I am not yet wed, and in a dozen years this babe will be breaking hearts with every glance. For that matter"—and he cut his eyes toward me—"her mother is still most fair!"

"Lay back, brother!" cried a mighty voice, filling the hall and jerking Leofwine upright like a doll upon a twine. Harold Godwine strode into his hall, a mantle of bright silk flaring from his shoulders and the crisp outside air swirling in with him. "Keep your eyes and your hands to yourself, Leofwine. The Welsh booty is mine!"

A moment before Leofwine had been a charming and self-assured young cock; with my eyes I saw him shrink a little and the luster go from him. For his sake I felt an annoyance with Harold Godwine—he drained the life from others, even his brother.

Harold saluted his mother and came straight to me. "I see you're still here," was his greeting.

"I was not aware I had a choice," I rejoined coldly.

He raised one sandy eyebrow and gave me a look I could not fathom. "We always have a choice, Edyth."

"My Lord Griffith did not think so! He did what he had to do and you slew him for it!"

"He had choices too—more than I."

"I am tired to death of you men who always pretend to be so abused by the very power you seek!"

Harold ignored my thrust and turned toward his mother. "You have not cured our vixen of her temper yet, madam! I thought by now you would have made an obedient daughter of her."

Both Gytha and I recoiled from that, but she recovered first. "I have daughters enough already, my lord! And daughters-in-law as well," she added, giving some special emphasis to her words. "It was my understanding that I was to be warder to this one, not mother!"

"Your distaste equals mine," I commented.

"Silence, both of you!" Harold roared in a battlefield voice. "Thank God there are still meek women and I know where to find them!" It was apparent that all present knew the meaning of that, save only me. Embarrassed glances were exchanged around the room, and I saw patent disapproval on the face of Stigand, Harold's priest and elbow-confidant.

"Since you brought up the subject . . ." Stigand began.

"I brought up nothing!"

". . . of Edith of the Swan Neck, perhaps we may assume you plan nuptials at last?"

Harold's scowl was savage. Tension crackled in the hall. All seemed to have forgotten me as some old argument was renewed.

"Edith has been hand-fast to me for twenty years, Stigand. If I had intended to wed her I would have done so long before now!"

"Nevertheless, it is a scandal, my lord."

"She is a fine girl," Gytha put in, "and she has borne you healthy children."

"Stop pressing upon me, all of you! Edith is a good woman and dear to me, as you all know, but she has always understood that I cannot make her my Lady. The arguments against it are as strong as ever."

"Your ambition is greater than your love, my lord," said Stigand sadly.

"My ambition is for the good of my country, Bishop. An advantageous marriage would strengthen my position at a time when the country requires me to be strong; marriage with a peasant would diminish me in the eyes of the Witan."

"I thought as much!" snapped Leofwine. "That was your reason for bringing Griffith's widow here, was it not? To pay court to her and assure yourself of her brothers' support when King Edward dies?"

Harold was whitely angry. "Do not speak of the King's death; it is a bad omen! Long may he live! Besides," he added in less ringing tones, "with Tostig on the north and Gyrth on the east, we have Edwin Aelfgarson quite surrounded in Mercia. I think he would see the wisdom of throwing his lot with us if need be."

Gytha had moved around the hall as this exchange was taking place; now she stood at my side, her voice hissing close to my ear. "You see how well he plans, my Harold," she said with a certain smugness. "It is true I would make merry to see him wed to Edith Swan Neck. She has long been like a daughter to me and her children are my grandchildren. But I do not question my son's wisdom in this matter, Stigand, nor should you. If he can make use of this woman"—she gestured to me—"then I am certain he is right to do so."

"I do not want to be 'made use of'!" I exclaimed bitterly.

Harold took notice of me then for a moment. I met his eyes and shouted at him, "I am not your property! I am Aldith of Wales, and I want to take my children and go home!"

No one spoke while Harold's blue eyes locked with mine. A force came from him to me then, across the empty space between us, and I felt as if he were really seeing me for the first time.

When he spoke his voice was careful, full of thought. "If you are not happy with us you should go home, of course, my lady. Unfortunately I cannot spare the men to escort you back to that wilderness where we found you, but I can do the next best thing."

I waited, a hare in a snare, waiting for the club to fall on my head.

"I can send you to your brother Edwin in Mercia; would that please you? After all, having killed your husband, I am responsible for you now. I must see that you are in a safe place and as content as may be while I am out of the country."

"Out of the country?" Gytha's voice rose in a question, but I cared naught about that.

"Yes, my lord, yes! Send me to my brother, oh, please do! I vow to cause you no trouble ever if you will just do that!"

Harold gave me a strange smile, involving only half his face. "Oh, you will cause me trouble, Edyth; make no mistake about that. I see it well enough. But if spending some months in your brother's household will make you happy, then it is easily done. I do hope the Earl of Mercia will be grateful to me for this gift!"

"He shall, my lord, I will see to it!" I was happy enough to make foolish promises.

"You said you would be out of the country, my son," Gytha interrupted, loath to leave the point and much disinterested in my travel plans.

"Aye, a goodly commission has come to the Earl," Stigand said. "King Edward is sending him on a mission to the Continent to attend to some matters for the Crown."

"I sail for Ponthieu in the spring," Harold added with a certain pride. "It was an honor I received even above my brother Tostig, who has of late stepped on some toes at court." His eyes sought mine again. "Will you miss me, my lady?" he asked in a bantering tone.

With the promise of my freedom, I did not want to take a chance on rousing his anger. Remember, I cautioned myself, men like a soft-spoken woman! You have given Harold Godwine reason enough to think you a shrew; do not displease him now!

"I do not know you well enough to miss you . . . yet, my lord," I replied, summoning up my old arts of coquetry and lowering my eyes.

"Ho!" exclaimed Leofwine. "A new conquest for the Earl of Wessex!"

Harold quirked one eyebrow upward again. I saw he was not much taken in by me. "Perhaps we can remedy that situation when I return, Edyth. No doubt I will have some business to do with Mercia, and I can call on you there. And bring you news of your children, of course."

Having dropped the club on my unsuspecting head, he turned away and strode from the hall.

Mercia

I RAGED, I CRIED. It did no good and gave me a headache. "If you insist on throwing a catfit," Harold told me, "I will have to deny you the company of your children at Christ Mass. It would be wrong to let you upset them by such behavior during the holy season."

So I spent the Yuletide being meek, sitting with my hands in my lap and my eyes gazing at far places. All my crying was done inside, where no one could see. With my sons I plaited the garlands of greens for the hall, and

Llywelyn was given the honor of lighting the fattest of the Yule candles, which was a great thrill for him. On Christ Mass night I sat like a guest at the Godwines' table and lifted my cup of polished horn in the wassail toast.

I would beg and plead no more. I could only hope that Harold would see the love I bore my children and relent.

But, alas for that hope, he was rarely at Arundel to witness my heartbroken devotion. Most nights the Earl's High Seat was empty beneath its crimson hangings at the end of the hall. It seemed that everyone knew where Harold was, but no one spoke of it openly— save only Gytha.

Once she remarked in my hearing, "The children should be here at this season, and their mother too. Harold has developed a nice sense of propriety rather late in life!"

The Twelve Days of Christ Mass ended too soon. On Plow Monday I was sent, alone and heavily guarded, to my brother Edwin in Mercia. Even my little Nesta, my baby, was kept from me.

So I was sent again across the land, north and west to the ancestral home of my father's father. And if I do not chronicle that journey it is because, in truth, I hardly noticed it, I was so sunk in misery and despair.

What good my freedom without my little

ones? Besides, this did not have the feel of freedom about it. It seemed more like exchanging one prison and one warden for another.

Edwin had changed so much, physically, that I scarcely recognized him. He had become a handsome young man, elegant as a peacock and seeming very self-possessed. When he came running out of Leofric's Great Hall to meet us, one would have thought he brought the loving welcome of a devoted brother.

"Edyth, here you are! Arrived as safe as a royal treasure, I vow, and looking very fine! The years have been kind to you, sister!" He held me at arm's length and looked into my face, and I into his.

The eyes were the same. Watchful, guarded, full of their own secrets. Edwin was one person on the surface and another inside, always.

"Some of the years have been kind, brother, and some have not."

"Yes. Well. We must see what we can do about making the future better for you, eh?" He patted my arm solicitously.

"My future will only be improved when my children are returned to me!"

Edwin's face revealed nothing, neither sympathy for me nor outrage at the kidnapping of his blood kin. "You must make the best of your situation, sister," he advised me.

"As I see it, Harold Godwine has already been most generous with you, all things considered. Women captured in the heat of battle are not always treated as honored guests."

So that was how the wind blew! "I was not his guest, I was his prisoner! I could not go to the privy room without a housecarle at my elbow, watching lest I try to run away! And now I have been brought here under the same conditions, and I suspect I will continue to be held like a prize of war, even in my own brother's house!"

Edwin smiled blandly. "Of course not, dear Edyth. You malign me by such hysterical accusations! I have taken my beloved kinswoman into my home after the death of her husband, that is all."

"And what about my children—your nephews, your niece?"

Edwin shrugged. "I certainly can't fight the Earl of Wessex for them, if that is what you are suggesting! He has chosen to hold his enemy's children, and I am in no position to oppose him, my dear. Surely you can see that!"

I can see, quite clearly. "You have not changed, my dear brother," I said with heartfelt bitterness. "It is quite obvious that you have made some sort of arrangement with the Godwines—to your own advantage, of course."

The fact that Edwin did not even try to deny my accusation told me how weak my position was. "Come into the hall, Edyth," was all he said, "and let me show you how comfortable your new home will be."

Well, I suppose it was comfortable. Like a cat, Edwin had always had the knack for finding the warmest bed and the sunniest spot. To the wealth of Leofric he had added an almost pagan profusion of furs and silks; even the stools had little velvet cushions on them. My chamber was larger and more amply furnished than my room at Arundel had been, and I noticed that Edwin had already adopted the Godwines' passion for featherbeds.

"You see, my sister; everything has been done to make you happy here." He said that with a completely sincere voice, as if he believed it and thought I would, too.

"And if I should desire to leave, Edwin? Would you make that easy for me, too?"

He pretended to be surprised that I could ask such a question. "But why should you leave, when you will have anything a woman could desire right here? Within reason, of course!" he amended hastily. "And where would you go, pray, if you did leave us? You have no Saxon kin living save only those of us in Mercia, and I can assure you, Edyth, our brother Morkere is like-minded to me in his desire that you stay with us! So where else could you go, a woman alone?"

"I have kin!" I flared at him. "Nearer and dearer to me than you and Morkere! I have kin who have not sold themselves to the Godwines! There are folk in Wales who love me and my children and would gladly give me shelter"

Edwin's smile was not sincere, but it was amused. "Ah, yes, the defeated Welsh. But some of them betrayed your Griffith, did they not?"

"Some of them were envious of him, yes," I admitted with reluctance, hating to give Edwin that point. "But there are still many who are loyal, I know, and now that there is peace I could make a good life for myself and the children . . ."

"Oh, Edyth, you keep coming back to the children!" Edwin put on an expression calculated to show deep concern; he must have forgotten how easily I could read him, for I was not fooled. "You must forget about the children for now, for your own good, and theirs! It will only fret you and cause you pain, and I can assure you it is most unnecessary. I have Earl Harold's word that they will be well treated, and you may be united with them in time." He paused. "If you are willing to be reasonable."

A price! Always a price on everything: myself, my body, my freedom, my children. Goods traded for value received. If we were simple rustics, ceorls living in a wattle and daub cottage with the chickens scratching on our floors, would we not be more free? I understood what Griffith had meant when he said he was the least free of his people.

To give Edwin some credit, I was treated most kindly, and at least I did not have Gytha's hostility to face. Edwin had recently taken himself a wife, a pleasant little body born to the lesser nobility among Leofric's thegns. Joan, she was named, and she did her best to treat me as a loved sister.

"What a lot you have seen, Edyth!" she would sigh enviously as we sat at our sewing together. "Imagine, having traveled to Ireland and Wales and been married to a King!"

"A Prince," I commented.

"Edwin said your husband was King of Wales!" Her eyes flew wide. She was still in that new state of matrimony where her husband's word was always believed.

"It is a matter of words only," I reassured her. "My Griffith was Ruler of All Wales, that is true."

"Do you miss him dreadfully?" Joan was so young she still asked questions like that.

"I cannot talk about him."

"Oh, you did love him, didn't you! Imagine that, a real love match!" She clasped her plump little hands beneath her chin and looked mightily pleased. "How wonderful for you! Even Earl Harold says he was a mighty warrior; he has always spoken of the Welsh Prince with respect."

For some reason that surprised me. "You have spoken often with the Earl of Wessex?"

"Oh . . . not often. But he was our guest here before Christ Mass, and my lord husband tells me the Earl often seeks his counsel."

Harold Godwine seek the counsel of a youth whose beard was still soft! Edwin had not lost his love of exaggeration!

I simmered like a slow pot on the hearth. I did my needlework—not so well as Joan—and tried to pass my time with the normal work of women in a manor house, but my children were always just behind my eyes. And how slowly the days dragged by!

Leofric's seat on the Avon River was at a crossroads frequented by travelers to Northumbria and Wessex, therefore we were goodly supplied with company and news. Then too, I think, a number of people found cause to visit the new Earl of Mercia just to gawp at his sister, the widow of the Welsh savage. Edwin seemed to take much pride in showing me off in that way, and there was little I could do about it. If I took refuge in my chamber with my maid and my loom the hours were too unbearably long, so I allowed him to exhibit me betimes in the Great Hall.

Then, in the full spring of the year, Morkere came to us hotfoot from his latest effort at court to attain an earldom. Save only Edwin's holding, all of England was in the grip of the Godwines, but Morkere seemed to think that the situation would change soon.

"The Earl Tostig of Northumbria is mightily dissatisfied that Harold was sent on the King's mission!" he told us excitedly. "Tostig feels that Harold is supplanting him as the King's favorite in order to be named his successor, and he is doing much to stir up a grumble at court."

Morkere still had that aggrieved whine in his voice. As I watched him, I found it hard to imagine him an earl of anything. But if Morkere were as rabbithearted as he had been in childhood, perhaps he was still a little in awe of his older sister and could be bullied or petted into aiding me in some way.

So I smiled brightly at him and listened with every appearance of interest to his recounting of the latest gossip from the West Palace of Thorney Island, where Edward of custom held his court.

"Tostig proposes to levy a heavy tax against the shires of Northumbria, to enrich his own pockets for the struggle he foresees with Harold. And his sister, King Edward's wife, has taken his side and is whispering in her husband's ear. When Earl Harold returns and learns of their treachery against him, we shall see Tostig set down as Earl of the north country and a new man will take his place!"

"What makes you think you might be that man, brother?" asked Edwin in a lazy drawl.

"I have your support, do I not?"

"For what it's worth, yes. But I use most of my efforts in my own behalf, brother; an earl must look out for himself and his earldom above all else. I cannot vow to help you unless it would be to the best interests of Mercia to do so."

I was surprised to hear so candid a statement from my brother. He had not dealt with me so frankly!

"Of course, it would be to your interest to support me in my claim for land!" Morkere exclaimed, pounding his fist on his knee for emphasis and then softening the blow at the last instant.

"I am not convinced of it," said Edwin. "This warfare between Harold and Tostig is dangerous. It would be better for us both, Morkere, if we kept ourselves well away from court until the thing is settled."

"It will not be settled until the King is

dead and the Witan has proclaimed his successor!"

"That cannot be too long; the old man is in shaky health. But even his death will not solve the thing. The Atheling is a mere child, too young to rule, and no man would trust another to act as his Regent. The Danish court has claims on the throne through the line of Hardecnut, and William of Normandy has shown himself interested in adding England to his holdings."

"So perhaps it would be best, brother, to sit back and bide our time, making no enemies and treading on no one's toes."

"It's well enough for you to say that!" Morkere was indignant. "You have the earldom of Mercia, a plump new wife and more riches than you can use! And what do I have?"

"A quarrelsome disposition," sighed Edwin. "I believe I know how Earl Harold must feel with Tostig yapping at his heels. Be patient, brother, and follow my advice; that is the best help I can give you now."

"Very well, then," said Morkere sulkily. "I see I must win my own without your aid!"

That night I had Gwladys fetch me a candle, and I made my way to Morkere's apartment after the household had grown quiet. I was pleased to see my brother still awake, nursing his grievances.

"And what do you want?" he greeted me with his usual surly manner. I chose to ignore it.

"To give you aid, brother. And ask for yours in return, of course."

Morkere rolled his eyes at me. "Are you going to try to talk me out of petitioning the King for a grant of land?"

"Oh, no! I think you are just as entitled to a fine holding as Edwin is"—that was true—"and I would be happy to argue in your behalf if you think that would help." Although God knows, I thought, what weight my words would have with anyone.

"So you are on my side. Wonderful. That means there are two of us in all the world."

"Nonsense, Morkere! Many of our father's thegns would support your claim, I know! And if I added my voice to yours, then mayhap the King would look with favor on your petition and create an earldom for you. Who knows, he might even carve a piece for you from our brother's holdings!"

That unlikely possibility cheered Morkere at last, and he gave me a reluctant smile. "What would you want in return for adding your influence to mine, sister? You would be chatelaine of my house, perhaps, until I marry?"

I waved my hand carelessly. "Nothing as

grand as that, I assure you! Just take me with you when you return to the court at Thorney, and I will speak to King Edward myself on your behalf."

Morkere watched me noncommittally. "And then . . ." he prompted.

"And then supply me with just a few men to ride to Arundel and get my children . . ."

"Good God, woman, you are mad! You would bring the wrath of Harold Godwine down on my head—is that your idea of helping me?" Morkere jumped to his feet and began pacing the chamber. I trotted after him and tugged at his sleeve.

"Harold would not know; he is on the Continent on the King's business!"

"But he will come back! And I would not have that man angry at me for all the earldoms in the land!"

"Then just help me leave here! Get me a horse, show me the road, give me two of your men-at-arms and I'll ask for nothing more! Please, brother!"

"You'll ask for nothing more!" he parroted. "Woman, you have already asked for too much!"

There was no help for me anywhere. Morkere went off to play politics, Joan began work on a gorgeous tapestry featuring her husband staghunting, and Edwin began to develop a little paunch.

In Wessex, my children and Griffith's were being raised by Harold's mother, and I paced the halls of Mercia alone.

The seasons waxed and waned; we had May Day and Whitsun and Lammas, when the first bread was blessed. On my birthday Joan gave me a mantle of blue silk with a golden collar—"The blue matches your eyes," she said sweetly—and Edwin presented me with a massive brooch inlaid with garnets. I suspect if they had been rubies he would have kept it for himself.

Then, as the days grew shorter and the swine were being fattened on beech mast in the woods, exciting news came to us from court. In the person of Morkere, who dearly loved to carry tales of bad news and tragedy, we learned that the heir of the native earls of Bernicia, the influential Cospatric, had been murdered. And some said his killer was the King's own wife!

"I sweat blood to repeat such a thing, but many think it is true!" Morkere proclaimed wide-eyed. "It is said she had it done to eliminate his opposition to Tostig. Tostig himself was with the King near Salisbury at the time, and protested that he was totally ignorant of the thing. But Cospatric's followers in Northumbria have led a great revolt against Tostig, and they intend to drive him from the land and declare a man of their own choice as earl!"

"How fortuitous!" said Edwin piously. "I suppose you have arranged to have your own name mentioned in that connection?"

"Better than that!" boasted Morkere. "I ride this day to York with the blessings of Harold Godwine himself, and I have every reason to expect that the New Year will see me as Morkere, Earl of Northumbria!"

Out of all that mickle-muckle only one thing had any meaning for me: Harold was back in England. Perhaps, perhaps, he would send my children to me. Or let me go to them.

One can always hope.

"So Earl Harold is home at last!" I interrupted in my eagerness.

Morkere shot me an annoyed look. "Yes, of course he is! And a long time he was about it, too! It seems he has been an unwilling guest of William the Bastard in Normandy these many months, and only just returned from the country!"

Harold, a captive? That was a novel piece of news! Even Edwin prickled his ears and begged for details.

"No one seems to know too much," said Morkere. "You know the Earl of Wessex, he keeps his own counsel. But it seems that he was shipwrecked or somesuch off the Norman coast, and William forced him to remain."

"For what purpose?"

"It seems that our Norman cousin was under the impression that he could force Harold Godwine to support his own claim to the English throne!" laughed Morkere. "He is not much a judge of men, is he?"

"Not if he thinks to win the bone Harold has marked for himself!" agreed Edwin. "What consideration could William hope to offer in return for Harold's support?"

That query started my own thoughts racing. Again I interrupted my brothers' conversation, and this time they both scowled at me. "Morkere, what consideration did you offer Harold Godwine in return for the earldom of Northumbria? It must have been a fine one if he would give you his brother's place for it!"

"Ah, well . . . I am not yet actually the Earl, you understand!" Morkere dodged. "I will have to have the approval of the King . . ."

"That is a foregone conclusion now," said Edwin, "with Tostig out of the way and Harold Godwine on the King's right hand. But our sister asked a wise question, and I would like to hear the answer myself, little brother. What consideration did you offer Harold in return for Northumbria?"

Morkere shuffled his feet and made a great to-do of hunting some misplaced morsel of food in his teeth. Edwin waited most patiently, arms crossed on his chest and eyes suspicious. "I trust," he said coolly, "you have not been so foolish as to pledge something involving me."

"Of course not! I only, well, traded something that is really of no use to either of us. But it will better both our positions, yours and mine!"

I felt the chill of unwanted knowledge settle over me. I knew only one piece of property that fitted that description. Morkere's words were not necessary; I read my fate in the way his eyes evaded mine.

"I agreed that we, as Edyth's nearest blood kin, would give her in marriage to the Earl of Wessex."

My miserable brother Edwin laughed outright, and I gritted my teeth with hatred of him for that. "Well done, Morkere! I suspected that was what he was after when he sent her to me with orders to keep close watch over her. He admires you, Edyth; the desire of England's next king is quite a plum for you!"

"I do not want it! I want no part of that man! How could you give me to him after all the wrongs he has done me!"

"Oh, come now," said Edwin in a reasonable voice, "he has not injured you so dread-

fully as all that. I grant you he had your precious Griffith killed, but that was war, sister;
there was nothing personal in it."

"He has taken my children!"

"And very wise of him, too!" interjected
Morkere. "He felt that you might not be over-
eager for this match, but with your children in
his custody you can scarce refuse him."

"Damn William!" I burst out. Both men
stared at me, uncomprehending. "If he wants to
make England a Norman province, didn't he
just kill Harold Godwine while he had him under his thumb? Why did he let him go?"

"Perhaps William was beguiled by Godwine's personal charm," suggested Edwin, "as
so many others have been." He smirked.

"I have not noticed any 'personal charm'!"
I cried. "I tell you I hate and despise Harold
Godwine, and rather than be married to him I
will kill myself!"

Joan, who had kept quiet through all this
as an obedient wife should—if she had no
spine—at last took my side. "My lord husband," she said timidly to Edwin, "if Edyth
has such strong feelings about this, perhaps it
would not be fair to force her into the marriage?"

Edwin shook off the gentle hand she laid
on his sleeve, as if it were an annoying black-
fly. "It is quite fair for all concerned, Joan! For

my sister, too, if she but had the wit to see it. A husband like the Earl of Wessex is not usually a widow's portion. For Morkere and myself, it will mean uniting our family and fortunes with the greatest power in the land. And for Harold . . ." Edwin looked me up and down, as if I were a cow at a fair. "I daresay Harold intends to enjoy his prize. And of course, with Edyth as his wife, he can count on the support of Mercia and Northumbria." He nodded to Mokere, who grinned. "So you see, dear wife, a more satisfactory match cannot be imagined!"

Poor Joan Dimwit, so easily seduced by Edwin's slippery tongue! She came from him to me with that same soft smile on her lips, anxious to make everything cream and roses. "Edwin is right, Edyth! This is really a stroke of great good fortune; can't you be happy about it?"

"I cannot be anything but bought and sold and traded!" I snarled at her. "If you would speak to me of happiness, then speak to me of the grave!" I brushed past her and stalked in fury to my chamber.

"Gwladys!" I startled the poor woman so that she dropped her needle and began crawling around on her knees, poking among the rushes on the floor and muttering to herself.

"Gwladys," I began again, more calmly,

"you have some knowledge of medicines and potions?"

"Aye, my lady." She stopped mumbling and looked up at me.

"So have I, but not enough for this. Tell me, in Wales do they have a brew that will bring sleep?"

"Aye, my lady, as well you know."

"Not that; that is quite insufficient for my purposes. I need much more sleep than just one night. I need to sleep until all the pain is gone and all the walls are down and I am free to be with Griffith again."

Gwladys scrambled to her feet, horrified. "You are talking madness, my lady!"

"All about me is madness, but I am quite sane, Gwladys. Sane enough to find life unbearable anymore and to want a way out of it, but too afraid of pain to drive a knife into my own bosom. You have served me well, Gwladys; serve me in this way too!"

"I could never do that! My Lord Griffith gave me into your service and charged me with your safekeeping always. He would never forgive me!"

So Griffith's hand reached out to me, even here. I could not stop the tears in my eyes or the burning in my throat. But neither could I go in marriage to Harold Godwine, loving

Griffith still! To be touched by another man, to share his body . . . impossible!

Impossible, too, to involve Gwladys in the last escape left to me. Better to make the arrangements on my own, poring over my trinkets to find bribes sufficient to send a page or scullery maid into the woods after the ingredients I needed. And then, when the stuff was mixed and hidden in a jar behind my bed, waiting for nightfall to do its deadly work, how could I test it but on myself?

Once more I waited until the household was quiet and my chamber echoed with the snores of Gwladys at the foot of the bed. Then—so stealthily!—I took my magic jar and crept from the room. I wanted to be under the stars, with the clean night wind blowing round.

That night of all nights no one even took notice of my going. Men slumbered in the hall, before the hearth, and my brother's steward lay full asleep on his bench just inside the door. I had only to gather my skirts in my hands and walk softly past him and I was outside.

But where to go? Edwin, for all his faults, had come from the same womb as I; I could not take poison and stretch myself to die an ugly death on his doorsill. So I carried my medicine down the steps and across the court, past kitchen and stable and out the postern gate, half-hidden in brambles.

Behind the manor the woods crowded close around the wall, then opened onto a gentle slope leading to a marshy stream.

There was a quarter moon, just enough light for me to pick my way along the path to the water. It seemed to me that would be a pleasant place to die, close to the running water.

But the nearer I got to the river the icier the wind became, and the woolen cloak I had wrapped around me seemed as thin as silk. Foolishness, to be unpleasantly chilled in the hour of one's death—what need of comfort then, anyway? The brew I had mixed for myself would be unpleasant enough to make me forget cold hands and feet! Nevertheless, by the time I reached the bank and felt the cold mud ooze through my thin slippers, I had begun to feel I lacked the courage for the thing.

The clicking I heard was my own teeth chattering. My body was shaking with cold rather than fear, but the effect was quite the same. If I had been a warrior I would have said I was unmanned, but at any rate the power to act was quite gone from me. I stood there, thoroughly miserable, gazing at the dark and rushing water and feeling cheated. "Next time," I vowed to the night. "When the night is not so bitter and

181

my hands are more steady, then I will be able to do it."

With a sense of anticlimax I turned and made my way back to the house. It seemed a much shorter road that time, although I tripped over roots and rocks I had not noticed before. I was able to return to my chamber as unobserved as at my departure, and I hid the jar of poison behind my bed once again, until such time as I would be able to make use of it.

I wonder what became of that jar? Mayhap Gwladys found it and did away with it, thinking to save me that way. Or perhaps it was never found and molders there still, in a dusty corner screened by cobwebs. For the time was somehow never right for me to use it, and at the end of the winter a large party of Harold's relatives and servitors arrived to prepare me for my wedding to the new King of England.

Pious old Edward was dead at last, and Harold Godwine had claimed the throne.

York

He came to Mercia with a large company of housecarles and body servants, men-at-arms and hangers-on. In short, he came with all the retinue of a king. The day before his arrival, a herald galloped up our road to make us aware of our forthcoming honor.

"King Harold of England has chosen to visit the home of his friend Edwin, Earl of Mercia!"

The household was thrown straightway into an uproar. Edwin, having been off on some business or other, arrived at about the same time as the King's herald, all atwit with plans for the tremendous impression he wanted to make on Harold Godwine. He wanted the stables to contain nothing but fat and glossy horses, all the fields to appear ready for the plow, and a day of intense sunshine and unseasonal warmth. Within ten minutes of his arrival, he had driven his wife to tears and me to my chambers.

"I am not at all interested in making a good impression on that man," I said to my brother over my shoulder as I left the frenzied activity in the hall, "and you would be well advised to leave me out of all this."

"But aren't you anxious to see your children? For a while they were all you talked about!"

My heart jumped in my breast. "Is the King bringing them with him?" Something in me hated referring to that man as the King.

"Ah, no," Edwin said with no real appearance of regret. "It seems they are being sent ahead to the city of York, to take their part in the nuptial celebrations."

Of course. The bait for the trap, just to be certain the bride arrived for the ceremony. Small wonder Harold was King; he planned his campaigns with such thoroughness.

And when he arrived with all his display

of wealth and power, that was part of a campaign, too. Shiremen and ceorls, farmers and tenants, they lined the road to see him and do him honor, and so of course Edwin mounted me on a horse and rode with me to the head of our valley to see all this and greet the King.

He wore crimson velvet and a fur-trimmed cloak that billowed in the wind of his horse's galloping. He came out from his party and cantered up to meet us alone, leaving even his guard behind. He rode with a certainty of himself that was meant to impress me, and it did, even against my will. Edwin's rare and sunny day sparkled around us, and the new King of England looked every inch a king.

It is hard to hate something that is beautiful and perfect. Griffith would not have hated Harold, seeing him like that in all his hard-won glory. Griffith would have understood and respected him for it.

"Well come, my lord." I bowed low over my saddlebow, keeping my face impassive.

"And my greetings to you, madam. Is all well with you?" If Harold were wooing me in hot blood, his voice was remarkably cool and formal!

Helpless I might be, but he could not force me to play his games. "All is not well with me, my lord," I told him while Edwin was still spouting his own greetings. Harold's eyes told me he considered Edwin as unimportant as I did. "My children are still motherless, and I am to be given into a marriage I did not desire."

For a moment I thought he would be angry, but then the skin around his eyes crinkled and he came close to smiling. "Your tongue is still icy, my lady! Come, have you no words of congratulation for me? I have come to you almost straightway from my hallowing, Edyth; I set aside matters of grave importance in order to gallop up the Watling Road like a beardless boy, anxious to press my suit, and you think no more of me than you would of such a stripling lad?"

"As I understand it, neither my admiration nor my cooperation is essential to this marriage," I told him. I gathered up my reins, ignoring the black looks Edwin was giving me, and said formally, "By your leave, sire?" Without waiting for his answer, I turned my horse and rode back to the manor.

I suppose he would have liked to bury a battle-ax between my shoulder blades, but he did not. Instead, he brought all his passel of people and was feasted that night in Leofric's hall.

Edwin had, of course, relinquished his own High Seat in favor of his sovereign, and I was placed on Joan's customary bench. We were fed and toasted as if we attended the celebration of a hand-fast marriage; I am sure the resemblance was intentional.

At dinner Harold made it obvious that he did not wish to discuss his recent excursion to the court of Duke William in Normandy. There were already rumors about that enforced visit. Edwin said that some of Harold's own men believed Harold had sworn an oath of fealty to William and vowed to support the Norman's claim to the English throne. If Harold Godwine had indulged in such double-dealing, he was wisely loath to speak of it, and he regaled us instead with the events of King Edward's death and his own succession.

"The King had been in poorly health for some time," he said, "but it seemed that Tostig's behavior was the final blow. It was not my desire to banish my own brother from the kingdom; when we were children together we were close as peas in a pod. But I could not, in good conscience, overlook murder for political advantage, even with my own brother and sister at the bottom of it!"

His blue eyes danced with fire. I wondered if he would consider my Griffith's death as murder for political advantage; he was slain to further the ambitions of one of the Godwine brood as surely as the dead Cospatric. But I kept my counsel and marked another score in my book against Harold: hypocrite.

"I spoke against Tostig, and my own sister, the King's wife, to the Witan. They would not act against the First Lady of England; she has built up a reputation for piety near as large as her husband's, and it protects her now! But they agreed with me that the greed and malcontent of Tostig had become a danger, so he was outlawed as his own subjects in Northumbria wished."

Harold was not eating as he spoke. A steaming joint lay across the trencher of bread in front of him, but he had taken no more than a bite from it. I could not credit him with such sensibilities that discussing the banishment of his brother could destroy his hearty appetite, so I concluded something must be wrong with the meat and left my own untouched. After all, this was my residence; if I were eating as usual in my chambers and sent back my meat untouched, no one would consider it an act of discourtesy!

"The Earl, the former Earl Tostig left England much in a grumble, I understand," put in Edwin. If Tostig were a sore subject with Harold, Edwin was too dense to notice, anyway.

"He took quite a large troop with him and sailed immediately to Flanders. Baldwin is half-brother to Tostig's wife, Judith, and no doubt has given him sanctuary and sympathy. But the sympathy should have gone to the King, who was heartbroken over the whole affair and took to his bed."

Harold dropped his voice, as one does when speaking of the dead and dying, and we all leaned forward a little without even being aware of it. The death of kings is a solemn thing, to be repeated in quiet rooms by the flickering of firelight, so that even the servants ceased their bustling and rattling of dishes.

"By the eighth day of Christ Mass we all knew the King was dying. The members of the Witan were summoned, his Lady slept at the foot of his bed and prayed continually until her voice grew hoarse. Stigand, Archbishop of Canterbury, attended the King, and his chamber was crowded both night and day. For two days he lay in the drowsing sickness, recognizing no one, but on the morning of the fifth day of the New Year his mind came to him again and he spoke to us.

"He told us that he had had a vision, and in that vision our whole land was conquered and laid waste by its enemies. He said this was to be a punishment for the wrongdoings of those in high places, and that there would be no salvation.

"We were all shocked and affrighted. I

thought he said these things because he was so disappointed in Tostig and some of the others, but Edward seemed to believe he had had a true vision. He clutched my hand and begged me to try and save my country, and I stood there with my head bowed and the tears on my face, not knowing what to say.

"Stigand tried to assure us the King spoke out of his old age and illness, but all around me I could feel fear creeping like a bramblebush. There was a sense of doom about the chamber, as if Edward had cursed us all, and I felt he had laid on me a burden too heavy to be borne. As I said to Stigand, I am but mortal; I cannot hold off Fate itself with sword and ax!

"The King would not let go my hand, however. Again he bade me defend the country, and then his breath made an ugly noise in his throat and Stigand hastened to give him the last rites. His old friend Edwin of Westminster administered the Eucharist, and even as the cup left his lips so did the King's spirit. I swear I felt it go! I actually felt his sense of relief at laying down the burdens of a life he had never enjoyed overmuch!"

As he spoke of the King's death, Harold made the sign of the cross upon his breast, as did we all. There was the appearance of genuine grief in his face, and I wondered suddenly if he had actually loved the saintly, bumbling old man, even after Edward showed his preference for Tostig. It was hard for me to think of that golden, impervious warrior loving and caring. To care is to be vulnerable, as my children made me vulnerable; as far as I knew King Harold loved nothing.

Harold continued his narrative; he was coming to the part he obviously relished telling. His voice lifted again and his eyes brightened as he told how the Witan had convened and chosen him as successor to Edward on that same day.

"No one spoke for the boy, the Atheling. No one supported the various claims of those others who feel they have rights here."

"We all understood that you were the King's choice," Edwin said. "He may have loved your brother, but Edward always felt the kingdom would be safest in your hands. All your earls supported you, my Lord!"

Harold grinned. "And so you are—*all*—my earls! My own brothers and you and your brother, my good Mercia. I owe you much, Edwin, and you owe me. Remember that." A look passed between them, and I saw my brother pale a little. I knew then that he feared the King even more than he rspected him, and,

191

perversely, that lessened my own fear of Harold.

"On the last day of Christ Mass, King Edward was buried in his newly hallowed West Minster, and that same day I was anointed King. Eldred, Archbishop of York, set the crown upon my head, and I dedicated myself to caring for the kingdom Edward bequeathed me."

How noble. How fine. I helped myself to a pickled egg.

"Your coronation was fraught with good omens, my lord!" Edwin burbled. "You must not dwell overmuch on the dying King's prophecy; it is as Stigand said. His mind was clouded. It was a splendid ceremony," Edwin continued to the table at large, "and the sight of our Lord Harold in white linen and gold surcoat heartened us all. When you turned to address us, with Edward's crown upon your head and the orb and scepter in your hands, my lord, it was like a fresh beginning for us all."

"Symbols of power only have meaning in hands that can hold onto them, Edwin," replied Harold. "The struggle is not yet over, even though I am anointed. There are many who will be loath to accept me as King, my own brother Tostig among them, I fear. The Northmen, the Normans, the adherents of the young Atheling—doubtless we shall hear from all of them in quick time. Only when all claims are silenced can we consider our land secure, as Edward wished.

"Therefore it is imperative that we present a unified front. The problem with Tostig has taught me a lesson; I would have no squabbling or treachery on my own doorsill."

Harold turned then and spoke directly to me with a forthrightness my own brothers rarely accorded me. "Edyth, that is much of my motive in this marriage. It is important at this time that all England be welded into one strong unit as it has never been before. We must be done with all this rivalry between earls, all this border warfare to add a few rods of land to some noble's holding. By joining the house of Godwine to the house of Leofric can do that!

"This afternoon, on the High Road, you said that this marriage did not require your cooperation, but it does, Edyth. I am doing what I genuinely believe to be best for all of us and for the kingdom, and I need your support as much as that of your brothers and their thegns!" He rose from his seat and came toward me, one hand extended as if in supplication. Earnest entreaty was in his voice and eyes; it would have been so easy to believe he meant what he said and was acting from the noblest impulses.

But the hand he stretched forward to me

had accepted my Griffith's bloody head as tribute, had lifted it by its matted hair as he
gazed into its lifeless eyes!

"Offer you support, my lord?" I let the bitterness I felt sit like bile upon my tongue and
flavor my voice. "I offer you nothing, nothing at
all. Whatever you may gain from or through
me will be gained without my help in any
way! You hold my children hostage, knowing
that I cannot endanger them by refusing to go
through with this hated coupling, but do not
ask any more of me than that! I will repeat the
marriage lines with you, Harold Godwine"—all
the company gasped when I referred to him
thus, ignoring his blood-bought title—"but I
will be neither your friend nor your ally!"

Harold stared at me, shocked that I
would speak to him in that fashion in the
presence of others. I was surprised at myself,
yet proud of the courage that welled up in me
with my anger. Edwin leaped from his seat
with an oath and would have struck me, I
think, had not Harold caught his hand by the
wrist and held it tightly.

"I will not have her hurt for telling me
the truth, Earl Edwin," he said in a deadly
cool voice. "If that is how the woman feels, I am
well advised to know it; there has been enough
treachery and hidden feeling." He looked at me.
"What about you, Edyth? If I insist we go

through with this marriage will you betray me, as my sister tried to betray King Edward and elevate Tostig over me?"

His gaze was so stern, so intense, that I could not break the lock his eyes had on mine. I lifted my trembling chin and spoke as proudly as I knew how. "In my lifetime I have seen enough of treachery to sicken me, too, my Lord. If you do insist, I will marry you, and I will not plot against you for any reason. Not for your sake, but for my own. I will not be a dog to hide under the table and snatch bones."

Harold continued to look at me for a long moment, holding Edwin's arm as if he had quite forgotten it. Edwin glanced from me to Harold and back again; I could imagine he saw himself losing the support of the throne and all that entailed. Then, gently, Harold released him.

"It is a strange vow for a woman to make to her bridegroom, but I daresay it is more valuable than many vows made with more tender feeling. I trust you, madam, and I believe you will do as you say.

"Earl Edwin, you will be so kind as to direct me to my chambers. I would be abed; we rise at cockcrow and ride on to York. You will bring your sister to me there as soon as you can have her ready."

He met my eyes again and made a courteous bow. "I shall see you in York, my lady. I trust I will find you quite unchanged?" With that curious remark, he turned on his heel and left the hall.

As it fell out, it took much preparation to turn the Welsh Prince's widow into a suitable bride for the English King. At five and twenty, I was much removed from the trembling virgin to be dressed in simple silks; seamstresses labored night and day to make me a trousseau of satin and samite and fine linen. Joan was as thrilled as if the wedding were her own; she certainly enjoyed the preparations more than I. Even Gwladys was all atwitter. More than once I had to remind her sharply that her delight in these things was a disloyalty to Prince Griffith.

"But he was a hearty man, my lady!" Gwladys defended herself. "He would not have wanted you to spend your life in a long face and purple mourning robes. Prince Griffith would have been pleased to see you safely wed again."

"Mayhap," I agreed, "but not to Harold Godwine."

"He is the King, my lady!"

"He is king of the Saxons and the Angles and the Jutes. I am now Welsh, Gwladys, by marriage and by choice. Harold is nothing to me. I will endure this thing in order to have my children again, but I take no pleasure in it."

There was one matter I took great interest in, and that was the subject of my marriage gown. Gytha had sent yards of saffron silk from Arundel, with instructions that it was to be sewn into my nuptial robes. She would! Knowing full well that in yellow I would appear like a jaundiced sheaf of wheat, Harold's mother had expressed her dislike for me in that meanly fashion!

I gave the yellow silk to an astonished footman and ordered a robe of green velvet, like the Welsh mountains in the spring. Blue was more becoming to me, but blue was Griffith's favorite and I would not wear it for Harold.

Harold had ridden on to York, with his dear friend the Bishop Wulfstan, to appear before the Witan of Northumbria and ask their support. The banishment of Tostig had not quieted the troubles in the North; Morkere would be Earl over a turbulent and touchy people, quick to imagine slights and slow to forgive. Harold sought to appease them through promises of support as well as the pageant of a royal wedding.

"He flirts with wasps," Edwin commented. The Northmen have always had little regard for the South; they think the southerners are weak and lack virtue. That was one reason they gave Tostig so much trouble, and I doubt they will find warmth in their hearts for the Earl of Wessex, even with a crown upon his head."

I thought to myself, You would desert his cause quickly enough as well, my brother, if the wind began to blow against him!

When all was—nearly—in readiness, Edwin sent word to York, and the date of my wedding and coronation as First Lady of England was announced to the people. No, I was not to be titled Queen; that is a fancy custom from the Continent, not in the Saxon tradition. Even the Irish use it, calling all their kings' wives queens, but the Saxons rightly understand that while there may be many queens, there can be but one First Lady. It is one Saxon custom with which I am in entire agreement still.

To my surprise, the King had left behind a wedding gift for me. I had thought I would be carried to York in a litter piled with wolf furs, guarded as usual by a troop of housecarles. But this time I journeyed, not under guard, but with escort, and though the difference may seem slight, it was very meaningful to me. I rode a palfrey, handsome and smooth-gaited, and I carried his reins in my own hands. My escort rode with their eyes on the countryside instead of on me, a great improvement. The cold north wind that cut into my cheeks was sweet with a freedom I had not felt for many months, and I felt a reluctant gratitude to Harold for restoring my dignity.

Until I reminded myself that it was he who had taken it from me in the first place.

Nevertheless, I almost enjoyed the trip. I had requested that Gwladys be given a pony that she might ride beside me betimes, and that request was speedily granted—as were all my requests of late. It was a comfort to be able to chat with her in the Welsh tongue when the mood was on me.

"Soon you will be chief maid to the First Lady, Gwladys, and no doubt we will spend much time in the West Palace of Thorney Island. It is said to be very grand; will you like that?"

"I have seen many great houses by now, my lady. I daresay the King's house will be the finest, but for a servant one is very like another. If you are pleased with it, so shall I be." She gave a little sigh not caused by the rough gait of her pony. "It matters little; none of them are Wales."

"You miss it as much as I do, don't you?"

"I was born there, my lady!" she exclaimed, as if that gave her an especial love for the place that I could not feel! "My heart-home will always be in the mountains."

I looked at the rolling fields on either side of us, their tender early greenness just breaking through the winter brown, and I knew that some folk thought them beautiful. "What was your home like, Gwladys?" I asked to pass the time.

"Oh, nothing so grand as yours, I vow! But it seemed good enough to me. I was born in a cottage at Llanberis, within sight of Snowdon itself."

"Your father was a shepherd?"

"Not him! He was a bard when times were good and people in great houses made free with their favors, and a warrior when there was booty to be taken. His father before him had fished in Colwyn Bay, but my father had no liking for the sea. He always wanted to better himself, he did, and it was a grand thing for him when I was taken as a young girl to serve at Rhuddlan."

Somehow I had never thought of Gwladys's life before I knew her. Yet servants have a life out of our sight, do they not, and hopes and dreams we may never know. Here was another world right at my elbow, and I never explored it.

"How old were you when you went to Rhuddlan?"

"I don't know, my lady; we did not reckon our ages much in numbers. But it was long before I became a woman."

"What could a small girl do in a great house?"

She smiled at my ignorance. "More than you think, my lady. I began by cleaning the garderobes and the privy house and caring for the ladies' napkins."

What a horrible occupation for a little girl! I tried to imagine my daughter Nesta at six or seven, cleaning up foulness or toting stained menstrual napkins to the laundresses. "Surely that cannot be all you did!"

"Oh, no. As soon as I was big enough to carry heavy things, I began to help in the scullery. One of the cooks taught me to speak in a proper way and behave myself in a lady's company, and then Prince Griffith gave me to you. Since then I have wanted for nothing, and I believe the Prince sent a fine gift to my family, too. If I were to go home tomorrow, they would make me right welcome in Llanberis!"

I rode through Saxon countryside and thought Celtic thoughts. We all began in sameness, naked babes covered with blood, and no one could tell a prince from a servant. Yet each turned out so differently. Humble Gwladys, grateful for what she perceived to be her high station as my maid; Griffith and Harold and Tostig and so many others, pawns in a chess game of ambition; the farmers we passed, the porters who struggled behind us with the carts piled with my dowry chests; the bishops, in their war to extract favors from God; and me, with my futile woman's rebellion—each one unique and different, center of a separate world. And who determines the outcome of each small life, the God of the Christians, the gods of the pagans, random chance, or . . . ourselves?

I rode for a long time in silence.

At Bedford we were joined by a large group of the thegns of Northumbria, come down to escort us into their territory and on to York. I was right glad to have their company in the gloom of the great forest of Nottingham; cottages were few and set far apart; and beneath the ancient trees was perpetual twilight.

When we reached the Derwent, the timbered bridge that stood across the river was found to be quite rotted in the center, and Osbert, who was once again captaining my escort at the King's request, decided that nothing would do but we must ford the river.

So of course a goodly portion of my dowry chests got wet, and much of my wedding finery would reach York in a bedraggled state. I made a big noise about it that accomplished nothing and put a crimp in my otherwise pleasant relationship with Osbert. Men do not always understand what is really important to ladies.

The cold March wind abated somewhat as

we neared the city of York. We slept our last night outside the city in the house of a cousin of the murdered Cospatric, and although we were treated courteously, it was easy to tell that hatred for the former Earl still ran hot. Harold had been crowned in the West Minster, but Tostig's brother was not yet wholeheartedly accepted as King in Northumbria.

"That bastard Tostig was bleeding us to death with his endless taxes!" I heard in the Hall that night. "When our cousin from Bernicia spoke out against him he was foully murdered; his blood is still damp upon the ground of Thorney Island! And Bernicia was not the only area to suffer; all Northumbria was aswarm with the Earl's spies, sniffing out hidden wealth and stealing it from us. We would have supported the Earl Tostig, had he been just, with our grain and our wood and our fighting men. But we will not accept the yoke of a tyrant! We are proud men here, not soft and fat like the thegns of Wessex, and if the new King abuses us we will break his plowblade for him!"

Shouts of "Aye! Aye!" rang down the Hall. I wondered how Harold hoped to fuse all these separate men into one people. I owed Harold nothing, God knows, but I felt it would only be honorable for me to speak up for him in this hostile assembly.

"I am not yet wed to the King"—I addressed myself to our host, Sihtric—"but I would have you know that the word he has given me he has always kept. As Earl of Wessex he has much wealth already; he does not need to increase his personal fortune at your expense. It was his vote which sent Tostig to Flanders and rid you of him, and it was Harold who gave you Morkere as Earl in his stead. Morkere is not a Godwine but mine own brother, raised in the land between North and South, and I trust you will uphold the Northmen's reputation for fairness and give him a chance to prove himself fit to govern." I looked Sihtric square in the eye.

"Aye, my lady. Let no man say the Northumbrians cry before they are hurt."

"Then you will withhold judgment on the King as well, until you see his mettle?"

Sihtric glanced round his Hall. I think he was not accustomed to having a woman speak publicly to him of these matters, but I had learned to be outspoken in the halls of Rhuddlan and was not likely to change my coat now. "Aye, my lady," he said at last. "We will give King Harold a chance, you may assure him of that. You spoke out bravely for him, and that must mean he is worth something; we will wait to see."

Over Sihtric's shoulder I saw Osbert, standing in formal salute by the door to the private chambers where I would sleep. My eyes met his, and I think he, ever so slightly, nodded his chin in a tiny salute.

At the hour of prime we departed for York. We entered the city through the southern gate, and Archbishop Eldred himself met us with an array of bishops and clerics in gold-threaded robes. The city was dressed with all the trappings of pageantry—feasting, music, day and night merrymaking on every street and Harold's personal standard of the Fighting Man hung outside the shops.

My brother Edwin was on the road shortly behind us with his own extensive retinue of Mercians, but for the first time in my life I outranked him. The Archbishop walked with our party, and I believe some of the lesser bishops remained at the gate to watch for the great Earl of Mercia.

We were escorted to a sizable house, which was now my brother Morkere's property, and met according to protocol by the new Earl of Northumbria himself. Earldom had not deepened Morkere's voice, but I was surprised to see that it had quieted some of the hungers in his eyes. There was a limit to ambition, then. For some.

"Well come, sister!" He grabbed both my cold hands in his and planted a damp kiss on my cheek. "We have been mightily busy getting all in readiness for this event, and I hope you will overlook . . .". He waved his hand about him, already very much the grand host begging his guests' indulgence for non-existent flaws in his hospitality.

"I am sure all will be satisfactory, my lord," I assured him. Already my eyes were flickering about, starved for the sight of certain small faces. "The children!" I reminded him. "Are they here?"

"Your children? Oh. Yes, I believe they are—but they are staying with the King, on the other side of the city. I am certain you will see them soon."

My heart went into my hose. My children were a treat promised me too often; I had almost quit believing in them. And now there would be yet another wait. "Morkere! Can't you arrange to have them brought here? It would give me such pleasure to have a few days to get acquainted with them again before I am wed!"

Harold's captain, Osbert, materialized at my shoulder. "I will fetch them to you myself, my lady," he said in his quietest voice. "I go this hour to make my report to His Grace, and I am sure that he will let me bring them back with me. I will give him my personal assurance that you will remain eager to do your sovereign's bidding."

"Why, thank you, Captain!" I extended my hand for Osbert to kiss and sent him on his way.

"You have won an ally in the King's camp," observed Morkere, quick to note such things.

"I feel I cannot afford any enemies, brother."

I was in my chamber with a passel of seamstresses and the head laundress, trying to repair the damage done to my wardrobe by its bath in the Derwent, when I heard the shouting of treble voices in the Hall. I flung my lapful aside and fair flew to meet them.

"Madam, madam!" cried Llywelyn, running toward me. Taller now, and so beautiful, his father's face laughing up into mine! Rhodri forgot what little dignity he may have acquired and shouted "Mama!" as he flung himself into my arms. I dropped to my knees and hugged both of them against me in an ecstasy of relief, smelling the fresh, cold air in their curls and striving not to cry. How big they were grown, what changes the year had wrought!

"There is one more waiting to be kissed, my lady," said Osbert's voice above me. I looked up and raised my arms for Nesta.

Baby no more. Griffith's daughter was a tiny little girl, as lovely as the legendary princess for whom she was named. In her face I saw nothing of myself, nothing of her father, only a beauty that was uniquely hers. I stared at her, quite in awe of what I had produced.

"She is a flower," breathed Osbert.

"Will you guard her for me always, Captain?" I asked him as I hugged her. "May I commend my daughter to your care?"

If I had not known it to be impossible, I might have thought the shine in the eyes of the burly Saxon warrior was caused by tears. "I will guard her with my soul, my lady," he intoned reverently, "and bless you for the honor!"

And so, with a lightened heart, I prepared to meet Harold in York Minster. The wedding was no more sought by me now than before, but my hours were so gladdened by my children's company that all things seemed bearable.

We are still together, I said in my heart to my husband. While I live, I will cherish the lives we created together, my Griffith, and you will always live in them. Harold Godwine will pay for having killed you by raising your children as his wards. The King of England himself will protect the family of Griffith ap Llywelyn!

York Minster

MY CHAMBERS SEEMED to be continually aswarm with people—more tiring women than I could possibly need, pages and squires, and maids and courtiers whose names I did not even know. They made the children fretful, so I took Gwladys by the sleeve and asked her to have a word with my brother.

"Which brother, my lady? Earl Edwin or Earl Morkere? They are both in the Great Hall, I think."

"It really matters not, they are alike as the

feet of a toad. Just say that I am tired of all this buzz about me and would prefer to have some peace to enjoy the children."

Gwladys trotted off on her errand, but she was soon back. "The Earl Edwin bids me tell you that you must grow used to it, for the King's wife is never left alone."

Here I was again, having my life run according to someone else's custom! "I will not have it! I am used to some privacy. Even at Arundel I did not have to dwell constantly in a room full of people!"

"I will see what I can do, my lady," said Gwladys with an air of resignation. But the crowd was never thinned much.

At Rhuddlan, the only sound in our chamber at night was his breathing, and mine.

The weather worsened. The days dawned cold and cloudy, with a bitter wind blowing down on us from Scotland. People dressed in the heaviest clothes they owned, and in my overcrowded chamber I was painfully aware of the odors of too many folk closeted together.

Then came a morning when the wind died down, the sun shone warm, and people stood packed together in the streets like birds in a pie.

It was the wedding day of the King of England.

Gwladys and the tiring women began working on me before cockcrow, as soon as I finished my morning prayers. First came a full bath, accomplished while I stood shivering and naked in a metal tub as an endless parade of servants carried leathern buckets of heated water to be poured over my body. I alternated between scorching and freezing. Bathing is, I think, a custom for the summer months, a pleasant dalliance in fern-fringed pools. But not in drafty, stone-floored halls in March!

At last Gwladys pronounced my tortures at an end, and a herbalist brought baskets of sweet-scented plants to rub my body dry. Then I was rubbed all over again, with scented oils, exotic and rare. Only when every inch of my skin was glowing pink and excessively perfumed did they begin to dress me.

Two shifts went on first: one of fine silk, next to my skin, and a glittering overshift of cloth of gold. Next the heavy green velvet cotte, and around my waist a girdle of gold and rubies, sent by the King. Now that I was warm again I could take some interest in the process; the girdle was exactly the span of my waist, and I wondered how Harold had come by it.

My hose were of wool, white and very soft. Shoes of buttery kidskin had been dyed to match my gown. A heady scent of cinnamon rose from the folds of the velvet as my body heated it, vying with the odors of the perfumes until my head spun. When I was clothed, Gwladys arranged my hair. I could hardly appear in the flowing tresses of a maiden, so it was plaited and coiled into two huge rolls, then fastened in gold nets over my ears. There was one part of me that would be warm in the March wind!

My face had been treated with masks of almond paste and honey, and my lips were rubbed with the lees of red wine. A massive collar of pearls replaced the gold Celtic torque I customarily wore; a cloak of forest green velvet lined with red squirrel was fastened around my shoulders. I was ready to go to the York Minster.

Attended by a vast retinue, our party walked and rode through the streets of the city. I was in an open litter, that all might see my face and any smiles I chose to give them, so I was generous in that regard. Crowds pressed upon us, laughing and toasting me with cups of ale. Though it was not yet midday, the people of York were more than a little drunk already. My soon-to-be subjects had, perhaps, more to celebrate than I.

Archbishop Eldred greeted me on the steps

of the York Minster, a magnificent poem in stone
that dwarfed the buildings around it. On his
arm, with my brothers at either side, I entered
the cathedral to meet Harold.

"I present you to your King," said Eldred
formally to me.

He was standing, quite alone, before the
high altar. He had dressed for his wedding in
a richly embroidered tunic, fine hose and leather shoes stamped with gold. A magnificent
cloak of ermine hung from his broad shoulders;
a crown of gold and gems rode his fair hair.
It was the first time I had seen him thus
crowned.

His face wore its permanent burn from sun
and wind that made his eyes seem such a brilliant blue. There was no tenderness in that face,
no womanly softness or flame of poetry. But I
could not mistake the strength that lay there,
nor the proud nobility. I felt sure my hatred of
Harold Godwine had not diminished, but I felt
a tiny twinge of satisfaction that he was so fair
to see.

The ceremony itself passed quickly. The
marriage settlement had all been agreed upon
in advance between Harold and my brothers,
the wedding gifts exchanged, and the scroll
of ownership for my dower house handed over
to my keeping. Nothing remained but the

speeches by which my brothers announced their intention of giving me to Harold and Eldred's blessing on behalf of the church.

The gift of myself was accepted by the regal figure in white ermine, who then held out his hand to me. When I took it, he forced a heavy golden ring upon my finger, then pulled me down to kneel with him before Eldred. Wulfstan took Harold's crown in trembling fingers as the Archbishop of York anointed us both with holy oil; then we rose again and faced the crowd of people packed into the cathedral.

Wulfstan replaced the crown on the King's head, and a velvet cushion, upon which another, smaller golden circlet lay, was handed Harold. He took this with great solemnity and lifted it high for all the people to see. Then he set it on my head, saying in a loud voice, from this day forward thou art Aldith, First Lady of England!"

I was so shocked at hearing him call me by my Welsh name that my eyes flew open wide. That was a gift I had not expected, and it touched me more than any other could. My heart raced in my breast. I tried to turn my head a little and look at Harold, but the unexpected weight of the crown reminded me of my new dignity and I looked forward instead.

Then I received my second shock. In the

first row of upturned faces was that of Gytha, Harold's mother, and beside her stood Harold himself! No, not Harold, but a young man barely come to beard, so like him as to have been Harold himself at that age. He could only be Harold's son, mayhap by Edith Swan Neck, come to witness his father's marriage to another woman. My heart went out to him for whatever pain he might be feeling, but, like his father, he kept his secrets closed behind his face.

The Archbishop gave a lengthy benediction which brought us all a-yawn, then we left the cathedral to a flourish of trumpets. A group of horses was being held at the foot of the minster steps. Harold gripped my arm with fingers like stone and guided me through the crowd toward them. He swung into the saddle of a restive chestnut stallion with an astonishing grace for a man of forty years, then held down a brawny arm to me and effortlessly pulled me up to sit behind him. People cheered; his courtiers mounted, and our wedding processional wound through the streets to the Archbishop's manor and our wedding feast.

The opulence of Eldred's house spoke much for the man. Not for him the simple life of Christian poverty and humility; Eldred of York dined on gold plate much more finely wrought than that of the Earl of Wessex at

Arundel, and his servants were so numerous I never saw a face more than once.

The oaken table set in the center of the Hall seated two score to a side, and it was so weighted down with food that no part of the wood showed. Our party drank the King's health in wooden goblets chased with gold while Harold drank from his own goblet, a legacy of the great Alfred. The banquet was lavish in the extreme. We began with eels stewed in milk, then beautiful whole salmon from Chester and thin wheaten cakes. There were three roast boars, swans, herons dressed with green peppers, jellied lambs' heads and joints of fatted beef. An endless stream of dishes from the Archbishop's kitchen provided pastries, blood puddings, cheese with loaves of white bread (never saw such before!), compotes of fruit and honey. The cooks must have much practice, I thought, to be able to mount such a royal feast.

The butlers—there were two: Harold's own, who traveled everywhere with him, and Eldred's—kept our goblets filled with ale, perry, mead, and some sour red wine from the Continent that Harold seemed to favor. As he poured it down his throat, I hoped, fleetingly, that perhaps he would be too drunk to claim his bride this night. But it was a foolish hope. The man's capacity was enormous. He drank more than anyone at table and did not show it by so much as a reddening of the face.

As each new food was presented he courteously selected the most choice morsel and offered it to me. I obediently ate from his fingers, seeing the approving nods of his courtiers from the corner of my eye. But my appetite was small, and my own hip-knife never attacked the fowls or the joint.

Harold lingered long at table, laughing at the coarse wedding jokes and responding in kind. If any of the ribald humor offended the Archbishop of York, he gave no sign; he laughed as loudly as my brothers when sly references were made to our activities a few hours hence.

When the torches began to smoke and servitors were carrying the remainders of the meal and trenchers of bread soaked with meat juices to the crowd outside, the King rose and took my hand. "We will take our leave of you now. Pray continue to enjoy yourselves with our excellent host, the good Archbishop"—he nodded to Eldred, who had fat glistening on his chin—"and we will bid you good morrow."

As I rose, my eyes met those of Gytha, hostile as ever, though a smile wreathed her thin lips. "Good night, Your Grace, and may your evening prove fruitful."

Bitch, I thought. The greatest pleasure I will

have this night is the knowledge that a woman you loathe shares your son's bed!

Minstrels continued to play, men continued to drink and roister, laughter rang to the rafters as the King's housecarles lighted us to our nuptial chamber. I was surprised to see that Harold had forbidden the usual press of laughing friends and relatives; he gave a certain dignity to an occasion which was usually far from dignified.

My tiring women—but not Gwladys—awaited me. They took me into a garderobe let off the chamber and there dressed me in the silk shift and golden corselet of a bridenight. My hair was loosed and combed to wave down my back; then I was returned to the King.

Our nuptial chamber was not just a sleeping apartment, but a timbered room as big as a cottage. A roaring fire had been fed sweet herbs, and the smoke that curled upward to the smoke openings was rich and fragrant. A giant bedstead held a stack of feather mattresses covered with new linen and hung round with velvets bearing the device of the Godwines. Chests and armor were piled roundabout; a brace of greyhounds dozed by the fire. At one glance you could tell it was a King's chamber.

His body servants had dressed him in a robe of plain linen so finely woven that the outline of his body showed quite clear. I kept my eyes cast firmly down. I was alone with Griffith's killer. Had I still my girdle and hip-knife I might have slain him then and avenged my love in the Welsh way, but his housecarles would have killed me without hesitation, and my children would not have outlived me by a day. Their futures and their safety depended on my going through with this.

"And now, Aldith, you are First Lady of England. What say you?"

"I give you thanks for bestowing upon me the name I prefer, my lord," I said as humbly as I could, still looking down.

He did not move toward me. "You were surpassing beautiful today in the sunlight. I had almost forgot how fair you are!" Did he intend, then, to woo me as a loved one? Such pretense was beyond me. I would force myself to keep the letter of our marriage contract, but I woud bring no womanly tenderness to the thing!

Harold reached out and touched me then, and I felt my unwilling flesh shrink away from him. His eyes darkened suddenly as I looked up, becoming narrow slits above his bared teeth. In the firelight he looked like a savage golden wolf.

"It is that way, is it, madam?"

"I cannot pretend a feeling for you, Your Grace. You know this was no love match!"

His laugh was harsh. "Nay, Aldith, no love match. But I did fear your spirit was broken and you would be a dull thing to bed. I am glad to see I was wrong."

Before I could move away, his hand shot out and grabbed my shift, jerking me to him. His other hand clutched my hair and pulled my head back. The eyes that glared down into mine were not tender, but they were not indifferent, either. They were hot as blue coals, and I remembered with a pang what joy the Vikings take in rape! Better for me if I had been humble and submissive!

The strength of the man was enormous. He ripped my shift from my body and hurled it away, holding me impaled on that hot blue gaze as he would impale me on his giant body. Truly I was terrified! He was hurting me wantonly, and he would hurt me more!

He was instantly and totally ready to take me; there was to be no preparation for me at all. He required no response, although I could feel my struggles excited him still more. I willed my body to be calm but it would not, my terror was too great.

He picked me up and threw me on his bed. I do not recall his removing his gown, though he must have done so. When he flung his body on mine, I thought I would never leave that bed alive.

At last he lay, spent, upon my aching body, and in a little while he was asleep. I eased out from under him, but he did not wake. Wrapping myself in the bed linen, I curled up in as small a ball as possible at the very edge of the bed. I realized then that I had not made my evening devotions, but the God I was accustomed to addressing had abandoned me, anyway.

Before I fell into an uneasy, exhausted slumber I had one last strange thought. Edith of the Swan Neck must not have satisfied His Grace of late.

London

IT WAS THE KING'S desire that we go on a royal progress, touring Northumbria that all of his northern subjects might see us and know their new sovereign. After the court was sufficiently recovered from the wedding festivities—the gaiety had been excessive for some —we were packed up and escorted to the city gates once more by Eldred and the officials of York.

My first experience with a royal progress was a mixed pleasure. The children did not go with us; after all, they are the off-spring of Wales, not England, and so I was to be deprived of their company once more. But at least I had the certainty of being united with them at the end of our tour, and I had faith that this would be so. It was my morning gift from Harold.

When I awoke well after cockcrow on the morning after our wedding I ached in every part. My greatest fear was that the King would want to repeat his performance of the night before. But no, he was already up and clothed, and when he saw my eyes open he actually smiled at me.

"Good morrow, Aldith! Was your sleep pleasant?"

"Mmmmmm." It was the only answer I cared to make.

Undaunted, he continued in a cheerful tone, "I've been waiting for you to waken. Now that you have, tell me what you wish as your bride gift. A jewel, a manor, an endowment for your favorite abbey?" He smiled most benevolently. For once the advantage lay with me.

"I am not an extravagant woman, my lord; the jewels you have already given me are quite sufficient, and the dower house whose deed I hold is really all I desire of property. As for an abbey, I must confess that I have no favorite; most of my devotions are private, between myself and God only. But there is one thing I would ask of you that would give me more joy than any other."

His face closed slightly. "What is it?"

I moved my body on the bed, tossing back my hair and lifting my face to the kind morning light before I answered. "Your word, my lord. Your solemn promise that I will never again be separated from my children against my will, nor have them used as leverage against me."

Harold stood quite still and looked at me, his eyes hooded like a drowsy horse. Then they opened wide again and his nostrils flared. "Well done, Aldith! I am happy to see I have misjudged neither your mettle nor your wits! Very well, my dear, you shall have your morning gift."

With that knowledge that is given to women in place of muscular strength, I knew that he was telling the truth and would not betray his promise. I nodded in acceptance of the gift; he reached forward and raised my chin that he might look into my eyes.

"We have each made a vow, Aldith; one to the other. You have sworn your loyalty, if not your love. I have given you sole possession of your children. On my word, Aldith, these vows do not depend upon each other, but only upon your honor and mine." He removed his hand from my chin, but his eyes still locked mine. "That will be enough," he said.

We left York on a day of tumbled gray clouds and a sniff of late snow. We were to make our progress in a great circle, passing through the more populated areas and towns as well as crossing the open countryside. Each night we would be guested at some thegn's house, observing the temper of the people and, we hoped, winning their allegiance.

The temper of the people was surprisingly good; they were not all as aggrieved as the lords of Bernicia. Toward Harold there was an attitude of grudging respect and we-shall-see; I was feted and praised like the greatest beauty who ever walked the land. My grandmother's reputation had traveled north from Mercia; more than one noble toasted me as "the heiress to magnificent Godiva!"

It was heady stuff.

The nights were different. Harold used me much; I marveled at his stamina even as I deplored his lack of subtlety. My nerves were tuned to different responses; I could not enjoy the embraces of Harold Godwine. But he was unlike my Griffith, he did not seem to need or expect me to participate; it was enough for him to celebrate his conquest of my body night after night.

Many mornings saw me seated most uncomfortably, even on my easy-gaited palfrey. Although I disliked being carried in a litter, there were times when I had to request it—and then bear the additional discomfort of dust in my face and a lack of pleasant conversation.

The Bishop Wulfstan rode with us, as Harold's confidant and personal priest, and I found I enjoyed his company as much as the King did. A learned man who was interested in everything, he told me the names of the trees we passed and the history of Roman settlement in Britain. Harold made a joke of it: "My Bishop is educating my wife for me again," he would laugh as the two of us rode side by side, Wulfstan talking and me listening.

The ubiquitous Osbert rode with us as well, and my brother Edwin and his party traveled with us for a while before they turned south to Mercia. Sometimes I was moved to wonder to myself, watching the faces about me, which was enemy, which was friend? My sworn allegiance lay with the King, albeit reluctantly. But in my heart I felt very alone, a mote in the eye of a storm. If I were in dire peril, whose strong arm might reach out to save me? Harold? Osbert?

None?

Through a twist of fate I was First Lady of England, yet I felt homeless and dispossessed.

Gwladys, given into bondage as a child, was more sure of her place in life than I.

Harold and the nobles talked of battles won and a kingdom to be held, speaking with the confidence of men who had never lost. But I knew how quickly all security can be wiped away; a word written on parchment, the slash of an ax, can do it. On those rare nights when Harold gave me peace in my bed I was tormented instead by nightmares, so that I awoke fearful and began the day under a cloud. Griffith would have noticed and commented on it; the King had larger issues on his mind.

By the end of the month, just as the countryside was greening and becoming worth the seeing, we finished our royal progress and returned to York. So happy was I to see my little ones again that even the sight of Gytha's sour face did not spoil the day for me.

"Your children have been raised as savages," was the greeting she gave me. "I understand that the King has most generously extended his royal protection to them, but does that not place a certain responsibility upon you, madam, to see that they are taught decent Saxon customs and behave themselves accordingly?"

I bristled. "My children are Welsh! I would not have them forget their father's heritage!"

Gytha sneered, an expression for which her

thin lips were singularly well suited. "A heritage of blood, madam! The elder boy, that *Thloo-ellen!*"—she mispronounced his name to vex me!—"talks night and day of his bloodthirsty sire! He would have us believe that a great army is forming in those godforsaken mountains this very minute, intending to swoop down on us all and murder us in our beds!"

So Griffith's boy had grown defiant in my absence! I was secretly pleased at his spirit, but alarmed at the danger such bravado might bring upon him.

I spoke to him of it in as much privacy as I could arrange during the day. "Llywelyn, you must restrain yourself from these brash speeches! Now you are a child, and people will tend to overlook what you say. But in a very few years there will be those who seize on your words and try to make something more of them. You could bring more warfare and bloodshed to your people, my son. Is that what you want?"

He stared up at me with his father's eyes. "When you are not here, my lady, we are sometimes insulted by these Saxon dogs!" His young eyes flamed with righteous indignation.

"I will remind you, my son, that I am a Saxon by birth! My inmost sympathies are not with these people; they have brought too much heartache on me in my lifetime. But it is important that we survive, particularly you and

Rhodri and your little sister. And to survive, you must avoid making enemies!"

He tossed his auburn forelock out of his eyes with a familiar gesture. "My father was not afraid to make enemies!"

I sighed. "Yes, and look what it got him. Even with all his strength he was betrayed and brought down—for nothing! Just to be a feather in Harold Godwine's cap!

"If anything happens to you children, his blood is wasted and his line dies forever! That is a treasure I guard, Llywelyn, as Griffith would have wished me to, and I will not let anything endanger it. Not even you! Now hold your rash tongue or answer to me!" My voice shook with my emotion and I do not know what was in my face, but Llywelyn fell silent and took a half-step backward. After that I heard no more stories about imprudent talk by my children, but sometimes I saw Llywelyn looking at me out of the corners of his eyes in a way that hurt me. I knew he felt I had betrayed his father's memory in some way, but of course I did not try to defend my actions to a child.

In that year the feast of Easter fell on the sixteenth of April, and with it the Easter Witenagemot was to be held in the West Minster. The great spring meeting of the Witan was formerly held in Winchester, the seat of the West Saxon kings since the time of Alfred. But it was Harold's intention to center the administration of his kingdom in London, which was so located that it could receive and dispense communications better than any other part of the country.

So, with all the wedding ceremonials behind us and the King feeling relatively sure that the strength of Northumbria stood behind him, we moved south to London and the West Palace on Thorney Island.

Our elaborate procession consisted, as usual, of the vast number of housecarles which were a permanent part of Harold's retinue, serving both as men-at-arms and as squires of the body if needed. They must be fed and equipped, so that meant many cart and pack animals. There was the king's steward and two butlers, his chamberlain and priest, as well as pages, heralds, equerries, cooks, wardrobe masters, herbalists, the physician, minstrels, mounted couriers, and any number of other dogsbodies whose functions seemed obscure. Yet Harold was considered to be a man of simple and restrained tastes—for a king.

We went back along Ermine Street, across the Humber and the Trent, to Watling Street and London. And everywhere we went Harold paid court to his people, even as he had on our wedding tour through Northumbria.

When we passed a cottage with its wind

doors unshuttered in that cool season, Harold straightway dispatched housecarles to cut down a giant oak and build shutters for the astonished ceorl who lived there.

At the village of Ouestraefeld the King saw that the townsfolk who lined the road to watch us pass were thinly clothed, and he left with them two carts of woolens and a bale of furs. And these things happened everywhere we went.

And, always, good Bishop Wulfstan was at his elbow. I believe Harold had courted the goodwill of Edlred by asking his blessing for our marriage, but he courted the goodwill of God through his friendship with Wulfstan. The Bishop was saintly, for truth, and his kindly goodness cast a spell. He even found the time to teach Llywelyn to read some simple Latin and instructed both boys in counting and geography.

I feared Harold might object to such favors being given, but he did not seem to pay mind to it.

It was sweet, that spring, riding down out of the north country. The light in the long valleys was bluish, the air clear and fine. Great forests of beech and oak marched like armies along the watercourses, bent on forcing out their rivals, the noble spruce. Game was everywhere: red deer, boar, all manner of wild fowl in the scrub on the hills and big fat salmon in the cold streams. The people were hardy and hard-working, more reserved and suspicious than those in the South. Interested though I was in seeing London, I almost regretted leaving Northumbria.

On our way I had made every opportunity to avoid Gytha, and she had done the same for me, but the afternoon before we were to reach London it chanced that we were riding together, with no one else close of our own rank. Feeling an obligation to make some sort of social remark, I commented on my eagerness to see London.

"London's single virtue is that it is an end to all this journeying for a while," Gytha sighed. "I am so tired of horse sweat and having my bones jounced! But I suppose"—she cast an eye toward me, suddenly spying a chance to play the cat—"a person such as yourself is used to living a rough life?"

It was too good an opportunity to overlook, even if it meant further alienating the woman. "Madam," I told her coolly, "the truly highborn always have greater stamina than the baseborn, and are able to bear a few discomforts without difficulty. The King's greyhounds have trotted gaily at his horse's heels since York, but I notice that Egbert's mongrel pack deserted us at the Ouse River. Mayhap, my lady, you have been misinformed as to the flawlessness of your pedigree?"

Enjoying the spectacle of Gytha speechless for once, I rode at a pleasant pace for some time, much puffed with myself. But the snake was merely waiting to strike back; I should have known it. As the shadows grew longer and we hastened to reach the monastery of Saint Paul, where we would spent the night, Gytha reined her horse close to mine again and hissed in a false friendly voice, "I am surprised that you are so eager to see London, Your Grace, considering."

"Considering? What are you talking about, madam?"

She tired to look mealy-mouthed. "Why, I know that I should not like to ride through Londontown and over the bridge at the river gate if my former husband's head were stuck up on a pole on that bridge!"

For a second time in my life I heard the sound of the sea roaring in my ears, and the world swirled away from me in a reddish blackness.

"She's awake, Your Grace," a dim voice said somewhere above me. I struggled to open my eyes, but when I did so the world swooped so dizzily that I closed them again. I realized I was lying in a little wooded glade off the road and people were leaning over me. The coolness of the glade made me shiver and brought back my senses a bit.

Bishop Wulfstan knelt beside me; I knew his soft, kind voice. "Please, my dear, open your eyes again!"

I did so. The King was there, too, standing with a flushed face and a bare head. "Aldith!" he spoke sharply.

I turned my face away. "Take him away from me, Wulfstan!" I pleaded. There was much whispering and tramping about, then the good Bishop knelt by me again and took my hand.

"The King is gone, my lady. But he was sore hurt that you sent him away."

"I would send him to the . . . I would send him away forever if I could!"

"Your Grace!" The noble Bishop was shocked. "The King cares for you very much! He was most upset when he heard you had fainted and fallen from your horse. And in your condition, a fall can be so dangerous!"

"My condition?" I came fully out of my swoon then. "You are mistaken, my Lord Bishop! If you suppose me to be with child you are muchly mistaken!"

His seamed and stubbly face sank in disappointment. "But if Your Grace is not . . . then . . . ?"

"I was told by the King's mother that Prince Griffith's head is on a pole in London!"

I cried out to him, letting some of the pain escape my soul through my lips. "She wanted to hurt me and she did!"

Wulfstan looked as wounded as I felt. "God forgive the woman! That was a cruel thing to do, my lady, whatever reason she may have had! Of course it was a frightful shock to you! You should have been prepared in a gentler way; I myself could have told you, at the right time, without putting it so bald!"

I felt sick. Not with the morning sickness of a life to come, but with the rotten sickness of grief still carried. "It's true then, Wulfstan? What she said?"

His eyes answered me.

They brought my children to me. Llywelyn smoothed my hair and kissed my cheek, bringing the tears to my eyes at last. Rhodri trotted up to me on his chubby little legs, thick as oil beakers. He showered me with wet kisses, then clasped his fingers in the ruby collar I wore and asked if he might have it. I heard one of the housecarles mutter to another, "The young Welsh puppy takes after his sire; I see he grabs what he wants free-handed!" In my tormented mind I entered a mark against that man.

The loveliest of my children, my little Nesta, was laid in my arms. In that crowd of sand-colored Saxons she glowed like a mountain rose. Eyes like velvet, with dark lashes spiked

like the points of a star. Pink cheeks, skin trans-
lucent as goat's milk, red lips always pouted for
a kiss. Wherever my children are is home, and
no price was too high to pay for their ransom! I
wrapped her silken curls around my fingers and
felt strength come back into my body. I would
give Gytha no more satisfaction that day.

"Osbert, give me your arm. We must not
delay the King."

A great crowd of merchants, reeves, bishops, nobles and doxies met us outside the New
Gate, together with the Lord Mayor. Some ex-
ceedingly dull things were said by all the important men present, which took up most of
the morning, and then at last we entered the
city.

I had last seen York as a town whose festival had ended, when even the drunkest villein
had sobered up and staggered off to his cottage
and his angry wife. Garlands of dried leaves
and early flowers hung dispiritedly here and
there, and pennons with the device of Godwine
were still nailed above door lintels. But the city
of London was very different indeed. It bore the
bustle and gaiety of a place where the festival
never quite ended, where there was always
more ale to be drunk and more girls to be
pinched.

The King's party formed itself into a parade within the shadow of the old Roman wall encircling the city. For the occasion I wore a crown, not the one Harold had set upon my head at York Minster, but a bulky gold thing with a sharp edge not sufficiently padded. I could feel it biting into my forehead. The trumpeters and heralds led off; the King, simply dressed but richly bejeweled, rode alone. Behind him paced the Mayor and Stigand, Archbishop of Canterbury. Then I followed at a slight distance on my palfrey, accompanied by the young wives of four of the crown stewards. One of the housecarles—not Osbert—held my horse's bridle, though the animal was quiet from the long journey and I could have handled him even if he was not.

Gytha was somewhere behind us. I hope she ate dust.

Harold's triumphal parade through London was to travel east across the Wall Brook and then double back along the Thames to the West Palace on Thorney Island. All of the city seemed to be an open marketplace, and merchants constantly besieged our caravan, begging the King's patronage. Harold was in a good humor and a generous mood; several times he ordered a halt while he selected laces and trinkets for me. But he did not proffer them himself; they were carried back to me by pages. Harold as a doting husband was something I did not expect or believe, but it pleased the spectators and delighted the merchants.

We had dinner at a tented pavilion on Cheapside Street. We were escorted to our seats by Stigand, who was both dignified and controversial. The table itself was raised on a high dais so that all might see us, and unusually high chairs were furnished as well, even fitted with the nicety of soft cushions. The King flung his aside with a snort of contempt, whereupon I immediately dispatched a page to retrieve it and add it to my own.

A great feast was served us even as cartloads of food were distributed to the rest of our party. I nibbled on some fowl boiled in sweet almond milk. Stigand urged me to try a concoction of onions, eggs and saffron which he was enjoying heartily. I tasted it, assured him it was delicious, and left it cooling on my plate, but at least we had engaged in some conversation.

Stigand was well known to me as the subject of much gossip, so that I was interested to observe him firsthand. I pretend to dislike such tittle-tattle, but I am secretly fascinated by people who have an aura of scandal about them. Stigand had been an ally of Harold's father while serving as Bishop of Winchester. At that time a man named Robert the Norman was

Archbishop of Canterbury. King Edward was known to be considering William the Bastard as his possible heir, and of course Archbishop Robert was sympathetic to the idea of having his countryman assume the English throne. In 1052, at the urging of the Godwine's, a popular uprising resulted in Robert's being driven from the country, and Stigand became Archbishop of Canterbury in his place.

My sympathies are with the outcast, so I was not prepared to view Stigand with friendly eyes. And, truly, nothing in his countenance encouraged me. The man had an almost reptilian head, with scaly skin and flat, cold eyes. There was none of Wulfstan's sweet saintliness about him; I understood why he was reluctant to let himself be seen in Rome when Pope Leo IX summoned him in reply to the deposed Robert's desperate appeal. Stigand chose instead to stay in England, where he had powerful friends, and was therefore condemned in absentia and excommunicated. Which made him an outcast too, I suppose, but that did not improve my feelings toward him.

Such was the influence of the Godwines that he continued to hold the archbishopric in defiance of the Pope, even after the death of old Earl Godwine the next year. Several more popes tried in vain to dislodge him, but the man was as fixed as a tick on a hound's hide, clinging to power and enlarging his sphere as the God-wines enlarged theirs.

In all that time no English bishop came to him for consecration. Even when Harold was crowned King he chose Eldred of York for the duty of coronation which customarily should have been Canterbury's. Yet Stigand remained a powerful presence; his lifelong loyalty to the Godwines gave him an influence that was hated but could not be denied. Looking at him, I was reminded of all the comely and loving faces that had surrounded my Griffith at Rhuddlan—and yet Griffith had been betrayed. What sort of man was Harold that he commanded the abso-lute fealty of the Fallen Angel of Canterbury? Was it possible that Stigand genuinely be-lieved, as so many others did, that England's future rested safest in Harold's hands?

Looking at Stigand I was frightened, for I felt that my life and my fate were totally given over to strangers. Wulfstan seemed to represent the forces of goodness; Stigand represented am-bition and implacable will. England must not be conquered by foreigners—I was in agree-ment with that—but when both good and evil were on our side, which would win?

Was there enough of Wulfstan in the King to win God's support, I wondered. But then

I had another, depressing thought; in a lifetime I have begun to learn that even the best man does not always win. There seemed no doubt that Harold would eventually have to fight for his country, and the outcome would not be determined by the simple forces of my childhood faith.

I lost my taste for food entirely and sat picking at my nails until the meal was over.

Mounted once more, we rode south toward the river. I turned in my saddle and managed to catch Osbert's eye; he spurred his horse to my side.

"Osbert, by what way do we go?"

"The London Bridge, my lady."

I tightened my grip on the reins until my horse tossed his head in protest, but I had to steady my nerves for the question: "Is that where they put . . . the heads . . . of England's enemies?"

"Yes, Your Grace." His expression was impassive.

"Then please send word to my lord the King and ask him to go by a different route, for my sake."

In a few minutes Harold had turned his horse and ridden back to me, scowling at this disruption of his plans. About us people swirled, a-buzz.

"Is the First Lady ill?"

"Nay, it is the heat of the sun; she wants a shady route!"

Coarse laughter. "It is the heat of the King's loins, I'll wager! I daresay the Lady carries an Atheling in her womb!"

Harold swung in beside me and the chatter ceased. "What nonsense is this?" he demanded, fierce and golden as a lion in the sun.

"My Lord, I rarely ask favors, but I beg you this once. Take some other way; do not go by the bridge!"

For a moment I saw annoyance and anger in his eyes at my presumption. Then he realized what I meant. His expression softened by an eyelash, only enough that I saw it, no one else. "Madam, you would understand that all folk must see me as King. This city supported my father; from it came his strength at court. London must be my conquest as well; we ride through all the town, as planned."

"And most particularly"—his eyes narrowed, and I felt the force of his will as he pressed it upon me—"most particularly must we *both* ride to the foot of the bridge! All the city folk, and all of the court must see that the past has no claim upon my lady."

"Please . . ." I began, horrified.

His voice was cold as he leaned toward me and hissed his command for my ears alone.

"You will do as I say, Aldith. You will ride with courage to the foot of London Bridge, and you will look upon whatever is there. You will give no sign of emotion, do you understand? No sign!"

The taste of Stigand's eggs and onions flooded my mouth. I could not speak for fear my dinner would pour forth and disgrace me. My head drooped over the saddlebow and I nodded, beaten by his will. Harold continued to gaze at me fixedly for a few moments to assure himself that I would obey, then he turned abruptly from me and spurred his horse. Miserable, I fell in behind him, and we rode down the Bishop's Gate Road to the bridge.

The smell of the Thames under an afternoon sun was equal parts of mud and weed and water. A number of people were gathered at the end of the bridge to greet him, including a band of German merchants come to pay their annual trading tribute of cloth, pepper and vinegar. To distract myself from the bridge I tried to smile at them, to take part in the exchange of courtesies. But it was no use. When Harold's attention was fixed on the crowd my head turned of its own accord, and I was gazing at the London Bridge.

A goodly wooden structure, spanning the broad and sluggish river. Wide enough for two wagons abreast to cross it, it had led into the walled city for hundreds of years. It marked the only route across the Thames to the south country, so almost everyone had cause to use it at some time. An ideal place for displaying the trophies of war.

They were there, pole after pole, the length of the bridge: an endless row of pikes topped by blackened objects like charred loaves of bread. The sun and salt air had discolored the heads of England's enemies; time and crows had rendered them unrecognizable. If one was my Griffith, I would never have known him.

The feelings I had dreaded did not come to me. There was no horror, no freshet of grief and rage. Nothing of Griffith ap Llywelyn awaited me on London Bridge; there was much more of him alive within me. All I felt was a sense of anticlimax, of aching letdown. Perhaps the worst nightmares are often so, faced in daylight. I had thought to meet my love here, in whatever agonizing form; instead I was without him in the dying afternoon, and in a few moments my life would go on with Harold Godwine.

My palfrey footshifted under me, disturbing my quiet emptiness. Harold rode up to me and laid a hand, not unkindly, on my arm. He looked along the strand where ships were tied up, his eyes swept the level green fields beyond and the pretty fringe of willows along the riverbank. "It is time to go on to the West Minster, madam," he said.

"Yes," I echoed, "it is time to go."

Thorney

Wʜᴇɴ Kɪɴɢ Eᴅᴡᴀʀᴅ ᴛʜᴇ Cᴏɴꜰᴇssᴏʀ built his beloved West Minster on Thorney Island, hard by the West Palace, he was using a location already sanctified by fire and blood. The Roman conquerors had built with stone upon the graveled part of the island where the footing was firmest. Legend had it that they were preceded there by ancient pagan rites, that the dark gods had been offered sacrifice on the mist-shrouded triangle between the Thames and the branches of the Tyburn.

By torchlight we came at last to the West Palace. A handsome timbered hall, it appeared similar, except in size, to the manor houses of the earls and more prosperous thegns. Beyond it loomed the stone abbey, the gardens and courtyards and clustered buildings into which Edward had poured his only kingly ambition. We forded the river at a place so shallow my skirts stayed dry; even those afoot needed hoist their garments no higher than their knees. "The Thames is silting up here," Wulfstan told me, "and Thorney Island is joining the mainland. King Edward always considered it a foolish expenditure to build a bridge which would soon be unneeded, and so we always arrive at Thorney with wet feet."

By the time we had been taken into the palace, I was so sick with weariness I did not even look around me. I longed only for Gwladys to put me to bed, or even lay me on a pallet in some dark corner. My very bones felt mushy with exhaustion.

Unfortunately, the vitality of strong men does not admit the frailty of women. Harold intended that we entertain immediately in the Feasting Hall, so a large meal and much drink was laid on straightway. I had no time to rest, only a few minutes alone with Gwladys to change my gown and brush my hair. At least I had a chance to remove that crown. Gwladys made mournful noises over the angry red groove it had worn in my forehead as she untwisted the locks of hair that had anchored it in place throughout the day. Doubtless the King thought I would appear before the court with the thing on my head, but I was determind to grind it underfoot rather than wear it again that day.

We returned to a festive scene. The Hall blazed with torches and an extravagance of candles. A high settle was arranged for the King, with a slightly lower one for me, both draped with swags of leaves and berries. Tables filled the center of the enormous room, and the wall was lined with mead benches beneath glowing tapestries. Gleemen circulated freely through the crush of nobles and courtiers, singing praises of the King and his Lady. I was scarcely seated when a bevy of young girls rushed up to me with a huge ale bowl. Shouts of "Wassail!" filled the hall.

Harold rose and lifted the great King Alfred's drinking horn in toast. It was the moment he had dreamed of: King and Queen of England, together in their palace, cheered by their subjects. Around him on the walls hung tangible signs of his wealth and power: the Flemish tapestries, the many huge bronze shields and crossed swords. At our marriage in York his face had been closed, remote; in bed it was savage; on our journeys, preoccupied. Now and for the first time I saw the strong features transfigured with genuine happiness.

Why, he is handsome! I thought.

At once I heard a sigh breathed behind me by some girlish voice: "The King is so beautiful!"

As Saxon custom decreed, I led the maidens as we carried the ale bowl around the hall to serve Harold's guests. Past tired, I put one foot ahead of the other and prayed I would not faint. One of Harold's pages walked before me, and a herald announced in a silvery voice the name of each noble as we offered the bowl. There were more strange faces than familiar ones, but I tried to smile on all while wishing the lot of them would just go away.

Food, innumerable smoking torches, the smell of sweat and ale, a dreadful pain in my back—I looked marveling toward Harold. He appeared much as he had that morning, fresh and eager. No wonder the man had achieved the throne!

I do not recall how or when it ended; only sometime much later I realized we were abed in a quiet chamber and Harold was snoring beside me. The weight of unspent sleep lay heavy on me, sodden, fog-colored. Oh, blessed darkness, that lies like a healing ointment on eyes burned with smoke!

When dawn came, I began my life as resident First Lady. The duties were little different from those I had performed at Rhuddlan, although I no longer wore a massive iron ring of keys. The King's steward was never far from me, and to him was entrusted the tiresome duty of locking and unlocking. Otherwise I was chatelaine of the West Palace, burdened with a thousand tasks a day. All that was done for the King's pleasure must be supervised, and the servants, like all servitors in whatever household, required constant urging. Thorney was constantly a-bustle with comings and goings; it was not uncommon for us to feed and bed a hundred guests a night. Butchers, cooks and yeomen began their labors long before cockcrow, preparing for the horde of messengers, petitioners and ambassadors to come.

A fortnight after our arrival, I was crossing the courtyard with Egbert and two porters on some errand when a wild clatter of hoofs sounded on the road. A moment later two men galloped at top speed into the yard, sawing their horses' mouths cruelly as they reined them in. One I recognized as the King's brother Leofwine; the other was the young replica of Harold himself.

The boy's big brown horse was plunging about, full of fight though sweated from his hard ride. An equerry dodged around his flailing front feet, trying to catch the bridle so the youth could dismount with dignity. But the horse was overexcited and would not be calm, so at last the boy leaped off like an acrobat, landing on his feet with a careless laugh. "I must take the time to tame that beast some-day," he commented as he turned and made directly for the King's private stair, Leofwine at his side.

I abandoned Egbert and hastened to the stables, for I knew Harold had gone there. I found him deep in conference with his saddler, but when he saw me he broke away and came to me.

"You are wild-eyed, Aldith; have you a bee in your skirt?"

I would not be baited; I merely told him of the new arrivals. It was the job of a page, but that way I would not have had the opportunity to ask the identity of the youth with my husband's face.

Harold was not affronted by my curiosity. "He has my look because he is my son, Aldith, as I'm sure you already knew."

"His mother . . . ?"

"Edith Swanneshals. Swan Neck. You know of her."

"Yes, Your Grace."

"You need no fear for your dignity, Al-dith; my mistress will not face you across the

Feasting Hall. But her sons are mine, they bear my blood, and they will be well treated whenever they wish to visit me." He spoke as if he expected me to protest, but for once I surprised him.

"I know that men have sons outside the marriage bed, My Lord, and it does not bother me. In Wales they are quite civilized about it; it is not considered an unnatural disgrace, My Lord. Griffith had sons long before he wed me, and I accepted it. I only wanted to hear you own your sons with pride, as he did."

Harold smiled. "Well spoken, Aldith. You behave with the dignity I sought in a First Lady." Then, to my immense discomfiture, his eyes raked down my body and up again. "Of course," he added, smiling in a different way, "dignity is not required in bed!"

Harold turned from me and strode off to seek his kin. I stared in rage at his leather-covered back. He had good qualities, I grudgingly admitted, but the bed would always be our battlefield. Dignity, indifference, coldness —these were my weapons against him and would remain so. If he wanted a hoyden, let him petition elsewhere. I would not surrender to him the Aldith of Griffith ap Lylwelyn!

The Witan convened for its Easter session. The noble and learned, the powerful and greedy, assembled from all over the kingdom to sit in solemn conclave, passing judgment and making laws. During the latter part of Edward's reign Harold had served almost as Vice-King, dictating so much policy that the members of the Witan were already accustomed to his authority.

As First Lady I was entitled by law to attend the Witenagemot if I wished, although my predecessors had bowed to custom and remained in womanly seclusion. But perhaps they lacked my curiosity. I donned a pompous wine red robe and took my place at the opening session.

When I told Harold I wished to attend he stared at me. "What interest can you have in laws, Aldith?"

"I understand Welsh law very well," I told him sharply, "and if my life is now to be regulated by Saxon law and the pronouncements of the Witan, I would like to understand that too!"

So I went. And it was very interesting, a sort of controlled and long-running argument that shifted from subject to subject. To underline his strong base of clerical support, Harold convened the Witan in the new West Minster, and an impressive ceremony it was. Bishops, abbots, earls, crown stewards and landed no-

bles crowded the nave while the King and the
senior officers of the Witan took the seats of
honor before the chancel.

Almost the first order of business was the
recognition and sanction of Harold's marriage
to me. All the members of the Witan agreed to
it and saluted me with formal courtesy, even
young Godwin, Harold's son, who was attend-
ing as squire to Leofwine. I did note that he was
the only squire so privileged.

But later on it developed that he had other business for the Witan to consider. It was
Godwin (I wonder who chose that name for
him, Harold or Edith Goose Neck?) who had
brought news of foremost importance from the
coast.

"Your Grace, I beg leave to address the
Witan," he said in a voice not yet firmly fixed
in its bass register. Harold smiled at him be-
nignly.

"Granted."

"I bring news of the Norman William, son
of Robert. A ship has come from Normandy
bearing tidings of the Pope's sanction of Duke
William's spurious claim to the crown of England!"

The Witan was thrown into an uproar,
and many things were said that were shock-
ingly improper in that sanctified house of God.
Harold, who of course already knew of this

from his private conversations with Godwin, sat silent on his High Seat and stared into some unseen distance. When at last a troubled order was restored, he rose and addressed the entire gemot in a calm voice.

"We have long known that Duke William intended to make our kingdom a province of Normandy. He is a resourceful man and a thorough one, so it is reasonable to assume he will use every means at his disposal to bring this about, and papal support is a mighty factor."

"But, Your Grace!" exploded Adelhard, one of the King's reeves. "Papal support would not be given without some strong evidence on the part of Duke William that he is entitled to make such a claim! There were many witnesses at King Edward's deathbed who heard him put the kingdom in your keeping; how can the Norman outweigh that?"

The buzz rose again in the crowd, but Harold silenced it with a wave of his hand. From the corner where I sat, half-hidden so that my female presence would not constantly offend the traditionalists, I saw Harold clench his jaw before he spoke. But that was the only sign he gave that his inner thoughts lacked serenity, and it would not have been visible from the front, anyway.

"When I was an enforced guest of Duke William," he said, with heavy stress on that word "enforced," "we spoke together many times of the possibilities of succession. By both frank and devious ways, he endeavored to win my agreement to support him in his blood claim to the crown. I told him that, as a cousin only of the royal line, he was not as entitled as—others—of better heritage and more intimate experience with the kingdom.

"When I left Normandy, William had no illusions that I thought him best fitted for the Crown.

"However, Godwin tells me that he has sworn to the Pope that I gave him my vow of support and agreed not to stand in his way."

The buzz rose to an angry roar again. Harold stood quietly through it, his eyes fixed on nothing but that inner vision of his own. In my own mind I was turning over his words.

"Then he is trying to gain the kingdom by a perjured claim!" cried an outraged abbot from the Chilterns.

"Duke William defies the wrath of God!" Stigand thundered, to be certain God heard of it.

There seemed to be no doubt that William would try to press his claim by force of arms. The Witan immediately gave the King its total support in the raising of both naval and land forces greater than any that had been put together in the kingdom before. Each of the earls, my brother Edwin speaking for both himself and Morkere, swore that every able-bodied shireman under his control would be summoned to defend the country.

There was almost an air of jubilation about what amounted to an undeclared war against Normandy. Even the clerics did not bemoan the possible spillage of blood, but vied with one another in their enthusiasm to support this noble defense of the country. Each man seemed to see it as a chance for some kind of glory.

I watched them as I would watch beetles swarming out from under a rock. Where would the glory be, I thought, if your heads were cleaved from your bodies? And I saw again my Griffith's blood rising in a red fountain from his severed neck.

Sickened, I rose and left the minster.

That night in the rare privacy afforded by our bed I asked Harold the question which had occurred to me as he addressed the gemot. "My lord, I heard you say that Duke William tried to make you swear him your support. But I did not hear you actually *say* you had never done so."

The huge body next to mine froze into stone. I do not think he ever breathed for a moment. Then he said, very carefully, "I did not lie to the other members of the Witan,

Aldith. I am the King; I do not lie to my council."

"But you allowed them to believe you gave no oath to William."

"What makes you think I did?"

"You did not say you did not."

He was very still again. When he spoke at last, there was respect in his voice. "You have too much mind for a woman, my lady. You hear what is not said, and that is often the most important thing. I wonder how many of the others heard it, too."

"It does not matter to them; they have chosen what they wish to believe. But as I am your wife I need to know the extent of your honor, Harold Godwine. Tell me."

I took a great chance that he would be angry with me, but he was not. The voice that answered me was tired, but full of relief as at a confessional.

"I promised William what was necessary in order to win my release from him and get back here. I felt it better to sacrifice my honor by making a false oath than to sacrifice my country by leaving her in the hands of incompetents. If I had refused to give William what he sought, he would have kept me there, helpless to protect this land, while he carried out his intentions anyway."

A weary sigh escaped him, one of the few

times I ever heard such a thing from Harold. "Now Aldith, think you that I have unforgivably compromised my honor—and yours as my Lady?"

There was a stone of sincerity in his question that told me he had asked himself that same question more than once. It had the pain of an old wound, never quite scabbed over.

I answered him as honestly as I knew. "My lord, I think you did what had to be done. You chose what you saw to be the welfare of this land over your personal honor, and that choice does not dishonor you."

The King reached out in the darkness and touched me; not my body, in the customary way; just my hand. For the first time since I had married him he took it in his and clasped our fingers together. So we lay, side by side, staring up into blackness. "I pray you are right Aldith," he said. "But I wonder. Dying, King Edward prophesied that England would be conquered as a punishment for the sins of those in high places. The others thought he meant them; I have always secretly thought he meant my perjured oath to Duke William.

"But he did not know of it, did he?"

"He was not told, no, but a man at the gates of Heaven may see things the rest of us do not. Perhaps he did know; how can I be sure?"

"He asked you to care for the kingdom!"

Harold would not take comfort. "The Crown rests this day on a lie, Aldith. Will all my land be punished for the sin on my conscience? Should I have chosen virtue over expediency?" Then he asked me a very strange thing. "What would your Welsh Prince have done, Aldith?"

He asked me seeking the truth, and I could not spare him, though God knows I wanted to in that bitter moment. "Griffith held his word sacred above all things," I whispered, miserable.

We did not speak again that night, and Harold did not let go my hand.

Next day, geld-writs were made by the King's chancellery, listing the payments to be levied for the hiring and equipping of the army, the Saxon fyrd. The districts which lay along the coast were ordered to prepare ships for the Crown's service; word was sent to every province to arm itself and make ready.

As the earls with the longest distance to travel, Edwin and Morkere set out for their respective seats even before the Witenagemot was adjourned. The remainder of its business, though important, was considered secondary to the task of assembling their thegns and raising an army. I bade my brothers farewell with no greater emotion than I had welcomed them, but I was somewhat pleased to note that they seemed a little less anxious to go out and kill people than some of their peers. Morkere expressed it rather plaintively: "I have not yet taken a wife, Edyth! I'm not ready to go to war and be killed!"

On the evening of the day the Witenagemot was adjourned, a festival of the Greater Litany, an awesome symbol like a warning of disaster as written by God's hand across the sky. Even as we assembled for the evening meal, a strange light filtered through the windows of the West Palace, so that we left our smoking meat and rushed out-of-doors to see.

An eerie green light lay upon the land. In the sky, just above the horizon, a thing like a star blazed, but it was no star! It was more like a flaming dragon with three immensely long tails, lashing fire across the heavens!

At the sight of the thing many of the servants, and some of the brave nobles as well, dropped to their knees and hid their eyes. After my first shocked sight of the awful light, I made the sign of the cross on my bosom and invoked the name of Jesus in terror, fearing that the world was ending even as I watched.

The King stood at my side. He did not cower or hide his eyes, but I heard him say hoarsely "Holy Mother of God!" and I knew he did not mean it as a profanity.

Later, men said that they saw all sorts of signs and portents in that April sky and always believed they had interpreted them rightly. But I know that that night none of us dared put a name to the thing or guess its purpose; we stared in awe and fear at God's firey sword slashing across the sky and waited like dumb animals for it to strike us dead.

Drifting on the night wind upriver came the sounds of Londontown, and the voice of the city that night was a moan and a wailing. We saw the glow of great fires being lit as the people tried to drive away the beast that hung above them, but it was to no purpose. It rose steadily through the sky, so slowly that we could not see its movement, but could only guess it from the change in its position in relation to the horizon.

Supper was forgotten; children were not put to bed that night. All the inhabitants of Thorney Island crowded into the palace courtyard, seeking safety in each other. Lowly porters huddled against pedigreed aristocrats and were not pushed away.

At last the King shook off the monster's spell sufficiently to summon his priests and bid them lead prayers in the minster. King Edward had died only eight days after the chancel was consecrated, and it would be years before the church could be completed as he had planned it; that night the men of God prayed for protection and forgiveness even as God's own baleful fiery eyes stared down at them through the still unroofed nave.

The world did not end. As a chill dawn wind rose to set us shivering, the weight of sleep became greater than the weight of fear, and one by one we abandoned our vigil. The King still stood in the courtyard when at last I excused myself and went to bed. I remember him yet, standing a head taller than the other men, with his face turned up to the sky and his hands hanging loosely at his sides.

"It is not something I can fight with my fists or my ax, Aldith," he said to me before I left him there. "All I can do is wait. God will act out His will in His own time."

I fell asleep before my head touched the bed, and when I awoke it was full day. A wave of relief washed over me; the terrible night had ended, we were undestroyed! Whatever that ghastly symbol was, it had not harmed us!

But then Gwladys came to dress me, and I saw her eyes abnormally large with fear. "It is still there, Your Grace."

"The three-tailed star? How can a star be shining in the daytime?"

She shook her head and pulled her shawl over it, as if in mourning. "I know not, but there it is!"

Incredibly, she was right! It was well past the hour of prime, the sun was high above the horizon, and yet we could all see the phenomenon still blazing above us, rising infinitesimally higher with each hour. Harold came to me, his eyes red-rimmed from lack of sleep.

"The scholars say it is a thing called a comet, a star broken loose from its moorings and flying through the sky."

"Will it fall on us?"

"No one can tell me, Aldith; there is a limit to what scholars know. Even Wulfstan is frightened of the thing and considers it an omen, but whether for good or evil he cannot say."

For a whole week our lives were a little unreal, bathed always in the eerie glow of the unnatural star as it slowly crossed the heavens. People would lose track of their conversations and break off speaking in midsentence as their eyes turned helplessly upward; dogs bayed and howled continually, and milk soured in the dairy.

But it never fell on us. At last, though we could not get used to it, we were able to pick up the thread of our lives somewhat and go on. Soothsayers began to arrive on Thorney Island in droves, each anxious to interpret God's sign for the King in return for gold or favors.

"I dare not listen to them," I heard Harold confess to Leofwine. "If the thing is a major sign it is either for good fortune or bad, and good fortune for one side would be bad for the other. None can tell me which way the die will fall, and I do not want to be influenced by mere opinion. War is coming—we all know it—and we can consider no outcome but victory. Send them away, all these self-appointed prophets, and let us make our own arrangements with God."

Harold had not been one to spend excessive time on his knees, thinking that his predecessor had done enough of that for two kings, but as long as the comet could be seen he devoted a goodly amount of the day to prayer. I think he hoped that God could be persuaded to show him a further sign, some proof that the comet foretold destruction for those who would try to seize England, but no such sign was given him.

At last the sky was clear again, and the shaken people began belatedly to prepare for May Day.

The Isle of Wight

Oh, MAY DAY WAS GORGEOUS that year! The people were wild with relief when the fiery dragon left the sky, and they planned such celebrations as had never been seen before. Poles were set up everywhere. Every flower, both wild and tame, was torn from its root and woven into a garland or thrust into a maiden's bosom. I never heard so much song or saw so many ale bowls, even at the drunken revelry that follows a wedding.

We all felt as if we had somehow escaped

266

a dire calamity, rescued from disaster by a special blessing richly deserved. England went a little wild that May Day.

"It is a pagan festival!" exclaimed Wulf-stan, pretending to be insulted when I co-quetted with him and asked if he would dance at the palace Maypole. (Some two hours hence I saw him, tonsured head agleam with sweat and a pretty girl on either arm, dancing as frisky a measure as the Morris dancers! It is my personal opinion that men of God have as much reason to be joyous as anyone else—more, mayhap, if they are as blessed as they think they are.)

When I found myself rather too tightly in the strong arms of Harold's handsome younger brother, Earl Gyrth, as we spun madly to the music, I allowed myself to enjoy my woman-hood as I had not for a long time. I flirted open-ly, I lowered my lids and looked up at him through my lashes, I bit my lips red and pouted them sweetly. When I caught him looking at them and moistening his own with his tongue, I giggled like a girl.

"You are a feast for a man, my lady!" he told me warmly. "Does my brother appreciate you properly?"

"Is any woman ever fully appreciated?" I laughed up at him.

"A woman like you—perhaps not. Methinks

it would take several men, working in turns!"

I bubbled with laughter, some caused by too much mead and some by too little dignity that night. "Are you applying to take a turn, my lord?"

His face sobered suddenly, and the arms that held me seemed harder than before. "Is there a position open?" he asked, with no laughter at all in his voice.

Until then I had been enjoying the game, a game I had not allowed myself since I fell in love with Griffith. But I thought Gyrth knew it was just that, a game; I did not dream he might take it seriously!

"Nay, sir!" I told him, still making myself laugh as I tried to maneuver some space between our bodies. "But if the position were open, I vow you would have first call on it!"

To my discomfiture, he would not match my banter. And his grip did not loosen. "So the King is not victorious in all things, eh, sister? He has not totally tamed you to heel, I see! But I have some talents he lacks, madam; all the gifts were not given to Harold! Perhaps I could arrange a little private demonstration . . . ?" He began to pull me toward the shadows, away from the revealing light of the giant bonfires that now held back the night. I glimpsed other figures entwined in dark places, and the embraces were fast losing their innocence.

"Please, my lord!" I did not want to fight him openly and make a scene, but I was beginning to realize that he was drunk and excited almost past the point of caring. I looked wildly around for help.

"The Earl seems to have misjudged his capacity for ale," said a voice in the darkness. Osbert, faithful Osbert, reached over my shoulder from behind and put his big hand right around Gyrth's throat. I saw the fingers tighten and Gyrth's face grow red, the eyes bulging. In a few short moments my brother-in-law went limp from lack of air and crumpled to the ground as Osbert released him.

We stood together, looking down. "It is odd how drink takes some men," said Osbert in an innocent voice. "They imagine things that never happened, and sometimes they faint away like giddy women."

He bent down and hoisted the unconscious man to his shoulder like a sack of meal. Then he straightened and smiled broadly at me. "He will waken in the morning with a head like a burst pumpkin and a badly fuddled memory, my lady. But I think you will have no trouble with him after this."

Osbert was right.

But Gyrth was not Harold's only brother

who coveted the King's possessions and power. Even as we danced in the palace at Thorney, Tostig was busy in Flanders, preparing an invasion fleet to sail against the King.

Unknowing, Harold had gone to Waltham, to the minster of the Holy Cross, his gift to the Church that had been consecrated six years past. Since the advent of the star with tails, Harold had been much involved with God, and he gave me to believe his trip to Waltham was for the purpose of supplicating that most powerful of allies. But the Early Gyrth, who was still with us and seemed to be harboring a smoldering though unspoken grudge, gave another name to the trip.

"He has gone to visit the Swan Neck!" Gyrth was quick to announce in the King's absence. And although I did not feel a drop of loving blood in my heart for Harold Godwine, I was startled to find the poison of jealousy coursing through my veins!

"What makes you think so, my lord? Did he tell you that?"

"He did not need to tell me, Your Grace," Gyrth said smugly. "Years ago he gave her a parcel of land near that spot, that he might combine God's business with a man's pleasure. He is very good at arranging things for his own benefit, is the King!" And I saw that Gyrth was much amused at my situation.

I was determined to say nothing of it to the King when he returned. Why should I? His romantic involvements were nothing to me! Yet the thing gnawed at my vitals like a ravening wolf, and I found to my anger that I thought of little else!

"I will not give him the satisfaction of thinking I am jealous of him!" I said firmly to Gwladys as she put on my hose.

"Of course not, my lady," she replied.

"He can have a concubine in every cathedral, it makes no difference!"

"It makes no difference," Gwladys echoed.

"I preserve my virtue for him, but of course there is no reason why it should work the other way round!"

"No reason at all, my lady. Men are different. Besides, you have told me often and often there is no love between you."

"None! I could not possibly love the King; he is as different from Griffith as peas from plums. And quit scratching my legs with your ragged nails, you clumsy woman!" I lashed out at her with my foot, almost knocking her off-balance as she knelt in front of me. "I do not understand why you have become so exasperating of late, Gwladys!"

"No, my lady," she said calmly.

Then the King returned, looking as innocent as a man who had spent his days and nights in prayer and fasting. But before the sweat was dry on his horse—and before I could ask him questions it were better not to ask— another and more sweated horse was in the palace stables. Riding hard from the south, a courier had come with news of a fleet sailing up the coast.

"It flies the flag of Flanders, Your Grace," the flush-faced boy stammered to his King, "and the standard of Northumbria. The pennons are the House of Godwine."

Harold swore with the mouth of a man who has not recently set foot inside a minster. "Tostig!"

"Aye, Your Grace, that is what they think on the coast. He has not yet put boats ashore in Sussex, but they are all afraid down there; they think he is forerunner to an invasion from Normandy."

"It would be like Tostig to throw his lot with William. In his desire to get revenge on me, he would rather give the crown of England to the Norman than see it on my head. Damn the man! When he was a child he was rash and reckless; now he is a fool!"

He called all his counselors to him; there was nothing for it but to assemble the fyrd along the coast and destroy Tostig and his fleet.

"I will lead them myself," Harold announced.

"He is your brother," Ansgar the marshal suggested tactfully. "Perhaps it would be better to send another against him . . . ?"

"If he were my dog and he were rabid, I would put him down myself and not send my friends to face him. I thank you for the thought, Ansgar, but I needs must tend to this matter myself. We prepare straightway for Sandwich!"

The preparations for war were significantly different from those for a royal progress. It was marvelous to see how much the King considered superfluous when there was a battle to be fought and time was precious. By nightfall his couriers were well on their way south, alterting the thegns of the need to assemble men, and a fully provisioned battle force was camped on the high ground of the island, to march at dawn.

Harold headed for Sandwich and the Kentish coast, where the Channel was narrow. As it fell out, Tostig was there before him, putting some of his troops ashore and harrying the land cruelly. Homes were burned, food and valuables taken, and some few good shiremen killed. As the English fryd drew near him, however, Tostig put his ships to sea again and sailed northward, apparently unwilling to face his enraged brother in open combat.

Harold turned south then, marching along the coast the way the raiders had come, giving aid and raising troops as he went. Tostig had first been sighted off the Isle of Wight, so the King made for that island, determined to camp there in expectation of the greater invasion force he felt sure would follow.

We spent some anxious days at Thorney until we received word that there had been no actual fighting. Gyrth and Leofwine had gone with the King, to my relief, as had his strapping son. So I was left to queen it about Thorney in prideful peace, giving such orders as I deemed necessary and with no man to say me nay.

I did not worry about him. I did not worry one moment about Harold Godwine, as I reminded Gwladys sharply when she stupidly accused me of being preoccupied.

The King had decided to set up his summer headquarters on the Isle of Wight, where he could best oversee the preparations for defense against Normandy. For it was clear that Tostig had sailed not from Flanders itself, of course, but from a Norman port. Harold intended to have the entire and rarely collected might of the English fyrd drawn up along our southern coast, with a powerful navy riding at anchor in the Channel; all the weight of England must sink southward to threaten the invaders with a solid wall of massed spears and determined men.

When his camp was firmly established, the King sent word to London that I was to be brought to him.

I was somewhat shocked. "He bids me join him in danger?" I asked Osbert.

"His Grace would not send for you if there were any danger, my lady, I am certain of that. But he is prepared to hold out forever in that place if necessary. No doubt he wants to conduct the business of the court with as much normalcy as possible, and that would include having the First Lady by his side."

I was vastly reluctant, but I had little choice. The children were not included in the King's summons, so I gladly left them in the safekeeping of the palace guard, far removed from the threat of war. It felt like leaving the own safe core of my being behind.

With Osbert as my personal bodyguard (is it not ironic, Griffith?) and a detachment of housecarles, I traveled with Gwladys and my necessary ladies-in-waiting across the London Bridge and southwest through Sussex to Chichester. I did not look up as we crossed the bridge, and I did not look toward Arundel as we neared Chichester.

A deputation of the King's men met us in that city and accompanied us to the Isle of Wight. The island had been turned into a complete military base; the King allowed himself little luxury on this outpost of his kingdom. We had a house much less grand than the West Palace. In truth, it was a scantily chinked timber cottage with only slight pretensions toward being a hall, and if it had not been early summer, the winds that blew through its walls would have been very unpleasant.

I had to remind myself sharply that I had not wanted to be First Lady of England. I must not regret the lack of a luxury I had not sought in the first place!

The King came to the dock himself to meet our boat, and I saw straightway that he was thinner, the lines etched deeper around his eyes. "It was good of you to come, Aldith," he said, taking both my hands in his.

"I came because I was commanded!" I reminded him tartly.

He ignored the thrust. "It is a time for massing one's resources, my lady. I would summon every strength I have for this confrontation."

I raised my brows at him. "You consider *me* one of your 'strengths,' my Lord?"

He almost, but not quite, smiled. "You are a strength I have not yet tapped, Aldith."

The words I did not want to say warred with my good sense and won. They forced themselves from my lips. "What about that woman who lives near Waltham Holy Cross

and raises your children, Harold? Is she another of your resources?"

The warmth vanished completely from his
eyes. "That is beneath you, madam."

"But you never discuss her with me!"

He stared at me. "You would prefer it if
I did? By God, you are a strange woman!"

"No! I do not want you to talk about her! I
do not want you even to see her! I . . . I don't
know what I want . . ." I trailed off mis-
erably, sorry for having started the whole
thing.

"I tell you this for the last time, Aldith, because I have neither the desire nor the energy
to waste on women's foolishness. I need you,
here, now, with me. You are strong; perhaps
you do not know how strong yourself. But as
long as I hold England, I need all the strength
I can muster to stand beside me. The woman
you speak of was my love from our childhood;
good she has been to me, and true, but hers is
not a strength like yours. She leans, like a vine
upon a wall, and in some times and circumstances that is charming. But if the wall is
taken away the vine falls down.

"Without support you continue to stand,
Aldith, and I count on that more than you
know. Now be done with this and do not speak
of it to me again."

He strode away, his shoulder rigid with inheld anger, and left me mortally confused as to my own feelings.

Heard at first hand, it appeared that Tostig had indeed come well prepared to do damage to his homeland. Thirty ships had comprised his fleet, including some of the Viking longships I remembered from the harbor at Dublin. A scattered few manor houses stood on the island; these Tostig had robbed and put to the torch. As soon as he had stripped the land of booty, he set sail again and began his ravaging of the coastline.

The King was most deeply angered by the fact that, in Sandwich, Tostig had gained additional men through bribe or threat. Good Kentish seamen had added their ships to his fleet and sailed northward with him; when Harold heard of this his heart hardened against his brother forever.

Gyrth was livid with rage, and Leofwine, whose earldom was Kent, wanted to put Tostig to the sword himself. "I feel like a maiden raped by my own brother!" he swore whenever the defection of the Kentish ships was mentioned.

"He thought the south country would support him," Harold commented bitterly. "This was our father's land, and Tostig thought his popularity here might outweigh mine. The dreaming fool! Thirteen years have I been Earl of Wessex, thirteen years have I cared for and courted these people! No brother of mine can wrest from me a love I have fought for and won!"

Gyrth's face flamed when Harold spoke those words in the hall of our house. I know not if Harold noticed or interpreted rightly his younger brother's discomfiture, but from that time on I became aware that the King placed his trust in no man save himself and Wulfstan.

And, strangely, in me. In the dark hours of the night we lay untouching while he poured out a recital of the day's doings and morrow's plans. I listened without comment or criticism, and I repeated nothing of what I heard to anyone, ever.

Afterward, unburdened, the King slept deeply and without dreams. Sometimes in the night he laid his hand on my hip, lightly.

Even as the business of war progressed, so did the business of nature. Since Thorney, Harold had not embraced me with passion, all his energies being directed elsewhere, but the First Lady has no privacy. Almost before I was aware of it myself, my ladies-in-waiting had commented on the cessation of my menses. "You were due a fortnight ago, my lady!" Gwladys chattered excitedly. "Have you yet told the King?"

"There is nothing certain to tell him, woman! I just made a long journey; it is only natural for me to be disarranged in my person."

"You never are!"

"Well, this is the first time, then! Let it be, Gwladys."

But she was right, of course. Even though I did not want to admit it to myself—it seemed such a profanation of the body that had belonged to Griffith—I was aware that I carried a child within me. Three had I borne; I knew the signs.

Gwladys did not believe my denial. She was very up-nosed at having such privy knowledge, and I knew she would not be able to keep the secret long. I would have to tell the King before he heard of it roundabout. But I felt a woman's desire to pick just the right time.

It fell nicely into my lap, a gift, strangely enough, from my brothers! Couriers came from the North with great news: Tostig and his treasonous fleet had put into the mouth of the Burnham River in Norfolk, pillaging the countryside; then when they wore out their welcome they sailed on to the Humber. But there they were met by Earl Edwin and a militia from Lindsey! Driven back aboard their ships, they made hasty sail for York, only to be met by Morkere and the Northumbrians.

All this armed resistance was too much for

the Kentishmen; they deserted and took their ships drag-tailed home. With his fleet reduced to twelve vessels and all his flags in disarray, Tostig beat a retreat for Scotland, and the north country was deemed secure once more.

"The earls of Leofric's line have proven themselves in battle!" Harold exulted in the hall. "Your family does you proud, Aldith! It was a good connection that I made there!"

My sense of humor was never besung by the bards in the hall at Rhuddlan, but I could not help enjoying a little play on words. "You have made another good connection with my family, my lord," I murmured with downcast eyes and secret smile. "And methinks it has borne fruit."

The King was no lackwit; he took my meaning instantly and his eyes blazed. "You are pregnant?"

"Yes, Your Grace." The joy I saw on his face was so beautiful that at that moment I did not begrudge him the use of my body.

"Oh, my love, you carry the Atheling'" He grasped my hands and pulled me off my stool, spinning me around him in a funny little dance totally lacking in kingly dignity. It was the first time I had ever heard him call me his love, and it quite shocked me. Again I was confused as to my feelings, and the spinning we were doing did not clear my head.

"Please, Your Grace, I am dizzy!"

"Oh, of course. I'm sorry, Aldith! Here, sit; bring wine for my Lady at once! Where is your maid; I'll have her come care for you immediately!" Harold fussed over me in a way that would have gladdened any woman's heart; it was impossible not to share his obvious delight. He insisted that the entire court be assembled straightway, even the officers of the fyrd, and the announcement made without delay.

"You will bear me a son, Aldith. I know it!" he exulted. "There will be no more of this tossing the crown into the air to see who catches it. The succession will be safe for my son, and the kingdom will rest united!"

It was impossible not to be swept up by such enthusiasm. Wales was being stripped from me, layer by layer, like a pearl soaked in vinegar, and daily I became more involved with England. Now I carried it within me. The Atheling, the Prince: the heir to the throne.

As my son Llywelyn should have been heir to Wales.

Pregnancy makes me happy. It puts a little wall around me that softens noises and brightens colors. This pregnancy dulled at last the pain of Griffith's loss and made me accept my new life even if it could not make me love my husband. But I felt easy in my skin, and my thoughts turned glowingly on the little being curled within me.

A new baby to hold. New, soft, toothless gums mumbling at my breast, for I would raise this child myself! I would allow no nurse; I had come to feel that each life was too precious to entrust to others. With that came a new desire to have my other children gathered about me; I hungered for my sons, and my daughter sitting warm on my lap.

I spoke of it to the King.

"If it would make you happy, Aldith, we will send for them soon. We shall not be going back to London, not for a while; if an invasion comes from Normandy, as I think it must, it will come here, and I must be here and ready."

"Would you send me to safekeeping with them?"

"No! I feel that you are safest right here, with me. There is no man I trust this day sufficiently to guard my son, save only myself."

"Osbert is faithful," I reminded him.

Harold's eyes twinkled. "I suspect Osbert has switched his allegiances somewhat, though I do not complain of it. His loyalty seems more to you than to me these days, and I am glad to see it; he is your complete conquest, Aldith, and I know he would not dishonor either one of us. But I trust the strength of my own right arm even more. You will stay with me, and as soon as I can spare a sufficient troop I will send for the children."

At night I sat naked on my bed, watching the swell of my belly and waiting for that first flutter of movement that signals new life inside. It was too soon, but I was eager; that little foot or elbow striking outward against my belly always gave me a thrill I cannot explain. Bishops speak of seeing saints; my most holy moment is that first signal from a new person.

The heat of the summer came and swelled around us, even as I ripened. At last my children came. With Osbert in stern and watchful attendance, the four of us went for long walks or stood in the summer wind at the coastline and watched the preparations of the burgeoning English fleet. The King had taken command of it himself, and we often caught a glimpse of his royal purple cloak flashing on one deck or another.

Rhodri was thrilled by the panoply of war. Osbert made him a little toy sword of wood, and he marched up and down with it, waving it in the air and making savage threats. When he came near to putting out his sister's eye, I took the thing away from him and broke it across my knee, which caused such a commotion that I boxed Rhodri's ears and sent the lot of them back to the hall.

Finding myself totally alone for once, I stood at the edge of the land and looked across the limitless sea. Somewhere over there was another fleet, other men preparing to kill, and other children, doubtless, playing at it.

I stood with my face toward Normandy and an innocent life cradled within me, and I wondered aloud if God felt as I did about the whole affair.

Even as I saw the tide come rushing in that summer day, the waves tumbling over one another in their eagerness to reach the shore, events were rushing forward too. Even then it must have been beyond control; we were sliding down an icy hill we did not even see, and the momentum grew greater with each passing day.

By the first of September, the King and his advisers had decided there was no further danger of an invasion from Normandy that year. Soon the storms of autumn would render the crossing unsafe; besides, the English fyrd was exhausted with their long and futile watch and anxious to be home, harvesting the crops they had barely planted when they were summoned.

In private, in our dark and secret world,

Harold confessed some misgivings. "I do not like disbanding the fyrd and leaving the coast unguarded, Aldith, but I cannot keep the men here to no purpose. Sooner or later I would have mutiny. While I still have the goodwill of every shireman and yeoman I must send them to their homes for the winter, and trust that in the spring they will not have forgotten the arts of war I drilled into them in this place."

Rather than subject me to an overland trip, Harold arranged that I return to London with him on his flagship. The seas still seemed calm when we set sail with the rest of the fleet, but before we reached Dover Strait a terrible wind came up and the sky turned black. How proud I was of the children then! Even little Nesta did not cry or hide her face in my skirts; she rode the pitching deck like a little sailor on her two small legs and laughed. We beat through the storm and made safe harbor without misfortune; my good sea-belly was not even affected by pregnancy, and I heard Harold boasting of it afterward.

But some of his ships were not so fortunate. Some of the supply ships foundered and were sunk, and as night fell a mast broke on a troop carrier and it lost control, eventually ramming another ship, with a goodly loss of men.

Weary and sick at heart over the losses, we reached Thorney Palace at last, anxious for a hot meal and our beds. The days at sea had been a great adventure for the children, but I was depressed by all the needless death and yearned for a quiet time away from the sight of water. I longed for the winter for peace that lay ahead and the birth of my baby.

Fulford

IT BEGAN WITH the splash of horses ridden at a gallop through the shallow crossing and a courier's hoarse cry: "Message for the King! Urgent message for the King!"

Gwladys and I were in the solar, consulting with the court herbalist about a tonic to reduce the slight swelling in my ankles. The herbalist recommended tea of comfrey; Gwladys held out for boiled sassafras and poultice of witch hazel. The matter was not yet resolved, the tempers, not tea, were coming to the boil when an urgency of trumpets rang through the palace. I left them to their medicaments and hastened to the hall.

The King stood before his High Seat, Ansgar below him and Stigand hovering close, quick to scent trouble. Reeves and officials crowded the hall, all listening tensely to the courier's news.

"It is the Norwegian King, Harald Hardraada, Your Grace! He has brought a whole fleet, sailing before the north wind, and they have already attacked Cleveland and Scarborough!"

Harold's face was grim, that muscle clenching in his jaw again. "We have some ships in the northern waters; were they unable to prevent this?"

The courier shook his head. "They were too few, Your Grace, and the Norseman has a whole invasion fleet! Nothing has been able to withstand him; he has entered the Humber and this very day may lie at anchor at Riccall, ten miles from York by road."

A horrified buzz ran through the hall. The suddenness of the attack was numbing; for so many months all thought and expectation had been centered on William of Normandy, it was as if the others who desired to control England had ceased to exist. But they had not, obviously. The greatest danger had not come from the South at all.

York! I pressed forward to stand with the King and face the courier, feeling a quick pity for his frightened face and travel-stained garments. "My brothers, the earls Edwin and Morkere—what of them?"

He shook his head again, and his eyes would not meet mine. "They are raising their troops, I know, but I cannot say how it goes with them."

"They drove Tostig from the country!"

Harold's voice cut in. "Harald Hardraada is not Tostig. He will not have embarked upon this thing ill prepared, and his men will not desert him in the pitch of battle. Mercia and Northumbria fought well before, but they cannot stand against Hardraada without aid!"

Stigand was white-faced. "Even now it may be too late, Your Grace!"

The King cut him with an icy stare. "It shall not be! Ansgar! We will leave at once! Give the orders for a forced march; we will attract such additional fighting men as we can along the way." His words were clipped and spare, his mind already sharp with generalship. He turned once more to the courier. "Are there others following you, bringing news?"

"Oh, yes, Your Grace!"

"Good, we shall encounter them on the road as we go. Hasten, everyone, each minute is precious. We will not sleep tonight on Thorney Island!"

Incredibly, that was true. By sundown every man who could be impressed into service was armed and provisioned, and reeves had ridden into London to draw more from their shops and houses. While the horses for the King's party were being assembled outside the stables another courier arrived, on a horse whose trembling legs had literally run it to death.

"The ships of Lord Tostig have come from Scotland and joined the fleet of Hardraada!" was the dire news the horse had been sacrificed to bring us.

I saw death in the King's face then. He strode to our chamber to finish dressing for the march, and I followed him on shaky knees, knowing that whatever happened now was in God's hands alone.

"They attack me on every side, Aldith," he said sadly as Sweyn Walleye fastened the King's heavy leather belt over his fine wool tunic. "I do not fear the Norwegian giant, but I wish to God my own brother did not stand with him!"

"You cannot kill him, my son!" rang a voice from the passageway. In another moment

Gytha herself burst in upon us, come hotfoot from her own apartments.

"Madam," the King began patiently, "we have discussed this before. When Tostig conspired with *your* daughter to murder an honored guest at court, he put himself beyond the pale and sacrificed his rights in this kingdom. Now that the kingdom is in my keeping, I must consider him as its enemy, not as my brother. He would destroy us all if he could; I fear his reason has become unhinged with greed and bitterness. I would have slain him had I caught him at Sandwich, with the blood of innocent townsfolk on his hands, and I will slay him in Northumbria if he fights with Harald Hardraada!"

"This is your doing!" Gytha whirled on me suddenly. "Before my son met you he had strong filial feelings; he did not hold blood ties so lightly! Now he no longer listens to my counsel. He has put aside my dear grandchildren as well as their mother, she who was like a daughter to me . . ."

"It was you who reminded me often enough that her blood was too humble for marriage!" Harold's temper was roused and redirected; I had never thought to see him turn on his mother as he did then. "I married a noblewoman, as you oft advised me, Mother, and you have never liked her for it! Your judgment is as rotten as Tostig's, and for all I know the treachery and madness in him were a birth-right from you! I am your sovereign, madam, and I will not have you come to my privy chamber and attempt to dictate to me! I will call an escort if I must to take you back to your apartments. I have no time for this!"

Gytha drew herself up with haughty, with-ered dignity, gave me one look that simmered with poison, and stalked out.

Harold looked after her somberly and then turned to me. "I will not see you again until this is resolved, Aldith. It is not possible to take a woman on a forced march like this, partic-ularly a woman great with child. Much as I want you close to me, I shall have to leave you here, as I leave my brother Leofwine to man-age the affairs of state until I return."

He looked deeply into my eyes. "Are you frightened for me, Aldith, or is that trembling lip for your valiant brothers?"

I bit it to keep it still. "I like none of this, my lord! It seems so sudden; we are all so un-prepared!"

"Perhaps it is better so, in some ways. We had months of waiting to fight and it came to nothing; it merely wore down the spirits of the men and used up the food supplies. Now at least we know the enemy awaits us and there is something solid to fight! My eyes grew so tired, Aldith, watching the horizon for those ships that never came!"

I walked with him to the palace gates. He was tall and strong in the gathering twilight, and I saw how all the men looked up to him with respect in their eyes. He made his farewells quickly and simply, a soldier gone off to yet another fight but certain of return on the morrow. As he swung astride his restive horse, I felt a compulsion to run to him, to place my hand on his knee and say . . . something. Something important that he must know and take with him, something I did not understand myself. While I hesitated, trying to shape the words on my tongue, he rose in the saddle and gave the command to move forward. Trumpets sounded; the night breeze from the river caught the standard bearing the golden dragon of Wessex and set it a-ripple.

"Now see there!" a voice exclaimed. "It is the fiery dragon from the sky, gone to lead our King to glory! It is a good omen!"

The people cheered as the horses clattered down the road and splashed into the shallows.

It was only three days later that the next couriers reached us, bearing chilling news. Tostig and Harald Hardraada had drawn up their troops at a place called Gate Fulford and pitched their camp beneath Hardraada's fearful banner, Landravager. There they were attacked by the combined forces of Edwin and Morkere, and a bloody battle had been fought. Several times the English thought to win, and drive the invaders back to the sea once more, but at last Hardraada broke through the center of Edwin's line and drove the English troops into the river.

The courier's description was horrifying. "So many of the dead Mercians were piled up in the water that the Norsemen walked dryfoot across the river on their bodies!"

And so it was at Fulford that the invasion of England had its first success and my brothers' armies were almost decimated. The victorious Hardraada marched on to York, and Harold Godwine marched across the country after him.

Stamford Bridge

WAITING IS WORSE than knowing. Grief rends the heart cleanly, that it may begin to heal; waiting shreds the spirit.

At Thorney we each searched for ways to fill the time between the coming of messengers from the North. I had innumerable womanly tasks I had been eager to get to, chores and projects that had been put off by our summer encampment on the Isle of Wight. But with time stopped, its hungry maw gaping to be fed, I could find nothing to put in it. I picked up my embroidery and put it down again, unable to concentrate. With Rotbert the steward at my heels I toured the kitchens, watching the preparation of food with unseeing eyes.

The children provided some distraction; Wulfstan had recommended a young cleric, one Hugo of Lewes, to tutor Llywelyn, and I often sat and listened to the lessons. The King had given Rhodri a tame hawk, and we occasionally took it out together in a fruitless attack on the sparrows. Dressing my daughter was a pleasure that could distract my mind for a little time as well.

But nothing held my attention for very long. My ear was permanently tuned to the sound of horses on the road, and I came to recognize that listening look on the faces of the others as well.

Gytha was distraught. In her grief, she lashed out at everyone, even her remaining children, so that Leofwine threatened to send her to a nunnery rather than encounter her uncertain temper in the halls of the palace.

"You did not take it so amiss when Harold marched against Tostig at Sandwich, madam," he reminded her.

"But this has a different feel about it! The King means to kill his brother, I know he does, I saw it in his face!"

I had seen it too, and it chilled me. I had

no reason to mourn Tostig Godwinesson—he was naught to me—but there was a horror about the confrontation that must be taking place. Brother killing brother; it was a bad omen for the kingdom.

Seeming dragfooted, the couriers came. We learned that the King had set his men a grueling pace as they pushed northward, and that he was drawing shiremen and yeomen from each territory they crossed. Word was being sent to the disassembled fyrd to gather itself once more and repel the invader, but there was no time to create the mighty mass which had needlessly awaited William of Normandy the past summer.

The fighting force of both Northumbria and Mercia was very greatly reduced; Edwin's thegns were beginning to straggle home, saying the north country was lost to Hardraada.

"Malcolm of Scotland had a hand in this!" Leofwine roared. "It is he who gave sanctuary to Tostig this time, then sent him out again to join forces with Hardraada, I am sure of it! He thinks to overrun us and take our land to add to his own; we will be nibbled away by our neighbors until nothing is left. At this rate, the Irish chieftains will soon be crossing the sea to claim their own bite of us!"

The lesser nobles steamed into London, hurrying to the palace to explain why they had, or had not, supplied the King with fighting men and provisions.

Leofwine was soon sickened of it and put Gyrth in charge of listening to excuses.

But, in truth, no one was deliberately failing the King. It was just that the situation was impossible. Armies could not be created overnight, or food grown to feed them. More than two hundred miles lay between London town and York; the haste of the march must surely weaken what troops the King had managed to obtain.

Then came word that Hardraada occupied York, and Tostig had been named by him as Earl of Northumbria once more. "It was not an unjust armistice," the courier said. "The city is not sacked, and in return for their support against King Harold, the Northumbrians have been promised a lasting peace."

My brothers, I thought bitterly. They go as the wind blows. My heart was heavy with disappointment in them, and I felt little better than Harold did about Tostig. "Earl Edwin was taken at Gate Fulford and is the prisoner of Hardraada, but Earl Morkere is said to have escaped. In his absence, Hardraada and Tostig will deal with those nobles who still live and can be found; a gemot to treat for peace will be held at the crossing of the River Derwent —the Stamford Bridge."

So they had not abandoned their land to the invader! Whiny Morkere and Edwin the self-seeking had not been party to a surrender. The court did not seem overly surprised at that, but they did not know my brothers as I did. In all the bad news from the North there was that spot of happiness for me: Aelfgar's sons had held true.

The courier who had brought us this news had passed through the Saxon lines at Tadcaster; that meant the fyrd had traveled two hundred miles in less than a week, marching day and night and dragging their supplies with them. Most of the men were afoot—only nobles and housecarles were mounted—and for the sake of speed food and armor were carried on the backs of the fyrd rather than in slow ox-carts. If Harold was already encamped at Tadcaster, he was within striking distance of the Norsemen; the next news we received must tell the tale.

So then we heard nothing.

We sat about the Great Hall and looked at one another. Leofwine paced; Gyrth fretted that he had not gone with his brother. "Waltheof and Bondig the Staller and Ansgar have commands with the King; why did he not take me as well?"

Archbishop Stigand, keeping the watch with us, tried to placate him. "The King has made London the capital of his kingdom, my lord. Those whom he had entrusted to guard it have as high an honor as those who march with him. Besides"—and he voiced the fear that hung unspoken in the hall—"if something happened to the King, you would be needed here to fill the regency."

Food was prepared and sent away again, untasted. Even the voracious Saxon appetite was dulled by the waiting. We all took turns walking to the courtyard and the main gates, bidding the warder open the privy door and then standing without, looking down the empty road and willing a rider to come.

A deputation of chapmen came from the City, reminding us that business went on even in time of war. Leofwine was abrupt with them but handled the matter well; we all gave it more attention than it deserved because it helped to pass the time.

Gyrth fumed again, "I should be there!"

I patted his hand. "It is no good to think of it, brother. Whatever has happened has happened already; no matter how it falls out, the battle must be over by now. It had been days since they reached Tadcaster; doubtless we will hear soon."

The hours passed, leadfooted.

We were in the King's chapel when news finally came. A herald burst into the nave, cried

"Victory! Victory!" looked around embarrassed, and dashed out again. I never heard Latin rattled off so quickly; the service was over almost before it had begun, and we all exited with sacrilegous haste.

"It was a surprise attack, a complete route!" was the joyous news. "Volunteers came to the levies from as far away as Worcestershire; men fell in with the King's fyrd every mile along the way. King Harold had seven full divisions by the time he crossed the Don, and everywhere men came to him swearing their love and allegiance!"

It was impossible, an impossible thing, yet somehow Harold had done it. He had created an army where none existed, and poured into them his own fighting will. We stared dazedly at one another, scarce able to credit our ears.

The courier, a young lad not much older than my Llywelyn by the look of him, was gray with exhaustion. Before he was allowed to continue, Leofwine sent for strong ale and meat for the lad and bade him sit on the King's own footstool to eat it. We all pressed around him, footshifting, desperate for him to continue.

Between mouthfuls of bread he did. "I was with the fyrd, coming up from southern Mercia, and I tell you it was a mighty thing! We were not allowed to slow, or be tired; we just went on and on, and when we lagged the King himself got off his horse and marched with us. If a man grew weary, the King took his pack and carried it himself. None of us could fail him after that!

"When we reached Tadcaster, we expected to see outriders guarding the way to York, but there were none. The land was as quiet as if it were at peace! The generals were jubilant; they felt Hardraada had so underestimated us that he had not even begun to make preparations for our arrival.

"And that was how it fell out. We rested well in camp, and people from the shire round-about came to us under cover of darkness and brought us good food and ale. They told us of the capitulation of York but four days past and marveled that we had arrived so soon. I marveled at it myself, as did we all!"

The members of the court crowded around the boy nodded in wondering agreement.

He continued, "When the fyrd was rested and ready, we were drawn up into our battle formations once more, and that evening King Harold took a detachment of guards and rode unafraid down the High Road to York.

"He met no guards, no sentries; the Norsemen and the Earl Tostig"—the boy's eyes darted fearfully around to see how we would react to

303

mention of that name—"had already gone with
the force of the army to a gemot at the Stamford Bridge.

"The city went wild with joy to see King
Harold ride through its gates once more. The
officials, the earls and thegns—all were gone
to Stamford Bridge, leaving only the people
themselves to see that England had come to
fight for them. The townspeople entered into
gladsome conspiracy to see that no news of the
arrival of the Saxon fyrd reached the Norsemen,
and King Harold rode back to us much heartened.

"Before cockcrow the next day we were on
the march. We went right through York, and
the girls threw flowers and kisses at us!" His
young eyes sparkled; this was a boy who had
already been seduced by the glories of war, I
could tell. Whatever blood he had seen spilled
since had not dampened his enthusiasm. And,
the way he told it, it did seem to be a thrilling
and joyous enterprise. Almost I found myself
wishing I had been marching with them, wearing hauberk and hose and carrying a glittering
spear in the bright sun!

"We went through Gate Helmsley and
some eight miles farther, so that by midmorning we were in the valley of the Derwent. We
could see that several roads converged there;
it was a good place to encamp an army and

arrange a peace treaty with the battle force spread out for all to see.

"We walked past fields where cattle grazed, and small boys fishing in the stony shallows of the river called to us and stood gape-mouthed as we passed. The land rolled gently; we began to catch occasional glimpses of a body of men in the distance. But they were spread about at ease, not drawn up into battle formations, and our captains ordered us to march double-time and reach them before they could be alarmed.

"We, my troop, had not yet reached Stamford Bridge when the battle was joined. King Harold rode in the lead, swinging his ax as he galloped, and the mounted knights rode with him. They poured down upon the startled Norsemen and killed them left and right. Up ahead of us we could see the battle standards, the Fighting Men and the Golden Dragon of Wessex, and a mighty cheer went up all along the fyrd when we knew we had caught the enemy and the surprise was complete."

"I wish I had been there! Oh, I wish to God I had been there!" Not Gyrth but Leofwine said those words, and every one of us felt them, I think. To see the Saxon fyrd come swooping down on the overconfident invaders—that must have been an hour of glory in God's eye!

"It was a hard battle," the boy went on. "Although the Vikings in their arrogance had

put aside their body armor, they were hard
men to kill! But the housecarles rode among
them with axes, and the foot soldiers came up
fast with pikes and clubs, and the air filled at
once with the cries of the dying."

He stopped to take a deep draught of ale;
we all begrudged him the missed minute of
narrative.

"Only one Norwegian guarded the foot of
Stamford Bridge, and before our foot soldiers
reached him he had slain a number of men.
They lay fallen around him like the petals of a
flower, and he stood in the center, bloodied
from head to foot and crying in a terrible voice
as he swung a sword about him. I hated to see
him go down—it was such a brave defense—
but go down he did, and the Saxon fyrd
swarmed over him.

"The river was deep by the bridge; no man
cared to ford it if he could cross dryfooted. So
we pushed and jostled one another in our
eagerness to get to the enemy, and someone
took from me my pouch of throwing stones.
I have a very good arm!" he added with pride.

"Go on!" Leofwine growled.

"Surely! Someone shouted that the slain
defender at the bridge was none other than
Harald, son of Harald Hardraada, and our captain sent a party to lay him aside, that his body
not be despoiled. Everywhere men were fight-

306

ing, hand to hand and breast to breast, and in the crowd there was often not room to swing an ax. Some of the foot soldiers had darts, and they did much damage with them. I had no weapon at all, having lost my stones, and the battle was too hot to allow me to find more. So I set about me with my fists and feet and did a right good job.

"My captain, seeing me unarmed, pulled me out of the fray and gave me his own knife. 'Go you ahead, Byrhic,' he told me, 'and give word to the King's men that the bridge is secure.'"

The boy's eyes drooped with weariness, but we could not let him be; every word he spoke was as gold to us.

"So you went forward, to the King's location?" Gyrth urged. "And how was it with him?"

"Oh, the fighting was fiercest there! The few Norsemen who had not put off their armor in the heat of the day were met with the main body of Saxon housecarles, and the flags of England and Norway were planted not five hundred yards apart. There was no mistaking the King—he fought like ten men, right in the thick of it—but I could not get close to him. I am but a cobbler by trade, my lord, I do not know the faces and rank of the great nobles. I did not know who to go to with my message or what was to be done with me after. So I yelled it out a few times into the general noise and then took the knife I had been given and attacked the nearest Viking." His eyes glowed. "I killed him, too."

We all smiled; it could not be helped.

He did not need further urging. The ale had restored his strength, and the excitement was peaking him once more. The words began to tumble out in a rush. "Up ahead I saw the flag of Hardraada, a great ugly thing with a cannibal crow upon it. 'Landravger' they called it. And near to it I glimpsed the Norwegian King himself. It could be none other; he stood as high as a horse, even a head above King Harold! And he wore the Viking helmet with the two horns. I tell you, it chilled my blood to see him!"

Gytha, who had spoken not one word during the lad's recital, spoke now. "And the Lord Tostig, did you see him there?"

He glanced toward her. "No, my lady, not at that time. But I would not have recognized him if I saw him, as I told you.

"The Norwegians had thrown up a shield wall, and I could see the Viking giant riding back and forth along it, giving instructions. Then someone hit my wrist a terrible blow, breaking something inside it, and I dropped my knife. Rather than stand defenseless I made off to one side, out of the heavy fighting, where there was a little rise in the ground and I could see well about me.

"Throwing spears were singing through the air from every direction. I had to duck betimes, but aside from that I was in no immediate danger. I saw a truce party gather, and there was a little break in the fighting. A noble came from behind the Norwegian shield wall and went to meet a mounted Saxon noble. All fell quiet to listen to what was said, but I could not make it out until I heard the Saxon cry, 'Then we will give Harold of Norway seven feet of English ground, or as much more as he may be taller than other men. And no more!' The rider whirled on his horse and cantered back to our side, and the fighting went on.

"I was watching the Viking giant when I saw an arrow find its mark in him. He staggered, drew himself upright, and then staggered again. A mighty roar was set up around him; his men crowded around to hold him up with their hands. But he was like a mighty tree gone rotten with age and struck by lightning. For all his size and strength, he could not prevail against the bolt, and so he fell, and I thought the crashing of that huge body must shake the earth around it!

"Seeing Harald Hardraada go down gave us more heart than anything else could have done. Even with my hurt arm I flung myself back into the fighting, yelling as I went until I nearly split my throat. I tried to stay close to the King and his housecarles, for that was the forefront of the fighting, and I knew when victory came it would be there.

"So it was that I saw that noble who had come from the Viking side to talk truce come forward again, and this time he brought with him Hardraada's battle flag. And I heard men who were around me shout that it was the Earl Tostig."

Gytha gave a moan like unto dying. No one else said anything.

"King Harold rode out to meet him," Byrhic told us, "and the others fell back around them. They met alone, with axes in their hands, and King Harold turned loose his horse, that he might fight his brother on equal terms. They stood knee to knee and spoke to each other a moment, but I know not what was said."

"I don't want to know," said Leofwine softly.

"They stepped a little apart, then, and went for each other in rage. Tostig fought like a berserker, slashing and flailing about him with his ax. King Harold stepped back and circled his brother weighing his huge ax in his hands and biding his time.

"Tostig seemed like a man insane in his

desire to sever the King in half, and he danced so wildly on the bloody grass that his foot slipped. In a flash the King was upon him; one swing of the ax, and Tostig's head rolled from his body."

We were all turned to stone, our breaths inheld, our hearts scarcely beating. Gytha sobbed and ran from the hall, and we could none of us look after her.

"The battle did not last long after that. The Norsemen had lost their King; the heart was cut out of them. They began to surrender in twos and threes, then tens and twenties, and before sundown the field was quiet save for the moaning of the wounded.

"I knew that messengers would be sent to London with the news of victory. I told no one of my injury but applied straightway, and put myself forward so boldly that I was given a fast horse and sent that same night."

"You have been a remarkably brave boy," commented Leofwine. "Is your wrist paining you now?" He reached out and took the lad's arm to look at it. The boy winced, but did not cease to smile.

"It matters not," he said. "I have ridden both day and night, sleeping only in snatches beside the road, and twice I have had to beg fresh horses along the way. And I tell you I felt no twinge of pain at all until this minute!"

"I believe you, boy," Leofwine smiled. "Now go with my squire there and rest."

The boy let himself be led away, casting a marveling gaze about him as he went.

The invasion was repulsed, the Viking force destroyed. Harold was safe, Tostig was dead. The giant from Norway was dead. A boy named Byrhic had fought well, ridden hard, and seen the royal palace. It was too much to take in; my head throbbed and ached and I wanted to laugh and cry.

Abbots and clerics, reeves and yeomen everyone seemed to be crowding into the Great Hall. The crowd spilled over into the passages and chambers and at last out into the courtyard, and Byrhic's tale was repeated again and again. We heard a cheer raised outside that echoed up and down the river. "God save the King! God save our good King Harold!" the people were crying.

I went to my chamber and had a fit of hysterics I could not explain even to myself; Gwladys had to put heated bricks at my feet and make some of her vile concoctions for me to drink before I could be quieted. And when I slept, it was as if I would never waken.

Would that I had not. I went to sleep feeling secure for the first time in months, feeling that the threat of war had been removed and we could have some sort of normal life. That

312

was foolish of me, I grant; normalcy is an illusion at best. My life had already taught me that and I should have remembered.

But I did not expect to awaken to find Gwladys's distraught face leaning over me, nor to hear her quavering voice tell me that an invasion fleet from Normandy had been spotted, crossing the Channel.

William the Bastard had set sail at last.

Waltham Abbey

THIS TIME there was no restraining Gyrth, nor Leofwine either. Armorers were summoned immediately, hauberks fitted and helms made ready. Every man on Thorney Island between the ages of twelve and sixty made preparations to join the English fyrd as it came south again to do battle with William. Riders were sent in desperate haste to the outlying shires reminding every thegn of his sworn duty to defend his King with every man beholden to him.

Llywelyn came to me. "I am not twelve,

my lady, but I am tall for my age, and I am good with a bow and quick with a knife!"

I stared at my eldest child in horror. "You will not fight, Llywelyn! You are a child!"

"Byrhic is but a few years older than I, and he had already been a hero at Stamford Bridge! He told me all about it!"

I made a silent note to myself to get Byrhic out of the palace immediately. We owed him a great debt, in truth, but I did not want him telling beguiling tales to my babes.

"You will not go, Llywelyn, and I wish to hear nothing more about it! There are pages in the palace older than you, and they are still reckoned too young to fight!"

He went away with his lower lip thrust out.

Messengers raced north to the King, heavy-hearted with their task of carrying bad news. It seemed a cruel jest to follow such a great victory with such a downward turn, but there was no help for it. We were invaded again; the King and the fyrd must be brought from the North to stand and fight once more, this time against a rested and freshly provisioned army.

It took but thirteen days for Harold to make Northumbria secure, find and free Edwin, locate Morkere and reseat him at York, and double-time his armies back to London, red-eyed and shamble-footed.

The entire city turned out to meet him. Shops were left with doors agape, kitchens wit¹ pots a-simmer at the hearth. I chewed my lip while my tiring women dressed me in a gown of brilliant blue and Gwladys plaited my hair into a coronet of golden braids atop my head. When I could sit no longer, I ran out the privy gate and down the shallow fording to join the mass of courtiers waiting on tiptoe and craning their necks for a first glimpse of the King.

He rode slowly along the river, giving his tired horse a long rein that it might stretch its neck and rest. In a ragged group of bright colors the thegns and housecarles, Harold's victorious generals, followed after him. Women broke from the crowd before the palace to run splashing into the water, careless of their lovingly chosen gowns as they called out the names of their returning menfolk.

Some of the women waited in vain, their eyes searching the road for figures that never appeared.

I waited at the edge of the river, feeling the damp mud ooze through my shoes. He rode straight toward me, sitting erect and seeing nothing. There was nothing in his face that I recognized. The eyes were not blue but gray and bleak; his mouth was narrowed to a thin line beneath a drooping straggle of golden mustache, and an unkempt stubble disguised the clean line of his jaw. I curtsied deeply as his horse drew abreast of me, but he did not even glance down. He rode on by me at the same slow walk, and I picked up my skirts in my two hands and followed him into the courtyard of the West Palace.

In the Great Hall he greeted us all with courtesy, but as remotely as if his spirit were still somewhere about the Stamford Bridge. The tone of his skin looked dead. Gytha would not come out to well come the King but kept to her chamber; he did not ask for her.

Those who had ridden with him—Ansgar, Eadwig, Waltheof and the rest—it was they who told us once more the story of the battle. It differed from Bryhic's version only in the viewpoint; a thegn sees a somewhat different war than a foot soldier does. But Ansgar added a note of interest to the tale of that lone defender on the bridge.

"It is a wooden bridge, there over the Derwent," he said, "and the planks of the floor are not closely joined together. The man who guarded the bridge fought so savagely and well that none could get past him until a Saxon secreted himself in a little boat and let it float down the river and under the bridge. Then he reached up between the planks and skewered the Viking on the point of his spear!"

In different circumstances it might have been a tale to laugh at; it might have brought many a hearty guffaw around a roaring fire. But we could none of us see anything funny in it; there seemed to be nothing left in the world that might start laughter anymore.

The situation was so grave it did not even have to be discussed. Without orders, the fyrd was re-forming itself as quickly as possible. Men who had been almost too tired to march home were struggling to find the strength to go and fight again.

When we went to our bedchamber, Harold dismissed all the servitors, even his squire of the body and my Gwladys. He had ordered the fire built up, though the night was warm for early October, and he sat himself on a stool in front of it and wrapped his arms about his knees.

"Come here, Aldith, and sit by me," he said. It was not a request.

I went to him timidly and sat down as he directed. I could think of nothing to say.

When at last he began to speak his voice was rusty and old; I could scarce hear it above the snapping and crackling of the fire. "I did not want to kill my brother, Aldith," he said.

"My lord, I should not hear these things! They are best said in the confessional, to your priest."

318

He ignored me. "I did not want to kill Tostig. But it was what he wanted. I saw it in his eyes that day at Stamford Bridge. It was some kind of triumph for him, getting me to kill him."

I tried to offer consolation. "Mayhap he thought that would wipe out the stain of his treason, set the scales in balance some way."

Harold shook his head but did not look at me; his eyes reflected only the flames. "No, it was not that. He desired the death stroke at my hands; it was some sort of victory to him. When I sent up to him before we fought I thought to offer him a chance for life, but he would not have it. 'You were the golden one, Harold,' he said to me. 'You were always the golden one.' That was all he would say. Then he attacked me with the ax and I had to defend myself.

"In the moment I swung the blade, and knew it would take his head, he knew it too. And there was joy in his eyes, Aldith. There was triumph!" Suddenly he buried his face in his hands, the great shoulders slumped forward in the firelight. "Why did he do that? Why, sweet Jesus, did he do that?"

I stood up and put my arms around that big, huddled figure as I would one of my children, and I cradled his head on my breast. I held him for long and long, feeling dry sobs

shake him and knowing from experience that
only time could bring him a measure of forget-
fulness.

If there were any time left.

One day only did the King plan to stop in
London. The fyrd would use the time to prepare as much as possible for the campaign
against the Normans, to regroup and take
stock of what assets it might still possess. The
King wanted a little time for himself, to go to
Waltham Abbey and pray.

In the morning, even before he had been
dressed, his mother came to our chamber. She
spoke with a low voice and would not look at
either one of us. "Send your wife from the
room, please, Your Grace. I would speak with
you in private."

Harold glanced at me. "There is nothing
you could say to me, madam, that Aldith need
not hear."

She lifted her head then and her eyes
flashed. "Why do you persist in calling Edyth
by that foreign name?"

Before I could give her a short answer,
the King replied calmly, "She prefers it madam. It is a small gift. Now, what did you wish
to say to me?"

She looked once at me, resentfully, then
half-turned her shoulder to me and spoke to
her son directly: "What was done with my

son's body? Was he given Christian burial, or have you fallen too low for that?"

Harold's face looked all sunken about the eyes as he gave her his answer: "Harald Hardrada I sent home to Norway on his shield, in honor of a great warrior. Your son I buried in holy ground in York; I did not disgrace him. You should have trusted me better than that." I heard his voice waver a trifle from the force of control he exerted upon himself, and I damned the woman in my heart.

She turned to go, slumped down and shrunken within her clothes. But at the doorway she stopped, and I saw that she could go no farther. She stood there unmoving, only trembling a little, and at last we heard her say in a whisper, "My son!"

I do not know which son she called, but Harold Godwine answered. He crossed the room in giant strides and had her wrapped in his arms so tightly I feared she might be smothered. He said nothing to her, nor she to him, but I could feel the healing flow between them. Sometimes the touch can say what the tongue cannot, methinks, and so it was with mother and son. And I was glad, for his sake.

When at last his arms loosed, she stepped from them and was gone into the passageway.

The King was not able to go that day to Waltham as he had wished. Hardly had Gytha left him when a page entered to tell us that an envoy had arrived from the camp of William the Bastard.

"Perhaps he wants to treat for peace?" I offered hopefully, but the King silenced me with a scornful look.

"If anyone should treat for peace it is I, Aldith! God knows I want no more of war. But you may be sure William sends me no soft words and false hopes; surely he knows our position by now as well as we do ourselves."

King Harold gave the Norman ambassadors audience before his High Seat, and much of the court was present to hear what was said. The monk Huon Margot had been chosen as spokesman, and he began straightway by addressing the King insultingly, without title. He reminded Harold that he had sworn an oath of fealty to William, vowing to support him as successor to Edward.

"Restore the kingdom you have stolen from my Lord," the monk cried in ringing tones, "and he will show you mercy!"

Ansgar the Marshal seized Harold by one arm and Gyrth grabbed the other, elsewise we would have had a pie made of Huon Margot on the table by dinner. While the King was held raving, William's emissaries made a hasty departure from the West Palace, and nothing was heard from them again.

It took long to restore the King to a reasonable temper, fit to lead the fyrd into combat. But at last the final arrangements were made, the final instructions given. I was commended to the keeping of the palace guard, with strict instructions that I was to remain safely on Thorney Island "until William floats belly-upward in the Channel!" But I had done enough waiting. Unbeknownst to the King, I had summoned my own allies and was making my own plans—as were others of the court ladies, though I did not know it at that time.

King Harold rode to his devotions at Waltham a day late. He returned in the evening, his companions with him; all seemed mightily shaken. The King did not even speak to us but went straightway to his private chapel and was closeted there long and long with only Wulfstan and his God.

A visit to Edith Swan Neck, if the trip had included such, could scarcely have had that result. I sought out Leofwine to speak with him of it, and so happened to be present when the two senior clerics from Waltham arrived at the West Palace.

They had been sent by the Dean of Waltham to accompany the King to the field of battle and to give him what spiritual aid they could. This was deemed necessary by the canons of the abbey as a result of what had happened during the King's devotions in the chapel that day.

The special pride of Waltham Abbey was the life-size crucifix in wood and marble, a gift of Tostig the Proud, which hung behind and slightly to the right of the high altar. Osgood, the elder priest, told us that the King and his party of thegns had taken part in the mass and then remained in the chapel to pray for success in the coming battle. Even after his friends completed their devotions, King Harold lingered on, accompanied only by Thorkild the sacristan.

Afterward, Thorkild reported to the clerics of Waltham that the King had gone to pray directly before the crucifix, throwing himself face downward on the stone floor and extending his arms at right angles to his body in the sign of the cross. And as he lay there, prostrate, the wooden head of the Christus turned slowly downward upon its neck until the eyes looked directly at Harold Godwine! Thorkild gave a gasp of awe and horror which startled the King, but he had not looked up and seen the crucifix. He completed his prayers and left the church, stopping outside to talk briefly with the Abbot. As soon as Thorkild recovered his wits he summoned his fellow clerics, and they all gazed in wonder at the altered figure which had once looked heavenward in its final agony. The face was now, truly, turned down.

The King was not told directly, but within minutes the news had spread through the precincts of the abbey like a blaze in grass. By the time Harold and his party set foot once more on the London road they knew of it, and the senior clerics of the church were already sitting in solemn conclave to try to determine the meaning of the miracle.

"It was agreed that we should be sent straightway after the King," Osgood concluded, "to accompany his body in this life and minister to it as it needed thereafter."

If I had had any lingering doubts as to my own intentions, that put an end to it. Harold Godwine had been my father's enemy long before we were met, yet he was husband to me now, and father to the babe that was only just beginning to kick within me.

Once, obedient and compliant, I would have done as I was bid and suffered another long agony of waiting. But the submission was gone from me; whatever fate lay in store I would know of it myself. "I will no longer be a piece in a chess game played by others!" I said to Gwladys in an attempt to convince her of the rightness of my decision.

She was not happy about it, but she worked in secret to prepare wardrobes for myself and the children, and she carried messages to Osbert for me.

On the morning of October twelfth, King Harold and a force of some four thousand men, including all the earls of the land save only my brothers, who had not yet reached London, marched out of the City and across London Bridge. In the wake of the fyrd came various parties of families, clerics and hangers-on, and a train of hastily assembled supply wagons too slow to keep up with the main force.

Farther back still, guided by the trail of dust that hung in the sky, a little family of freedmen rode on unusually fine horses. Osbert and several of his most trusted men-at-arms were the men of the family, Gwladys and I the women, and we were accompanied by two small boys and a tiny girl.

In my mind as I rode lay the great weight of all the things I had not said to Harold Godwine. Which is harder: to unsay the misspoken word or to replace the word left unsaid? Our official parting had been brief and correct, conducted in the presence of the entire court and a troop of waiting housecarles. Harold's last words to me had been: "If things do not go well with us in the South, take the children and go with all haste to the stronghold of the Earl of Mercia. I will try to meet you there later."

I could only agree, and say the formal

words of "fare you well" and "God be with you." There was no opportunity to tell him that I had been mistaken about the quality of the man, and that my hatred had been transmuted into something else.

I do not know if he would have even welcomed such news; it would probably have meant little by comparison with the Norman invasion.

After the battle there will be time, I promised myself again and again, like a talisman.

The fyrd was well ahead of us; I did not want the King to learn I had so thoroughly disobeyed his orders. But we did not travel alone. Down every crossroad and cowpath people came streaming afoot or on horseback, turning south toward the coast. Farmers set aside their harvesting and took to the road; Angles and Saxons and square-headed Jutes, freedmen and bondmen and squires, smiths and carpenters and swineherds and beekeepers—the population of all southern England seemed to be on the move, drawn to the coast.

"This is a mistake, Your Grace: I regret letting you talk me into this!" Osbert gritted through his teeth as he rode beside me. Nesta sat before him on the saddle, playing happily with the hogged mane of her "father's" horse.

"Perhaps, Osbert, but I can do nothing

else. Our world is changing hour by hour, can you not feel it? These people can"—and I waved my hand to indicate the scores of our fellow travelers—"and like me, they must go and attend the birth of whatever is coming."

"A free England is coming, united under the standard of the Fighting Men and safe forever from foreign intrusion!" Osbert prophesied with the ring of trumpets in his voice.

"God grant that you are right, good Osbert, but there have been so many signs . . . the comet, the crucifix at Waltham . . ."

"Those things are open to different interpretations, my lady! Can you not see them as signs of victory? It was the Golden Dragon of Wessex that flamed across the sky, the same figure that ripples on Godwine's banner! And I doubt not that the Christ on the crucifix mourned the soldiers who will die in winning our victory! After all, the King destroyed the entire Viking force at Stamford Bridge; does that not prove that the heavens themselves are on his side?"

Mayhap. But if that were true, what voice had roused all these people from their farms and shops and set them on the road to Hastings, making the long journey in an eerie near-silence? If they had been going to see a great victory, would they not have been laughing and singing, making jokes and walking quick-step?

But they were not. We, all of us, followed the fyrd to its destiny in quietness, our eyes fixed somberly on the far horizon.

Hastings

We went through Crayford, with the rank smell of the river always in our nostrils; we crossed the Medway at Rochester and followed the south branch of the High Way. By the time we reached the outermost edge of the Andredsweald, darkness was upon us.

"Even by day this is a dark and dangerous place, Your Grace," Osbert warned me. "I strongly suggest we camp here tonight and continue at cockcrow."

"Will we arrive in time?"

He smiled slightly. "For sure, my lady. Battles are rarely fought when the two armies first espy one another. There will be some negotiations, camps will be pitched and battle plans made, and a suitable battleground must be chosen. Even if the fyrd marches all night, it will be the day after tomorrow before both sides are prepared to take to the field."

Osbert was right about the Andredsweald. A few yards inside the forest and you could not see your horse's ears in front of you. I was glad to wrap myself in my cloak and lie upon the earth at the wood's edge, where I could at least see the stars.

When the sky was still ashy gray, we were up and mounted once more. Rhodri was fretful—he had not slept enough—but Nesta was happy to continue her flirtation with Osbert and my brave Llywelyn was excited at being allowed to ride with Osbert's men, feeling very military.

The cold darkness of the forest closed over our heads. The air grew thick and heavy with the smell of living and dead things, green ferns and rotten wood. Even more ancient than Nottingham was the Andredsweald; the Romans had cleared only a part of it during their long occupation of our land, and the forest had relentlessly claimed its own and more, clutching at the hills and valleys with oaken fingers.

The coast road ran through the wood in a serpentine, so different from the broad High Ways of the open country. The way was still paved with Roman stone, though much broken now, and if we did not stray off into the trees there was no danger of getting lost. As the day progressed, dimly seen through the heavy foliage, we began to meet people coming the other way on the road.

They proved to be refugees, fleeing the burning and pillaging of the Normans on the coast. They had encountered the fyrd well ahead of us and given Harold's sentries news from the scene of the invasion; now they were passing their news to other travelers and doing right well at it. Each group they spoke with gave them food or ale or blankets; with luck they could replace some of their lost fortunes, such as they were.

At midday we shared our meal with a woodcutter who owned a small cottage on the southern border of the forest. "A fine little place it is, too," he boasted, "all snug and out of the way!"

"If your home is so fine why have you deserted it?" I asked him. "Have the Bastard's men burned you out?"

"Not likely!" he laughed. "They could never find it, so well is it tucked into the hollow where I built it. But they have done a goodly

amount of damage to the countryside roundabout, raping and stealing and killing more
cattle than they can ever eat! It sickens me
to see, it does. I had my share of battles when
I was young—lost an eye to a spear and lived
to tell of it!—and I want to see no more killing. I'm off to the North for a while until all of
this is over."

Osbert was indignant. "King Harold needs
every man in the shire to join his armies and
repel the invader. Do you not think it would
be better for you to turn round and march the
other way?"

Our mealguest looked at us through his
one good eye. "If I thought so, I would do so,
boy. But I will tell you a tale. When the Norman ships first came ashore it was at Pevensey,
down the coast a way, and the shore where
they landed was all mud.

"Men who were there say that the Normans waded ashore, carrying their armor with
them, and among them was this Duke William.
But as he reached the edge of the land the
Duke put a foot wrong somehow and tripped,
sprawling face downward in the mud."

Llywelyn laughed aloud, Osbert and his
men chortled, and even Gwladys gave a giggle.
"It is not funny to me," the old man continued,
"and I will say why. It is told that when Duke
William got to his feet his own men laughed,

but he took no notice of them. He stood there, with his face all smeared and his hands covered with mud, and he held his fist up to the sky. 'Thus I take England in my own two fists!' he cried, and all his men cheered.

"Now, I have lived long, mayhap longer than I should have, and I will tell you this. A man who can turn bad into good like that will not be easy beaten. It is a dark sign. The battle will be terrible, and I think I will take me up to some cousins of mine near Ox Ford until the thing is settled.

"By the by," he left us as a parting gift, "you are well come to the use of my cottage if you like! It's a goodly one, though hard to find; I'll tell you the way to it."

So it was that Osbert was given careful and complicated directions to the woodcutter's home, and his description of it proved to be right in one respect. It was marvelous hard to find. But a filthier, damper, more uncomfortable dwelling I never saw in all my days. Had it not been so close to the final encampment of the English fyrd I could never have considered using it.

We slept that night wrapped in our cloaks and coarse blankets, lying on a dirt floor that smelled more moldly than the forest itself. I lay awake long and long, listening to sounds

I could not recognize and wondering what thoughts were Harold's on this night.

The endless night did end. Light crept through the cracks in the flimsily built walls and the smoke hole and I could hear the first sleepy morning songs of the birds in the Andredsweald. Our daylong trek through the forest had left me sensitive to each separate little voice, and I lay awhile just listening. Then I rose silently, so as not to wake the others, and walked tiptoe from the hut.

The chill of the night had grown deeper with the coming of dawn, so I wrapped my cloak of coarse brown wool about me in the rustic fashion, pulling it over my head like a shawl. My identity well disguised, I climbed out of the hollow where the cottage nestled and looked about.

The place was some six or seven miles inland but quite high, for in the distant dawn I could see the gleam of the Channel. At my back and all about me stood the trees, joined by massive walls of rhododendron, their leaves dark and leathery with the approach of winter. Before me the forest opened onto a rolling, grassy upland. The air, though cold, was sweet. Unbidden, the thought came to me, This is a pleasant place to die.

At a distance I could see the ruins of several burned buildings, a farmer's holdings put to the torch by the Normans. Directly ahead of me, toward the Hastings Road, lay a broad meadow unspoiled by frost but trampled and ruined by thousands of marching feet. The land rolled upward to a ridge in the distance, and fell away on one side of that to a low and marshy area. Between the ridge and the edge of the forest where I stood rose a little hill crowned with oaks.

On that hill, brightly colored in the morning light, stood a silk pavilion usually pitched for ladies of quality. As the day brightened I thought I recognized the pennon fluttering from the staff; it was Gytha's colors. I was not the only one of Harold's women come to see the battle.

Black-robed figures moved about the hill; monks, perhaps from Waltham. And then I saw that there was a second pavilion on the far side of the first, a tent which sported no royal flag. Was it possible that Gytha had brought the Goose-Necked woman with her?

My face flamed in anger, and I quite forgot the need to remain out of sight. I longed only to rush across the dewy meadow and up that distant hill, and rake my nails down the face of the woman in the second tent. How dare she come to this place!

Then my baby moved within me, and my

anger sank to a bed of glowing coals. It was not the time for recklessness. I stepped back into the shelter of the wood's edge, and as I did so I heard Osbert say, "You are up early, Your Grace."

"Not early enough, mayhap. I see the fyrd is already encamped along that ridge yonder; preparations for battle seem to be already made."

"I stood watch by the road, Your Grace, while you slept. Men came through the forest pell-mell all night to join the King's forces; there may be seven thousand men with the fyrd by now. And the King has chosen an excellent position, as you can see." He stretched his arm southward, pointing out to me those details of military strategy I would not otherwise have understood.

"Lacking strength of numbers in both archers and mounted warriors, the King has spread his men along the top of the ridge to minimize the fire of Norman bowmen, who must shoot upward. That same position will make it more difficult for the Norman knights, who wear heavy armor and ride horses lacking in agility."

"Does the ground drop sharply beyond the ridge, Osbert?"

"You cannot see it from here, Your Grace, but I have come this way before, and I can as-

337

sure you it does. The King has been wise to come so quickly and get here first; he has placed his army directly across the road the Normans would take if they sought to reach London. They will have no choice but to stand below him and fight, for if they try to ride around him there is impenetrable undergrowth on one side and a marsh on the other."

Directly athwart the road we could see the standards of Wessex and Harold Godwine, flickering in the rising breeze. Side by side the Golden Dragon and the Fighting Man guarded the way to the heart of England, and beneath them the tents of the nobles stood out against the skyline.

We could see, and smell, the smoke from the cooking fires; shouted orders drifted to us on the wind with the occasional whinny of a horse. But we were too far away to make out details; we might have been watching the scrunnage of a nest of disturbed ants. For a moment I envied Gytha her well-situated observation post—but not her companion.

Osbert continued to point out the advantages Harold had acquired. "The marsh is called the Sandy Lake, and the ridge is named for it in the Saxon way—Senlac. A quagmire lies hidden in that marsh, one which the King knows well enough but William's men may not have yet discovered. The land we protect will protect us in turn, my lady; you will see. Many Normans may perish in that place before this day is through!"

One Merfyn, one of Osbert's men, came up to us then. As a man of Kent, he was quick to point out the Kentish flag at the west end of Senlac Ridge. The brave Kentish thegns had been honored to receive the Normans' first attack by way of their position. Were they tired, those waiting warriors? Or did they relish the killing light as it came in from the sea?

Never have I understood this about men. Taken one by one they do not want to die, they make a louder outcry than their wives at the smallest injury. But when they talk of battle while sitting safely before their own fires, their faces shine with love. What pleasure do they find in the stink of another man's blood? Those who kill can be killed, as every wife and mother knows. And when death comes in battle it is not glorious at all. It is hideous and vile and full of screaming, and men cry for hours for their mothers while their lives seep into the soil.

Yet a man will get up out of his marriage bed to go and seek that senseless pain, or to inflict it on a stranger who bears him no other grudge. I see nothing to recommend it.

Now we could see more men-at-arms coming out of the forest or running down the road,

skirting Gytha's hill and hastening to join the
English line. Shire levies, mostly, armed with
their scythes and forks and clubs. No matter
what happens, there are always those who arrive late. Griffith used to say that had the world
ended in the year 1000, as the soothsayers pre-
dicted, some men would not have come to the
Last Judgment until 1002.

"There is something strange about that," I
heard Osbert say to Merfyn.

"What is strange?" I strained my eyes to see
the distant line of moving men.

"The sun is coming out of the Channel
now, Your Grace, but it strikes no sparks from
body armor!"

"Which means . . . ?"

"If a sufficient number of our men were
equipped with ring mail and hauberks, as they
were at Stamford Bridge, the sun would cast
glints on the metal. But I see very few! I fear
there is not enough armor to go around, and
many just fight in only their leather tunics!"

My eyes were not so good as Osbert's, but
I had detected another shortage. Even at that
distance, the great Saxon shields of limewood
should have been visible, their kite shapes out-
lined against the brightening sky. But there
were not as many as there should have been.
And the stragglers who were moving up to join

the ranks carried simple planks, or even shutters torn from their houses.

"We had to leave too much armor in Northumbria," Merfyn said sadly. "It was impossible to come back at the pace the King set and carry all of that as well."

So that was the price of the victory at Stamford Bridge. Harold must lead his army to battle hiding behind their own shutters.

I left them and went back to the hut to see to my children. They were all awake, and Gwladys was feeding them a gruel of barley and honey, and some pounded nuts. I sat down on a small three-legged stool to warm my hands at the fire.

Llywelyn came to me and leaned against my shoulder, and I could smell the sweet-salt of his childish skin. His breath was a little rotten still, from sleep, unlike the milky scent of babies. "Did you see the King, madam?" he asked me.

"No, the fyrd is some little distance from here. There is a wide ridge running across the Hastings Road, and they are encamped there. It is too far to recognize men, but I think I spotted the King's tent."

"Will we go to watch the battle when the Normans come?" Some of the eagerness for war had gone out of Llywelyn's voice. I wondered if he remembered seeing his father's head with naught but space beneath it.

"I will go to see it, son, but I am depending on you to stand guard here and care for your brother and your womenfolk."

"Womenfolk? You mean Nesta?"

"And Gwladys, you must cherish her as well. You are *the* Llywelyn now; I trust you to keep everyone safe and hidden until I return."

His radiant smile rewarded me. "I can do that, my lady! You need not worry at all!" Brave, sweet lad. God spare you. God spare us all.

I paused a moment longer to give instructions to Gwladys. "I will take Osbert and go as close as he dares to the battle, that we will know its outcome straightway. Keep the children dressed warmly and be ready to flee. I do not know how long it will take, but when it is over, I will come back here. Keep quiet, light no fires, and put out that one on the hearth. On forfeit of your life, let no one suspect we are here!"

A strong injunction for that loyal soul, but I intended that there be not the smallest disobedience. She was undone by my words and clutched my cloak, begging me not to go.

"You forget yourself, Gwladys! Of course I will see the battle! Did you think we came all this way so that I might cower in the woods like a hind? My place is by the King! When the battle ends I must be the first to reach him; I have things to tell him that can wait no longer. He dreamed of unifying all England, and I would have him know that I understand that dream at last. And love him for dreaming it, even as I deplore the slaughter to come! Think you that he will understand that, Gwladys?"

The woman looked at me wild-eyed. "I do not understand it myself, Your Grace!"

To my own surprise I laughed. "Perhaps I do not either. But no matter now, it will sort itself in time."

Osbert awaited me outside. With one hand always on his knife, he led me by some trackless path at the very edge of the forest until we reached a point almost even with Senlac Ridge. Our view was better than that of Gytha and that other woman on their hill, and so long as we stayed within the cover of the trees we were unlikely to be seen. The whole west side of the ridge was clear to our view, and we could now see its steep face and the Hastings Road beyond it.

The fyrd was drawn up in its battle position. Along the whole front of the ridge stood the loyal housecarles, the most skilled of English warriors, holding their shields pressed edge to edge to form a shield wall. Behind them, shoulder to shoulder and ten deep, were the rest of the housecarles and armed ceorls. Theirs was the most terrible of weapons, the mighty battle-ax brought to England by the Danes. No man could live in its deadly path, as I well knew. A skilled axman could cut his enemy in twain so quickly and cleanly that the man would continue to stand upright for a bird's breath before falling dead into separate islands of cooling meat.

Soldiers not carrying axes awaited the Normans with spears and longclubs, to the heads of which round stones had been bound with thongs. "Skullbreakers" Osbert called them.

"Do you wish you stood with them, Osbert?"

"I am doing the task the King assigned me, my lady," he answered simply. "Caring for you."

The thegns were easy to recognize, being horsed and helmeted. My eye was drawn to one who wore plainest garb yet towered above the others as he sat on his chestnut destrier. The horse was footsore, picking its way over the broken ground gingerly, but Harold of England looked almost as fresh as if he had not driven an army twice the length of England in three weeks.

He was riding toward the summit of the ridge from the direction of Gytha's hill, whence he had no doubt gone to seek his mother's blessing before the battle. (And another blessing, too? From a raddle-necked woman with patient eyes?) He had to kick his tired horse to make it canter up the rise to the summit, where the Fighting Man waved in front of the headquarters tent. He made as if to dismount, but just then someone grabbed his horse's bridle and gestured wildly toward the south. Harold rose in his stirrups for a better look, and I steadied myself with a hand on Osbert's shoulders as I mounted a fallen tree to improve my own view.

Up the rutted road from the Channel, a sea of a different kind poured toward us. Wave upon wave of metal armor gleamed in the sun. Hundreds and hundreds of huge horses bore knights protected from head to hip and preceded by a mass of bowmen and infantry.

One group of knights detached itself from the main body and took up a position on a knoll some three hundred yards from the foot of Senlac Ridge. "The Bastard and his barons have picked themselves a good vantage point," commented Osbert.

It was now well into the morning; the sun was up and the mist had all burned off. The two armies came together, not with a clash of weapons, but with a raucous burst of hoots and jeers. Each side taunted the other with the wildest insults as they strove to work themselves into a killing rage. From where we stood I was spared the words, but the meaning was clear enough.

Just when it seemed that the Normans would charge at last, a wondrous thing happened. A path fell open through the heart of their ranks, and a fellow clothed as a minstrel came galloping out of the mass of Norman soldiers onto the open ground between the two armies. His horse was most gaily caparisoned; bells jingled on its gilded reins. When the rider reached the foot of the ridge directly beneath Harold's standard at the summit, he reined his charger back on its haunches and hurled his lance high in the air.

English and Norman alike, the men stopped their shouting and stared agape. The amazing minstrel caught his lance by the blade with his ungloved hand and immediately tossed it high again.

"The man is mad!" Osbert exclaimed. Mayhap he was, but it was a glorious madness. For that my Griffith would have applauded him, and written a triad about it later.

A third time he threw the lance, and we watched it spin silver, end over end, in the sun.

But whatever finale he had planned for his amazing performance was not to be, for the horse chose to play a part of its own. With a lunge it tore the reins from the rider's hands and bolted straight for the ridge, leaping up the slope with prodigious bounds. In a few heartbeats it had carried its hapless rider to the center of the Saxon line. The poor fool swung his lance about him desperately but vanished almost at once beneath a press of men and axes.

As if that were a signal, the battle was joined at last. The morning came alive with a hellish roar. Screams, yells, curses, the clash of metal and the thud of wood, the neighing of horse and the long singing hiss of arrows in flight.

Behind the shield wall the Saxons stood firm as the Norman arrows came up at them. Most of the arrows glanced harmlessly off their shields and fell back onto the slope. A few men were wounded in their knees or feet, but when one fell another immediately stepped into his place.

The Norman archers reached into their quivers and fired a second volley, then a third, with little more result. When our men did not return their fire, the Normans eventually found themselves reaching into empty quivers while their needed arrows lay beyond their reach on the sloped face of the ridge. So did the King's first strategy succeed.

The Norman infantry moved up to take the

place of the bowmen. Above them the house-carles raised their battle-axes, and the fighting became savage.

The axes cut through helm and hauberk as a knife cuts through rotten meat. The Bastard's men fell back with their heads split open, showering blood and and brains around them. Our thegns hurled their spears with skilled accuracy, and many tore through the Norman chain mail. One mounted knight raised his helm for a moment, as I watched him, and made to wipe the sweat from his eyes. Instantly a Saxon javelin spitted through his neck and he tumbled off his horse.

Trumpets and horns sounded continually; orders were being shouted from all sides. I doubt if the fighting men really heard any of it. The general noise was so great no individual sound stood out clearly.

This was muchly different from the limited warfare I had seen between Godwine's men and Griffith's, in Wales. The war horses, the heavy armor, the great masses of men—but above all that ceaseless racket. Every man at Senlac Ridge must have been yelling constantly, save only the dying, who shrieked and moaned.

The Normans fought well, but the English fought better. At last we could see a faltering in the Norman charge. "Men become reluctant to press forward when they must climb over the piled-up bodies of their comrades," Osbert explained.

Never had I seen so much blood. The axes created a crimson world, a nightmare place where everything was blurred by the constant red spray. The coppery sweet smell of it came drifting to us as the breeze played fitfully across the battleground.

Harold sat calmly on his horse, directly beneath the Fighting Man. He sat as if relaxed, his huge ax resting across his shoulder. It was still too early in the fight for him; his blood-lust was not yet sufficiently roused. He merely watched the battle closely and called out orders or encouragement to his men.

Then it happened that a few soldiers on both sides began to lose their nerve, throw down their weapons, and run away. Some Saxons fled toward our wood and fell with Norman arrows in their backs. We saw Normans making for the marsh, but then our view was cut off and we did not know what happened to them.

Osbert's experienced eyes saw something mine had not. Harold's brothers, the earls Gyrth and Leofwine, had been in the thick of the fighting at the shield wall. Just as the first charge of Norman cavalry succeeded in reaching the foot of the ridge, Osbert gave a cry.

"Lord Leofwine has fallen!"

"Where? Oh, Osbert, are you sure?"

"Yes, Your Grace. I could pick him out in any throng. He pushed forward to meet the Norman horsemen with his ax, and a foot soldier got to him unnoticed and cut him through the body with a sword!"

Poor Leofwine! Good and kindly, brought down by a faceless stranger.

The Norman charge gave ground, but I saw gaps appear in the shield wall that were slow to fill.

"There is Duke William, my lady . . . there, on the black horse, beneath the banner of the cross. He flaunts the papal blessing for this enterprise!"

As a new charge galloped up Senlac Ridge the axes met them. The helmeted knight Osbert identified as William of Normandy had a horse cut to pieces under him, and a cheer went up from the fyrd. But he scrambled straightway to his feet, caught the bridle of the nearest riderless horse, and was back in the battle. The Bastard was no coward. Armed with that spiked iron ball they call the mace, he fought as savagely as any, and soon I lost sight of him in the press of men and horses.

Having seen William in the forefront of his knights, King Harold gathered his reins and rode down the ridge at last, his mighty ax singing its terrible song about him as he went.

The tales of his prowess were true; I saw men fall before him like scythed wheat.

The strain of standing so long and the tension of the day were giving me a headache. I could feel a throbbing pain behind my eyes. It was impossible for me to go lie down somewhere—anything might happen if I took my eyes from the field for a moment—so I bade Osbert fetch me water from the supply he had cached in the woods.

As soon as he was out of sight I attended to a call of nature and then seated myself on the fallen log. Once I was no longer standing, my feet and legs began to ache cruelly, and I longed to lie on the leafy earth, but I dared not.

To the west of the English position lay a steep gulley, through which flowed a stream. Looking across the open ground behind our soldiers, I saw a group of Norman knights come charging right through our line and, unable to stop, ride their plunging horses straight over the lip of the gully and fall from sight. It was as if the earth had swallowed them up. The foot soldiers who followed them through the break in the line were terrified. In a frantic scramble they raced headlong down the slope of the ridge and into the marsh.

Above the din of battle came a new sound:

the echoing scream of injured men and horses at the bottom of the gully. It was answered by the hysterical shrieks of the foot soldiers, who panicked and ran as from some supernatural occurrence. Not having my vantage point, they could not guess what had happened to the nights, and they must have been sore affrighted.

In a few short minutes the loss of the horsemen had been enough to turn the tide of battle in our favor. Normans by the hundreds, knights as well as infantry, caught the contagion of terror and fled. We saw the noonday sun on the backs of the invaders.

Osbert rejoined me then, but I impatiently pushed the waterskin away. "See, Osbert, see there!" I waved wildly to call his attention to the action before us.

Apparently the Bastard's men thought he himself had been killed, for now we saw him galloping into the mass of deserters, snatching off his helmet that they might see his living face. Back and forth he rode, trying to rally them to return to the fight. It was a courageous act, for without his helmet he was a tempt-target.

Seeing the Normans in flight, the Saxon line, which had stood like a rock until then lost control. For three hours they had stood under a terrible attack; now they saw a chance to get revenge, and they broke ranks to race in pursuit of the enemy. Whooping with glee, our shire levies followed the Normans into the marsh to take terrible toll of them with club and spear.

I could see both armies, breaking ranks and milling about in confusion. The only men who seemed to hold steadfast were our own officers, struggling to re-form the shield wall along the ridge. The frantic commands of the housecarles carried clearly: "Return to your posts! Re-form the line! *Re-form the line!*"

By now a great number of our soldiers had abandoned the ridge and were either in the marsh or beyond Senlac, out of my sight. But the terror which had unmanned the Normans seemed to be over. William's efforts began to succeed, and he and his officers stemmed the Norman retreat. His men turned back to stand and fight, now that the English had left their protected position on the heights. In hand to hand combat, our tired soldiers stood little chance against the fresh Normans and their superior equipment.

Most of what followed I could not see clearly, but I could guess at it from the maneuvering taking place around the command post under the standard of the Fighting Man. We had to be suffering heavy losses; the officers were desperate, and the trumpets blew Recall incessantly.

Harold galloped up the ridge, gave hasty orders to the thegns, and was gone again. After an endless time our men began to return to their places, but there were not nearly so many as had gone joyfully whooping after the Normans. The unarmored shire levies who had gone into the marsh did not come back at all, nor did the King's brother Gyrth.

"Why don't Edwin and Morkere arrive with reinforcements?" I asked Osbert time and again.

His answer was always the same. "I think they hang back, Your Grace, because their levies were so reduced in the campaign in Northumbria. But they will be here, surely!"

Under a sky as blue and tranquil as that of a May day, men screamed their lives away in that bloody place, trying to win a piece of land no victor could carry home with him. And when all these men are dead, their bones turned to dust and their names forgot, still the land will be here under other blue October skies.

I found myself exhausted, and when Osbert offered me a honeycake and ale I took them gladly.

When we finished our little meal, Osbert tried to get me to go back to the hut, but of course I would not. As he knew beforehand. While our decimated army regrouped, we, too, prepared ourselves for the next phase of the battle. On Gytha's hill I saw two tall women standing before her tent, waiting also.

At last the trumpets sounded Charge, and it all began again.

The afternoon became a long blur to me. The yelling was as dreadful as ever, but it came from fewer, tireder throats. The clash of arms and stench of blood seemed to have filled this place forever. Our men stood in their solid defense line once more, but the Normans broke through it again and again, and each time there were less shields on the wall.

Sometimes I could see the King's bare golden head and swinging ax. Once or twice I glimpsed Duke William, each time on a different horse. We were slaughtering his horses, at least!

Ansgar the marshal dragged a Norman knight from his horse not too far from where we watched among the trees. The two of them struggled on foot, each man seeking an advantage that would allow him to kill the other. The Norman had lost his sword somewhere; all Ansgar had left was the broken shaft of a javelin. Neither wanted to get within the reach of the other and so they circled round and round, like chained bears put in the pit to fight.

Ansgar grabbed up some scruffy little bush and lashed the knight across the face with it,

then jumped back. I saw his teeth gleam in a
ferocious grin. The enraged Norman closed
with him and was rewarded with a knee in the
groin. Rolling on the ground, grunting and cursing, they looked much as my brothers had in so
many childhood scuffles. Then a red pool began to leak out from beneath them, and when
Ansgar stood up I could see the splintered haft
of the javelin driven through the Norman's
mouth and up into his brain. The man died so
close to us we could smell the odor of his
bowels opening. Ansgar reeled with fatigue
above him, then righted himself and went off to
catch the Norman horse.

My brain was scalded with the sights I saw.

Again I saw the invaders break and retreat,
much as they had done in the morning, and
again the English ignored their orders and
raced after them. The outcome was the same as
before. The Normans led their pursuers some
distance away, then turned on them and cut
them down. In their reckless courage, the Saxons and Angles died, and fewer returned
each time to Senlac Ridge. By now the Normans knew our men would follow, even to
their doom, if they thought their enemy was
retreating. A cold and calculating brain used
this knowledge to great advantage, and the
Saxon leaders were powerless to prevent the

suicide of their own men. Each feigned retreat meant further casualties.

It was a pitifully small group by now, the English fyrd. Where just that morning they had stood in a grand army the length of the ridge, now they were a small knot of desperate men. Harold pulled together what remained of his troops and formed them about his standard, with the remaining shielded housecarles along front. They were the wall against which the Norman sea must break, and their steadfast courage was the King's last defense.

Dead and gone were the shire levies who had rallied to Harold's standard from all the corners of the land. Men from York and Gloucester, from London and Lincoln and Lindsey, their broken bodies littered the Hastings Road. In their coarse peasant robes, the dirt from their fields still under their nails, they sprawled dead in the marsh and on the slopes. Some of them had been cowards, and many of them had been foolish, but their massed numbers had been the backbone of the army and now they were gone. The ceorls with their spears and their skullbreakers were gone. Even the Kentish men, famed for their skill in warfare, were gone.

All that was left of Anglo-Saxon England stood together. The standard of the Fighting

Man still rode the summit; there were just not enough fighting men left beneath it.

But so great was their determination that they fought on, unslacking. They could not win, but they would not lose. Then William the Bastard bethought him of a new stratagem. Orders were shouted, and the archers were brought up again and massed at the foot of the ridge. But they did not shoot at an upward angle against the massed shields. No, they aimed their arrows almost straight up, so they flew up all at once in a dense black cloud, arched high above our line, over the protective shields, then fell swiftly down into the English ranks.

I do not know how many were hit, for I saw only one. Harold of England took an arrow in the head and fell, with a dreamy slowness, to the bloodsoaked earth.

His own men stepped back from him in shock and horror, and I could see clearly what happened next. With his own hands, he grasped the arrow by its shaft and pulled it out of his eye socket. He writhed on the ground in agony, but before anyone could touch him he was on his feet again. Somehow he found the strength to shoulder his ax one more time, and he went between his own housecarles and met the Normans coming up the slope. His stunned troops followed him, but it was obvious he could not last long. The English line was broken completely now, and even Duke William had ridden to the top of the ridge. I saw him sitting on yet another horse, directing a group of knights to capture our standards and end the battle.

They carved their way with flashing swords to the King of England. I watched him fight, and go down, and struggle weakly to rise again. The hacking blades closed over him.

The war ended then, for England and for me. Sick to my soul, I turned my back on all of it and stumbled through the woods to my children. If Osbert accompanied me I cannot recall it; I neither heard nor saw anything.

The woods were black, as if the sun had set.

Wales

I LAY ON THE FLOOR of the hut, only half-aware of the activity around me. Voices spoke, figures bent over me, but I could not answer them. Even the voices of the children were abrasive and unwelcome; I tried to push them away with my mind.

"Your Grace! Your Grace!" Someone had been shaking my shoulders for a long time. I fought to focus my reluctant eyes and saw that it was Osbert. Beyond him Gwladys hunched, crying into her apron.

"Night has come, my lady, and the Normans are scouring the countryside for survivors. What do you wish us to do?"

Osbert's tone was that of an uncertain child, seeking authority. At first I was puzzled to hear him thus; then I remembered. Authority was dead on Hastings field.

With great difficulty I forced my aching bones to sit me up. "The King, Osbert; what have they done with the King?"

There were actual tears in the housecarle's eyes, and I heard Gwladys sob aloud. "They cannot identify him, Your Grace."

"What do you mean?"

He looked around the room, lit only by one feeble torch, as if hoping to find someone else who would say the words he did not want to say.

"The Normans stripped all the English bodies, my lady. And they are . . . they are"—his voice choked—"very badly hacked up. No one has been able to recognize King Harold."

"Mother of God!" Bile flooded my mouth, and I retched onto the filthy floor.

But I could not afford the luxury of weakness. Harold was dead; everyone in that woodcutter's shack looked to me to tell them what to do. Our lives depended on it. The lives of the children of two kings depended on it.

I dug my nails into my palms until the

pain cleared my head a little. "You say the Normans are searching for survivors? Is there a chance they will find us here?"

"I doubt it, Your Grace. Men have already passed by quite close without noticing the place; even at a little distance it seems part of the trees and brush. But if we took to the road now they would be on us in a twinkling."

"William would not treat kindly with me, as . . . as Harold Godwine did. My children and I would doubtless live out our lives in some damp Norman keep." There was nothing more I could do for Harold, but much I could do for his unborn child.

"The Bastard shall not get us, Osbert. We will stay here until his army moves on to enjoy its conquest elsewhere, and then we will go someplace where he will never send to look for us. Doubtless he does not know I am here now; even the King did not know. He will assume I have been left in safekeeping somewhere, for him to pick like a ripe plum at his leisure."

My mind was churning, picking over the plans that had been forming beneath its surface even as we came through the Andredsweald. There had always been the foreknowledge of this moment within me, I think. All that I had learned must come together and save us now, and chart a future for my children. A safe future. Free of the heritage of blood.

I forced my voice to be brisk. "Gwladys! Compose yourself, woman, and listen to me. Have you still those relatives you once told me about, in the mountains of Snowdonia?"

She looked at me wonderingly. "Aye, my lady."

"And they would well come you, and give you shelter?"

"Aye . . ."

"Think you they would also extend the Welsh hospitality to a family of poor English freedmen, fleeing the Normans and anxious to build a new life for themselves?"

The woman stared at me as if she were simple-minded. "But, Your Grace . . . !"

"Do not call me that ever again! I am no longer First Lady, Gwladys! I am no longer a Lady at all, just a simple lowborn woman with my husband, here"—and I took the arm of the astonished Osbert—"and our children.

"*And that is who I shall remain;* do you understand me?"

I do not know who was shaken more, Gwladys or Osbert. But at last it was agreed. Such identifying belongings as we had with us would be buried forever in the dark of the forest, save only Griffith's ruby and the ring Harold had put on my finger in the York Minster. These I would hide on my person in such a way that they would not be found if we were robbed and searched. Osbert gave his housecarles, save only Merfyn, who had an eye for Gwladys, permission to leave us and make their own ways home. The remaining horses we turned loose; they were fine enough to give us away.

Osbert caught a farmer's nag running loose in the woods and tied it up at a distance for me to ride when we left. "You cannot walk to Wales, my lady, not in your condition!" he said gently.

When the sickly dawn broke over Senlac Ridge, I bade Merfyn go as near as he dared to the battlefield and see if he could learn if the King had been found. When he came back he was drag-footed, and I thought the news was bad.

"No, King Harold has been found, my lady. Duke William has taken his body and says he will give it decent burial, but he will not return it to the English."

Harold Godwine. Once more in William's custody.

"How was he identified, Merfyn?"

It was obvious that that was the part he was loath to tell. "I met one of the Earl Gyrth's men; he told me that the monks from Waltham went to Duke William and asked for the King's body. He sent them to try to identify it, but they could not. They went to Gytha, but she could not even try."

Poor Gytha; I pitied her then as I had never done before.

"And so, who found the King, Merfyn?"

He footshifted and would not meet my eyes. "No one knew you were here, my lady . . ."

"Aldith! Call me only Aldith, Merfyn, and mind you do not forget!"

He looked most uncomfortable. "Yes, uh, Aldith. At any rate, no one knew you were here, and so, uh . . ."

"And so?"

"Edith Swanneshals went down to the field. The monks carried torches for her, and she walked among the English dead, bending over their naked and butchered bodies and going dry-eyed."

I felt sick.

"At last she stopped, my friend said, and cried aloud, sinking onto the ground. She cradled what lay there in her lap and would not be comforted. It is said she recognized the King by signs none other would know."

He did not have to add that. I did not want to know it!

"And so the King's body was wrapped in linen and carried to Duke William, but then he refused to give it to the monks after all. We can only trust he will treat it kindly; we are powerless to do more!"

Merfyn's voice rose in an agony of helplessness and regret. Behind our eyes, I think we all watched that woman moving slowly among the dead, her face ghastly in the torchlight.

The Normans have begun to pull out. Osbert had seen their divisions moving slowly up the road toward London, and I shudder for those who encounter them along the way.

We will not follow the London road but cut cross-country, as the local folk do. It will be a long journey, and the cold weather will reach us in earnest before we see the mountains of Wales rising ahead of us. But I feel my babe strong within me, and I know Osbert will keep his vow to the King and care well for us.

Along the way, to pass the time, I will begin to instruct my children in their new heritage. Can the sons of kings be taught to live without slaughter, to put aside ambition and forget the claiming of thrones? We shall see. I want my sons to live, for the sake of life itself.

I am coming home, Griffith.

Get the whole story of
THE RAKEHELL DYNASTY

__BOOK ONE: THE BOOK OF JONATHAN RAKEHELL
by Michael William Scott   (D30-308, $3.50)

__BOOK TWO: CHINA BRIDE
by Michael William Scott   (D30-309, $3.50)

__BOOK THREE: ORIENT AFFAIR
by Michael William Scott   (D90-238, $3.50)

The bold, sweeping, passionate story of a great New England shipping family caught up in the winds of change —and of the one man who would dare to sail his dream ship to the frightening, beautiful land of China. He was Jonathan Rakehell, and his destiny would change the course of history.

THE RAKEHELL DYNASTY—
THE GRAND SAGA OF THE GREAT CLIPPER SHIPS
AND OF THE MEN WHO BUILT THEM
TO CONQUER THE SEAS AND CHALLENGE THE WORLD!

Jonathan Rakehell—who staked his reputation and his place in the family on the clipper's amazing speed.

Lai-Tse Lu—the beautiful, independent daughter of a Chinese merchant. She could not know that Jonathan's proud clipper ship carried a cargo of love and pain, joy and tragedy for her.

Louise Graves—Jonathan's wife-to-be, who waits at home in New London keeping a secret of her own.

Bradford Walker—Jonathan's scheming brother-in-law who scoffs at the clipper and plots to replace Jonathan as heir to the Rakehell shipping line.

__THE MER-LION
by Lee Arthur (A90-044, $3.50)

In Scotland, he was a noble...but in the bloody desert colosseum, he was a slave battling for the hand of a woman he hated. James Mackenzie intrigued royalty...the queen of France, the king of Scotland, the king of England, and the Amira Aisha of Tunis. But James Mackenzie was a man of destiny, a Scot whose fortune was guarded by THE MER-LION.

To order, use the coupon below If you prefer to use your own stationery, please include complete title as well as book number and price. Allow 4 weeks for delivery